To Bed the Bride

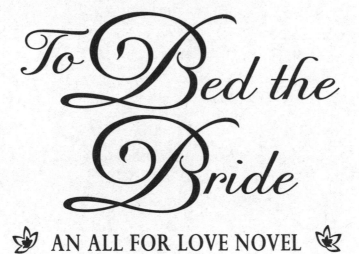

To Bed the Bride

 AN ALL FOR LOVE NOVEL

KAREN RANNEY

AVONBOOKS

An Imprint of HarperCollins*Publishers*

TO BED THE BRIDE. Copyright © 2019 by Karen Ranney LLC. All rights reserved. Printed in the United States of America. No part of this book may be used or reproduced in any manner whatsoever without written permission except in the case of brief quotations embodied in critical articles and reviews. For information, address HarperCollins Publishers, 195 Broadway, New York, NY 10007.

First Avon Books mass market printing: December 2019
First Avon Books hardcover printing: November 2019

Print Edition ISBN: 978-0-06-295265-3
Digital Edition ISBN: 978-0-06-284109-4

FIRST EDITION

19 20 21 22 23 LSC 10 9 8 7 6 5 4 3 2 1

Codicil to the Last Will and Testament of Archibald Hamish Craig

As previously stated, the estate of Hearthmere, including lands, cattle, sheep, and the Hearthmere bloodline, is left to my beloved daughter, Eleanor Elizabeth Craig.

Since she is still a minor child, I entreat my younger brother, William, to act as trustee for Hearthmere and custodian of Eleanor until such time as she reaches her majority. Should he wish to accept this position, details of which are found in separate documents, he will be required to live with his family at Hearthmere in order to provide a home for Eleanor. When Eleanor reaches her majority, if she wishes, and solely at her discretion, my brother and his family shall continue to live at Hearthmere.

In consideration for his services and that of his wife, the estate shall pay him an annual sum agreed upon in separate documents until such time as Eleanor reaches her majority.

It is my wish that Eleanor, having been deprived of a mother from birth, will be surrounded by family who will love and cherish her.

Family is everything.

Chapter One

September, 1868
Hearthmere, Scotland

"I won't leave if you don't want me to. If you're afraid to stay here by yourself I can postpone my visit."

Eleanor Craig looked at her cousin, trying to tell if he was serious. Jeremy had never offered to do something unselfish.

"I'm not afraid, Jeremy. Besides, there are twenty-five people here. I couldn't be alone if I wanted to."

"Yes, but they're servants."

She bit back a comment. Her cousin had never seen servants as people. It wasn't his fault. The attitude was one her aunt had espoused and verbalized often.

They aren't our kind. How many times had she heard that comment?

"They're employees who work at Hearthmere," Eleanor said, trying not to sound irritated. "They were loyal to my father and yours."

"Why shouldn't they be? They get away with too much. No one's here to tell them what to do."

"Mrs. Willett does an admirable job."

"Mrs. Willett is just a housekeeper."

Jeremy hadn't wanted to accompany her to Scotland, a fact that was evident only hours after their arrival. When he'd announced that he was thinking of visiting Edinburgh, she'd been overjoyed. At least this way she wouldn't have to hear him endlessly complaining about one thing or another.

"You really should go," she said. "See your friends. How long will you be staying?"

"A week, maybe two."

Two weeks without Jeremy would be a blessing.

Hearthmere was a jewel of a house, but it was not equipped with all the creature comforts her cousin preferred.

"Go. I insist," she said.

"Mother wouldn't be pleased if I left you here. Alone."

His look was speculative, almost as if he was trying to decide if she would immediately write her aunt and inform her that he'd abandoned his prescribed role of protector to hie off to the city.

Eleanor smiled. "I'm not alone, Jeremy. I'd feel much better if I knew you were having as much fun as I was. I won't say anything to Aunt Deborah."

He shook his head. "How you can abide this moldering pile of bricks, I don't know."

Once again she bit back her comment. Hearthmere had been the Craig family home for four hundred years or more. As a Craig, Jeremy should understand that, despite the fact that he tried to pretend he wasn't half Scot.

Granted, there were places needing repair, but the house was filled with history. You couldn't walk into the Clan Hall, for example, without feeling the spirits of long-dead Craigs surrounding you. The gardens were laid out on plans that had been prepared hundreds of years earlier. The curtain wall, part of the original castle, had been built as protection from enemy clans and the English and now served to shield the courtyard from the worst of the westerly winds.

Her annual visit to Scotland was something she looked forward to all year. She came home not only to check on the house and the staff, but to refresh herself in a way. She dreamed of living here again just as she had before her aunt had upended the family and moved them to London.

"It will be our little secret," Eleanor said. "No one else needs to know."

"You're certain?" Jeremy asked, already turning to leave the parlor.

She nodded. "You mustn't worry about me. I'll be fine."

With any luck she hadn't revealed her relief to him. Jeremy was like his mother in temperament, always finding fault with arrangements or people. The two of them seemed to enjoy complaining, never understanding how tiring it could be to hear.

The longer he was gone the happier she would be.

"I'll be back in two weeks, then," he said. "In time to escort you home, Eleanor."

Home? England had never been home to her and London even less so. She didn't make that remark, however. Over the years she'd learned when to speak and when to keep silent.

"You'll be leaving in the morning?"

"This afternoon, I think. The weather is fair, although that's always hard to tell in Scotland. One moment it's sunny. The next you're deluged."

She'd always thought the same about English weather, but once again she kept her comments to herself.

Jeremy was more than willing to forget that his father had grown up here. He seemed to have forgotten his heritage the moment they moved to England and especially after his mother had married again.

His stepfather was Hamilton Richards, a wealthy industrialist who made soap, various kinds and types of soap that he shipped all over the world. He had no children of his own and welcomed all of them into his family and his home with sincere generosity. Ever since, both Jeremy and his sister, Daphne, had forgotten they were Scots.

She watched as Jeremy walked out of the parlor. He'd probably already given orders for his bags to be taken to the carriage.

Their conversation had only been for show. Jeremy didn't really care about leaving her behind. The regrettable truth was that her cousin thought more of his own pleasure than anyone's convenience.

If Hamilton hadn't been as wealthy as he was, perhaps Jeremy's life would've been different. At this point, Jeremy would've had some sort of occupation, rather than spending most of his time gambling and drinking with his friends. Hamilton, however, was willing to finance Jeremy's adventures.

Daphne's husband wasn't nearly as wealthy as Hamilton, so there were times when she came to the massive London home, met with Hamilton in his library, and left with a smug smile on her face. With any luck, his fortune would outlast the Craig children's greed.

Eleanor had benefited from Hamilton's kindness, too. Her aunt had been all for denying Eleanor this trip to Scotland. It had been Hamilton who had convinced Deborah to allow it.

"Let her see the place," Hamilton had said. "After all, she'll soon have her own establishment."

Eleanor was grateful that her aunt's husband had interceded. She hadn't wanted to have to send for her solicitor. He'd been the one to originally insist upon the arrangement.

"She is a Scot, Mrs. Craig," he'd said to her aunt. "If you will not agree to remain in Scotland as was our arrangement with your husband, then Miss Craig must be allowed to return home periodically."

Her aunt had fussed for a few moments before the solicitor spoke again.

"If you will allow your niece to visit Hearthmere for a month each year then I see no reason why the annual stipend should be allowed to stop, at least until Miss Craig's majority. Just one month out of the year. Surely that wouldn't be a hardship?"

Up until then, Eleanor hadn't realized that her aunt and uncle had been paid to care for her. She'd been allowed to come to Scotland for a month for the past four years. After her aunt had married Hamilton Richards, but Deborah had continued to allow the attorney's arrangement. At least until this year, when she'd shortened it from a month to only two weeks.

The time in Scotland had always been bittersweet, only because she had to ultimately return to England.

"You can't live there, Eleanor," her aunt said, every time she returned. "Your life is here in London."

Only because she had no choice in the matter.

Every time Eleanor came back to Hearthmere, whether escorted by Jeremy or her aunt and her husband, it was the same. Wishing they were gone to leave her alone to savor the house settling in around her, almost as if it welcomed her after an absence of eleven months.

She'd never seen a ghost, although tales of them abounded in Scotland. She wished, however, that there were ghosts haunting Hearthmere and that her father was one of them. She'd sit at his knee as she had as a child as he'd tell her another story about their ancestors, the brave men and stalwart women who had lived here, loved here, and spent their lives protecting Hearthmere. She would walk with him through the house, visiting rooms she hadn't seen for a year. His library. The Conservatory her great-grandfather had built for his wife. The aviary and then the chapel. The stained-glass windows and arched ceiling still had the power to steal her breath, no matter how often she opened one of the double doors and stepped inside.

It felt like she was only half alive in London all these months, waiting impatiently for her arrival home. Once here, she could feel a stirring of her blood as if everything was slowly waking. She wasn't Deborah Richards's niece. She was Eleanor Craig, daughter of Archibald Craig, of the Clan Craig. She knew her history from the smallest fragment of battle flag in the Clan Hall, to the sword she'd once thought coated with rust up near the ceiling. Her uncle had been the one who told her the truth.

"It's blood, Eleanor. One of our bloodthirsty relatives evidently smite his enemy. Or is it smote? Regardless, they left the blood on the sword."

She missed her uncle. He'd died five years ago while walking from the house to the stable complex. Less than three weeks later his widow had swept up her two children and Eleanor and returned to London.

If her father hadn't died in a tragic accident, and then her uncle, she might have been able to stay here, instead of moving to England. A foolish wish, to be able to turn back time and circumstances.

She was the only one in the family, she suspected, who wished things had stayed the same. Her aunt was blissfully happy and Daphne and Jeremy appreciated all of the advantages they'd been given, thanks to their mother's second husband.

The minute Jeremy's carriage reached the last turn, heading for the main road, Eleanor grabbed her skirts with both hands and made her way quickly out of the parlor and through the corridor, up the stairs to the room she'd occupied ever since she was a child.

Her cousin Daphne had once told her that since she was the chatelaine of Hearthmere she should occupy the large suite in the corner. Perhaps one day she would.

After closing the door softly behind her, she raced to the armoire, tapping along the left side, just as her father had taught her. This piece of furniture had a secret panel, but it wasn't the only one. Her desk had a secret drawer, too. So did her father's massive desk in his library.

The space wasn't all that large, but it was big enough to hide her riding skirt. Not the one that went with her habit, sewn by one of the finest seamstresses in London. No, this style she'd devised for herself when she was ten. She'd taken one of her older skirts, sewn two tight seams, then cut the skirt in the middle. Only her father had known what she'd done and he'd approved wholeheartedly.

"A woman's saddle is a danger," he'd said. "It's flimsy and won't do you any good. The harpies don't have to know you've learned to ride astride."

They'd ridden together just after dawn every morning. For years she'd awakened with the same bright excitement until she was eleven and realized that those days were gone and would never come again.

This time she would ride just as she had with her father, as she had on each of her annual visits.

Standing, she grabbed the top half of her riding habit and paired it with her altered skirt. After pulling on her boots, she ignored the chaplet and the hat with its veil. She was going riding this morning, not like they did in London's parks, but across the glen and down the roads until she and Maud grew tired.

In her sitting room was a block of ornamental panels along one wall. She pressed the third block, then used her fingertips to open the secret door even farther.

Hearthmere was a treasure trove of secrets and she knew them all. Her father had taught them to her one by one, revealing another magical aspect of the house on every birthday. She learned about this set of secret corridors and stairs when she was ten. There was no need for a lantern or candle. Arrow slits, once part of the old castle, lit the space.

She made her way down the stairs, listening. There was an exit into the large pantry, but that was too close to the kitchen. A great many of Hearthmere's servants congregated there in the mornings. The last thing she wanted to do was pop out and shock everyone. Instead, she took the next exit leading to an anteroom close to the library. Holding on to the door for a moment, she waited until a maid passed before stepping out.

She left the house and made it past the milking shed before she was noticed. Two young boys heading in the opposite direction waved to her and she waved back.

Turning, she looked at Hearthmere sitting on a knoll of earth, blocking out the view of the horizon, its two wings stretching out like arms to enfold anyone who came close. A long time ago a castle had stood there, home to the first Craigs.

The gray stone was the color of London fog. The white-outlined windows looked like dozens of eyes, ever vigilant. All the chimneys reminded her of organ pipes, but instead of sound they belched smoke, especially from the kitchen. The house lived and breathed on its own without her interference, sheltering those who worked at Hearthmere, who kept her father's legacy alive. Strangers were welcome here and travelers were greeted with a hot meal and sometimes a bed for the night, all in the name of Archie Craig.

Hearthmere was, on the whole, self-sustaining. There were crofters on a huge swath of land that wasn't managed under the home farms, and both cattle and sheep were being raised on the rest of the acreage.

They employed twenty-five people, some who worked in the house, but mostly those who managed the horses.

As she looked at the house, pride soared through her. She would always be a Scot, regardless of how many years she lived in England. Her father was a Craig and his father before him, a long line of men that stretched back hundreds and hundreds of years.

Family is everything. Her father had said that to her repeatedly. She didn't understand how her aunt and her family could so easily toss their heritage aside.

She would never abandon Hearthmere.

Chapter Two

At the crest of the hill, Eleanor stopped to appreciate the view. Below her was the main stable building, consisting of over fifty stalls. The construction mimicked that of Hearthmere, the gray brick and white trim a perfect match to the house. Behind the stable was a series of paddocks and corrals, chutes, and rings to exercise the horses. Farther still was an oval dirt track her father had constructed to train the horses.

Hearthmere Thoroughbreds were known for their gray coloring, and had won at The Oaks, The Derby, and most of the English races. Their winning times had improved the sport to the point that Hearthmere Thoroughbreds were synonymous with the best of the breed. They'd had requests to purchase available horses from all over the world. Only those buyers known to her father or uncle were considered, the health and well-being of their horses being of paramount importance.

Their winnings were compiled in her steward's monthly report. Every year they made more than the previous year. The profits were spent on improvements to the stables as well as buying more blood stock. When a foal was born she was informed of it, the birth heralded as important and recorded in her father's large ledger. She wasn't supposed to call it what it was, his stud book. Such an inelegant term would have been shocking said in mixed company. She wasn't supposed to know a great deal that she knew, which was a shame because she could have had some

rousing conversations about racing with several of her more boring suitors.

Michael didn't seem inclined to gamble, which was probably
an asset in a future husband. He wasn't interested in the Hearthmere bloodline, either, which was disturbing. Despite her bringing up the subject on numerous occasions, he seemed not to want
to discuss her home.

She'd met her fiancé at a ball. He'd been pointed out to her by
Jenny Woolsey, who'd become her friend by dint of having attended most of the same social functions. The poor thing was
always laced too tightly and had the misfortune of perspiring
when anxious.

Perhaps as a result of being shunned by the other girls—as
well as potential suitors—or because she was naturally obser-
vant, Jenny could identify most of the guests at the various events
they'd attended. She knew a man's title, if applicable, and what
his yearly income was rumored to be. She'd spotted Michael immediately.

"It's the Earl of Wescott," she said, her voice excited. "He's recently returned from the Caribbean."

Eleanor had given him a quick glance, but she hadn't paid him
much attention. After all, he was an earl and she hadn't aimed
that high. Yet by the end of the season they were engaged. Her
entire future had changed.

"My dear girl," her aunt had said, "aren't you the sly puss?
You've managed to acquire the most eligible man in London, perhaps all of England."

She'd never been the focus of her aunt's attention, let alone her
praise. Eleanor found herself bemused by the situation and the
speed at which it had happened. One moment Michael had called
upon her aunt's husband, and the next she was being feted for her
charm, poise, and grace.

Not to mention being the object of speculation and endless
rumors wherever she went.

Now she began the long trek down to the stable complex, noting changes that had been made in the past year. She knew about all of them, thanks to her steward's monthly reports: the new fencing in the north pasture, the construction of an area for the foals to be trained.

Mr. Contino's office was in the middle of the long stable building. She nodded to several men she knew, and stopped and had a conversation with a few of them before finally hesitating at the stable master's door.

"Good morning, Mr. Contino," she said.

She normally didn't simply show up at Mr. Contino's door without a prior announcement. He didn't like to be startled and was apt to take out his irritation at her verbally in Italian. She'd never learned the language, but she was almost certain Mr. Contino swore at her from time to time.

He'd come from Italy, around Genoa, she'd been told. The man was an expert when it came to horses, at least according to her father. From the records her steward had sent her, Mr. Contino had continued with his expertise in the years since her uncle's death.

The stable master had only tolerated Uncle William, but he'd had a genuine affection for her father. Archie could be found here at any time of the day or night. After dark, the two men would open a bottle of her father's favorite wine. During the day it was the strongest coffee, never made more palatable with a touch of cream.

Mr. Contino had been given rooms on the third floor of the house, but preferred to make his home above the stable office.

"He likes being close to the horses," her father had explained to her.

She'd wondered how the stable master had tolerated the smell of the stable before realizing it was probably like Daphne's perfume. After a while, you no longer noticed how dreadfully overpowering it was and how it even seemed to flavor anything you ate.

"What is it you want?" The man's heavily accented voice

sounded annoyed, but that was Mr. Contino. He always sounded annoyed.

"To speak with you," she said, stepping into the doorway.

He'd cleaned his office since she'd last seen it. Instead of a series of bridles and bits being strewn over the top of his desk, everything was neatly hung on hooks on the opposite wall. The two chairs in front of the desk were empty of blankets and a saddle—another change. Two large ledgers were spread open on the surface of his desk. When she appeared, he laid down his pen and scowled at her.

"You're late."

"Late?"

"You're normally here in July," he said. "It's September. Where have you been?"

She smiled. "I almost didn't come at all," she said. "As it is, I'll only be here for two weeks, not the full month."

He didn't say anything for a moment. When he did speak she wasn't surprised at his comment. Mr. Contino had never approved of Deborah.

"Your aunt?"

Not really. Michael had made the decision that she was only to remain here two weeks this year.

"He's going to be your husband, Eleanor," Deborah had said. "If Michael says that he only wants you to stay in Scotland for two weeks, then it's a decision you should obey."

Michael wasn't her husband yet. Nor was she sure she liked the idea that he could decide—without any input from her—where she was to go and how long she was to stay. According to her aunt, that was marriage. A wife could not directly contravene her husband's orders. Instead, she had to be inventive and clever. In other words, a woman had to be cunning in order to achieve her own wishes and wants.

Evidently, being duplicitous was simply a trait of smart women. Eleanor wasn't altogether certain she agreed with that, either, even if it was the way of the world.

Mr. Contino made a gesture toward one of the chairs in front of his desk and she entered the room and sat, trying to get up her courage.

"It's better to do something unpleasant right away, lass, than let it blister." Her father had given her that advice.

"I'm to be married," she said.

Mr. Contino was the first person she'd told at Hearthmere. Yet she didn't doubt that the rest of the staff knew. Somehow, they always ferreted out important information and there was nothing more important than this. Not because of her. She was well aware of who she was and how unprepossessing. But she was engaged to a peer and that pulled her out of nondescript status and shone a spotlight on her.

"He's an earl. It's quite a remarkable thing, really. I never thought to attract the attention of an earl. Or any member of the peerage."

"Like will seek out like," he said. "It happens in the animal kingdom and it happens among people."

She didn't know what to say to that. She certainly wasn't a member of the peerage. Nor was she entirely certain she wanted to become a countess, for that matter. Now Daphne, that was a different story. If anyone should have been a countess, it was Daphne.

"We survived your uncle," Mr. Contino said. "We can survive a husband."

Although her uncle had grown up at Hearthmere, he hadn't been the least interested in the Hearthmere bloodline. He'd made incredibly stupid decisions that she and Mr. Contino had to reverse behind his back. William Craig was more suited for his avocation—writing poetry.

"Can I saddle Maud?" she asked, standing.

"She's ready for you." He stood, too. Although Mr. Contino was shorter than she by nearly a foot, he always seemed larger, mainly because of his personality. "We've exercised her well since you've been gone, Miss Eli."

His use of her father's name for her almost pushed the smile off her face. No one else called her that.

"Thank you, Mr. Contino."

He only nodded in response.

Without another word she left the stable master's office and headed toward Maud's stall.

Maud was a Highland pony, a garron, originally purchased to breed with one of their Arabian stallions. Her father thought that the result would be an attractive offspring with greater speed and an amenable temperament. Unfortunately, Maud had never produced a foal, but her father hadn't sold the pony. Instead, she'd become Eleanor's mount.

As a garron, Maud was tall, a chestnut with a full body and well-built quarters. Her eyes, set wide apart, were intelligent and knowing. Her head was arched and her mane was long, as was her tail, which fell nearly to the ground.

Maud wasn't a young animal, but she hadn't developed any significant signs of age. Although Eleanor wished she could have brought Maud to London, it wasn't the right place for her. She was better off at Hearthmere where there weren't crowds and endless noises to startle her.

Eleanor left the stable, heading east. She wanted to explore slowly, giving both Maud and herself time to be reacquainted with their normal route.

She hadn't expected the sheep.

Normally, Hearthmere's flocks were taken to the pastures south of the house, not here. But these didn't look like her sheep. They raised black-faced Scottish sheep at Hearthmere, not animals with white, elongated faces and sharp, pointed ears. Perhaps she should have paid more attention to the steward's last report. Had they begun raising a different breed?

She debated retracing her steps, but she wanted to go onward. She tried guiding Maud through the white bleating cloud except that they weren't parting for her. Instead, they milled around her, keeping her from making any progress on the road.

Maud didn't like the animals being so close to her legs. Twice she skipped to the side. Dismounting, Eleanor grabbed Maud's reins, deciding to lead her through the flock rather than attempt to do so mounted.

She thought the sheep would part for her if she pushed her way through them. The opposite was true. They seemed to relish bumping against her and announcing their displeasure in a high, irritating, whining bleat.

Abruptly, the sea of white thinned, leaving her staring at a black-and-white dog with a huge ruff and a set of impressive teeth. Like the sheep, he was not pleased with her appearance, but unlike the flock, he was poised to attack.

Chapter Three

Logan McKnight had always known that sheep weren't quiet animals. They might move in a cloud of fleece and feet, but they weren't silent. On the contrary, they were loud and in an annoying way. They bleated in tandem and then separately. Just when he got used to the rhythm of their noise, they changed it again.

However, he hadn't known about the spitting.

A few of the ewes had sized him up from the first day and decided that he was wanting. Without warning, they'd spew spittle on him if he ventured too close. He learned to keep his distance.

Thank heavens for Peter and Paul. Without the two border collies, he didn't know where the flock would be right now. Not headed toward the upper glen, that was certain. They'd probably be halfway to the Hebrides.

Some of his contemporaries—should they be unfortunate enough to spy him in his current role—would say that he was hiding. He preferred to consider this time away from London as a sabbatical. He needed a week or two in the Highlands to clear his mind and maybe clean his soul.

As long as the sheep obeyed the dogs' commands he could follow along and act like he knew what he was doing. At night the dogs herded the sheep into a tight circle and remained on guard, one of them at Logan's feet and the other in front of the flock.

The solitude had originally been a balm to his nerves. Lately, however, he almost craved the sound of another voice—other than his as he rehearsed a forthcoming speech. The dogs never offered comment, although the sheep didn't seem to approve.

He hadn't seen another human being in days. Nor had he seen a newspaper in all that time, a fact for which he was grateful. He didn't want to read about himself.

The time hadn't been wasted, however. He'd had time to think, and at first his thoughts were filled with what had happened in Abyssinia. Then his mind traveled back a few decades to the freedom he'd experienced as a child. It had been years since he'd felt that carefree.

This was, perhaps, the closest he'd come in a long while, acting in Old Ned's stead while the shepherd visited a sick relative.

One of the dogs barked. Logan turned his head to find Peter standing rigid on the road, staring down a horse and rider.

ELEANOR STAYED WHERE she was, conscious that Maud was as unsettled as she felt. Although the mare was exercised every day, it was in a closed corral, not the countryside. This experience of the sheep and now the dog was unusual—and frightening—for her and she was reacting with her normal skittishness.

The dog's eyes hadn't veered from them.

"All I want to do is pass," she said to the dog. "You needn't look at me like I'm your lunch. Go away."

The dog didn't stop growling. In fact, he took a few steps toward her. If the sheep hadn't been milling so close she would have backed away.

"I mean it," she said in a more forceful tone. "Shoo!"

"He's only doing his job."

She looked up to find a man standing there holding a crook, and a knapsack, watching her.

"You'll never get him to move with a command like *shoo*," he added.

Eleanor was torn between feeling ridiculous and being justifiably annoyed.

"This is a public thoroughfare," she said. "One not set aside primarily for sheep."

"I agree."

"Then you need to move them so that I can get by," she said.

"Wouldn't it be easier for you to simply go around?" His accent was that of Scotland. Stronger than hers, given her five years in London.

He was smiling at her. A very charming smile as it turned out, one that she told herself not to notice overmuch.

Although he was dressed in a cream-colored shirt, open at the neck and rolled up at the sleeves, he didn't look like a shepherd. First of all, he didn't have a beard and his black hair was closely cut. Except for his attire, which included loose trousers showing several stains—one of which appeared to be blood—he looked like any of the men she'd met during her two seasons.

She didn't make a habit of paying attention to a strange man's appearance, but this shepherd made it somewhat difficult not to notice him. He had a rough-hewn appearance: black hair ruffled by the wind, a broad face with strong features, a nose that was almost too large for his face, and a mouth still arranged in a smile. His was a stubborn chin that warned her this encounter might not go to her satisfaction. Nor did he look the least bit abashed by the situation.

Surely he knew that she was his employer?

"Our sheep are never moved here," she said. "You've taken them too far afield."

"Have I?"

"You have. You should rectify this situation immediately. No one needs to know."

"Don't they?"

She shook her head, wishing he would do something about the dog. Every time she directed her attention somewhere else, the dog moved closer to her. If she wasn't careful, the border collie would be only inches away.

"You needn't be afraid of him."

Anyone with half a brain would be cautious of a growling dog, especially one as large and as ferocious as that one. To make matters worse, now there were two dogs, the second one circling around and actually coming closer to her and Maud than the first animal.

"You really must call them off," she said. "Right now."

"Do you always give strangers orders? I've counted three so far."

"I'm your employer," she said. "I'm Eleanor Craig of Hearthmere."

"Are you, then? I'm pleased to meet you, Eleanor Craig of Hearthmere, but you're not my employer."

"Of course I am, and those are my sheep. Now do something about them," she said, trying not to look at the dogs. Instead, she focused her attention on the shepherd, surprised when his smile faded.

"You really are frightened, aren't you?"

She wanted to protest that she wasn't afraid, but it seemed ludicrous to make that claim when she could feel herself shaking.

"Are you going to command them to move?"

He whistled. Only a two-note whistle, and both dogs turned and came to sit at his side. Why hadn't he done that from the beginning if it was so easy? Why had he thought it necessary to put her through such distress?

"Miss Craig, those are not your sheep. They belong to the Duke of Montrose. In fact, you're on the duke's land."

She'd come farther than she thought.

"Are you very certain they aren't my sheep?"

"Yes."

"Then by extension, you're not my employee."

He smiled. "Indeed, I'm not."

She'd sounded imperious and dictatorial, and in a few words this shepherd had made her feel small and petty.

"Will you move your sheep so that I can pass?"

He studied her for several long moments. She half expected

him to question her further. Instead, he took a few steps toward her, the dogs accompanying him. When she stiffened he stopped where he was.

"Are you afraid of all dogs or is it just these two?"

"Yours are sufficiently big to warrant some caution."

"You have the wrong impression of them. They're exceedingly gentle dogs."

To him, perhaps. They didn't look gentle to her.

She shook her head, remaining still. Maud had settled a little behind her, the mare acting as a living bulwark from the rest of the sheep.

The shepherd gave the dogs a command and they remained where they were as he approached her.

"Please make them go away."

He startled her by putting down the crook and knapsack on the road and moving behind her. When she glanced at him over her shoulder he only smiled once again.

"Trust me, Miss Eleanor Craig of Hearthmere."

Why should she? He was a stranger to her, one with some degree of arrogance.

When he put both hands on her waist she made a sound too much like a shriek. The dogs stood, ears alert.

"What are you doing?"

"I'm convincing you that they don't mean to harm you."

"But you do?"

"Don't be foolish," he said.

"Foolish? Please, let go of me."

"I shall, in just one moment. Sixty seconds, that's all I ask."

He was standing much too close and he still had his hands on her waist. They might have been dancing, except that she'd never seen this kind of pairing.

"Call them," he said.

"What?"

"Call the dogs. Peter and Paul. Call them."

"I'll do no such thing," she said. "Don't be ridiculous."

"They're waiting for your call."

She glanced at the two dogs. They hadn't looked away from her this whole time.

"I'm not going to call them. I want them to go away. I want *you* to go away. Please release me."

"You're shaking," he said, stepping back and dropping his hands. She turned.

"You're the most obnoxious man," she said.

"I've been called far worse, Miss Craig."

She ignored that remark. "Your dogs are vicious."

His laughter was insulting. "Only if you're after one of their sheep. Then I wouldn't want to tangle with Peter or Paul."

"They would be better named Terror and Intimidation."

"You haven't been around dogs very much, have you, Miss Craig?"

"Enough to know those that are well mannered and those that are not."

"Peter and Paul are extraordinarily well mannered, but they're working dogs. You can't have them sit on your lap and take treats from your lips."

"I don't want to have anything to do with them," she said.

His smile startled her again. Did he know how attractive he was when he smiled? She suspected he did, just as he was aware of his . . . Her thoughts ground to a halt. What was there about him? Something almost brutish, but that wasn't the word. She had the feeling that he was a fighter. A warrior. He reminded her of a Scot of old. She could almost see him in a kilt, his chest bare but for a swath of tartan. Instead of a crook, he might be holding a club or a sword, bloodied from recent battle.

This man, this warrior, might have wolves as companions, not appreciably different from the dogs that accompanied him now. Instead of sheep, clanspeople would be surrounding him, looking to him as their leader.

How ridiculous, to envision a shepherd as a leader of men. Or perhaps not so ridiculous after all, given what she'd learned in her two seasons. Men were sometimes like sheep, adhering to all sorts of societal rules that on the surface looked idiotic. Some men, however, chose to go their own way. Like this man might.

Which was Michael?

That thought had the effect of dousing her in cold water. How could she be wondering about another man when her fiancé should be uppermost in her mind?

Chapter Four

The shepherd startled her by reaching out and rubbing Maud's nose. The mare seemed to like his attention, behavior that struck Eleanor as peculiar since Maud was aloof with most people.

"She's a beautiful animal."

"She's from my father's stable," she said.

"Your father is a great judge of horseflesh."

"He was," she said. "Hearthmere horses are known all over the world."

He glanced at her, caught her gaze, and held it for a moment before she looked away. His eyes were brown, a warm brown that seemed to hold humor in their depths. Did he think the situation was amusing? No doubt he did. And her fear? Something else to ridicule.

"I've never been a horseman," he said, still stroking Maud. "I've never made the time."

She didn't mention that he hadn't the money to purchase a horse, being a shepherd. Besides, what would he need one for? His legs carried him well enough.

"I doubt your sheep would welcome the presence of a horse," she said. "And Peter and Paul no doubt would object."

She really shouldn't pay any attention to his smile. It had the effect of warming her from the inside out.

"What's her name?" he asked, his hand flattened on Maud's neck.

"Maud." Then, even though he hadn't asked, she filled in the rest of the story for him. "It's from the Tennyson poem," she said.

"Maud acts as if she's never seen sheep."

She really didn't want to have an amiable conversation with this man. Instead, she should leave, right this minute.

"She's exercised at home, in a small paddock."

He looked at her again. It was the confrontation, of course, that made her feel so very strange at that moment. Or the fact that she'd been warmed from her ride. That was the explanation for the rush of heat she suddenly felt.

"I didn't expect to meet a beautiful woman on an extraordinary-looking horse today."

How dare he say such things? It was the height of rudeness, yet at the same time she couldn't help but feel a tiny frisson of pleasure at his words. She certainly wasn't beautiful, and saying that was intentional flattery on his part, no doubt to accomplish something nefarious.

He whistled and the dogs moved. She held herself tight as they circled around her, one on each side. With deft nips here and there and a growl toward one enormous ewe, they separated the flock, leaving the road clear.

"Can I help you mount?"

She didn't turn toward his voice. It would be best if she didn't notice him at all.

"I suppose you could find a large enough rock if you walk far enough. Or a fence. However, I'd be more than happy to give you a leg up."

Even the man's conversation was scandalous. No one mentioned limbs in mixed company.

She glanced at him. As she watched, he linked his hands and bent toward her.

"Wouldn't this be easier?"

Yes, but she was torn between pride and an increasing sense of embarrassment. Still, accepting his help would be better than having him watch her walk Maud all the way home. Maud was too tall and the stirrup too high for her to mount without assistance.

She nodded to him and placed her foot in the cup of his hands. Standing close to him made him seem even taller and larger than before.

In seconds she was back in the saddle.

He moved to her side, and put his hand at the top of her boot, nearly on her leg. Her bare leg.

"I approve of your alteration," he said. "I've often thought that a lady's saddle was ludicrous in the extreme. Not to mention damn dangerous."

He moved closer to her, then raised his hand to encircle her wrist, almost as if he wanted to imprison her.

Looking down at him, she shook her wrist free.

"Will your rudeness know no limits, shepherd?"

"I'm not entirely certain, Miss Eleanor Craig of Hearthmere."

She didn't know what to say to that. This insufferable man had the ability to strip the words from her.

"You have no manners."

"Perhaps you could stay and lecture me on proper behavior," he said. "Or are you still too afraid of the dogs?"

"I was not afraid," she said, lying.

"Very well, you weren't afraid."

They looked at each other and it seemed like a hundred words or more passed between them, each one unspoken. A conversation of thoughts, perhaps, one filled with curiosity on his part and confusion on hers.

She would return home and banish any thought of the shepherd and this entire interlude. It would be like a dream, something she imagined. Or recalled later to wonder if it was real.

"Goodbye, Miss Eleanor Craig."

Never had she met a more irritating person in her life or a more confounding one. A shepherd who didn't speak as one. A man who complimented her too fulsomely and looked at her with admiring eyes. He'd touched her intimately and didn't look the least bit apologetic for doing so.

Instead of saying another word, she left him then, sending Maud galloping home, determined never to come this way again.

SHE WAS ANGRY at him and he couldn't blame her. Something in his nature had been awakened by the mysterious Miss Craig. He wanted to see what she was like beneath that facade of utter politeness. He'd never felt like goading a woman into rage before and the fact that he'd done so with her was a surprise.

He hadn't lied. She was beautiful, but he'd never been attracted to women of her sort. First of all, she wasn't a blonde and he was normally only attracted to blonde-haired women. Secondly, she'd evidently been reared with all those rules about decorum and civility. Granted, that had been his upbringing as well, but he'd found that it was sometimes better to roll in the mud than pretend the mud wasn't there. He liked scrappy people who said what they meant and meant what they said, who weren't afraid to let a few impolite words fly if it meant getting their point across. He liked sincerity and people who told the truth. Those like Miss Craig, however, hid behind all those rules and lessons.

She hadn't liked him touching her. He hadn't meant to, but her reaction—an instantaneous flare in her lovely blue eyes—had fascinated him. He'd rarely gotten that reaction in the past, but then, he wasn't known for teasing women.

He remembered the Craigs of Hearthmere. Archie Craig had died some years earlier. He must have been Eleanor's father. He'd heard something about the breeding farm, but he couldn't remember what now.

Eleanor. The name suited her. She looked like an Eleanor with her patrician features. He'd been surprised that she was riding astride at first. However, the more he observed her the more he realized how skilled she was. Eleanor was at home in the saddle, a great deal more than he was.

When she was standing beside her horse, however, he was much taller. She was the perfect height for him to bend and kiss her.

That thought made him smile. He couldn't help but wonder what the very proper Miss Eleanor Craig would have done if he'd swept her into his arms. No doubt she would have screamed or struck him. If nothing else, she would have probably lectured him about smelling of sheep.

Logan turned and made his way back up the hill, the dogs following. With a series of whistles, he gave them their commands.

She'd turned white at the idea of meeting Peter or Paul. The border collies were well trained and he hadn't lied to her. As long as she wasn't a threat to their sheep, they would welcome her as one of their friends.

In two days his secretary would come and he'd go back to London. He doubted that he'd see Miss Craig again. Strangely, that realization disappointed him. Yet he didn't have time for a woman in his life right now. He didn't even have time to speculate on a relationship.

A pity that. At another time, he might have pursued Miss Eleanor Craig, just to see those blue eyes snapping at him again.

Chapter Five

"Did you have an enjoyable morning, Miss Eleanor?"

Eleanor sighed, wishing she'd been able to slip up to her room before being seen by Mrs. Willett.

Clara Willett had been installed in her position as housekeeper by Eleanor's aunt, having been recommended by two friends. The fact that the woman, English by birth and inclination, had remained in an isolated house in Scotland was due to two things: she was paid extraordinarily well and she was in love with Mr. Contino. Eleanor couldn't help but know the first fact, since she oversaw the expenditures every quarter, but she wasn't supposed to know about the love affair.

One of the maids had passed that information along to her last year, and ever since, she'd noticed telltale signs of their relationship. Sometimes you don't see what's right in front of you until it's pointed out by someone else.

Mrs. Willett was one of those women whose age it would be difficult to pinpoint. Her hair was not quite blonde but was most definitely lighter than brown. Her face was full but not plump. Her eyes were her most commanding feature, being a pale blue. Her lips were almost always pursed just a little, as if afraid of giving the appearance of being accidentally pleased.

Her bosom was prominent and always covered in her dark blue housekeeper's uniform. Eleanor wasn't certain if it was something her aunt had started or a personal preference of Mrs. Willett, but the woman was never seen without her uniform with white cuffs and collar. Occasionally she wore a brooch and sometimes the collar was lace, but most of the time it was a serviceable cotton.

If the housekeeper and Mr. Contino were engaged in a torrid love affair—the nature of the relationship being shockingly passionate, according to the maid—it was done with the greatest discretion. The two didn't chase each other through the corridors of Hearthmere at midnight. When Mrs. Willett referred to Mr. Contino, which wasn't often, it was by his last name in the frostiest of tones. When he had occasion to comment on her, it was "the housekeeper." Everything was quite proper and aboveboard.

As long as Hearthmere was running smoothly and her father's horses were in excellent condition, Eleanor saw no reason to mention her knowledge to either of them.

"Yes, I did, thank you," she said now, wishing she didn't look so mussed. She'd curried Maud herself, half in apology for leading her through a sea of sheep. Her forbidden skirt had traces of dirt on its hem. She had the feeling, thus unproven, that Mrs. Willett sent her aunt letters during her month in Scotland, no doubt filled with information about what Eleanor had been doing and saying, changes she'd made, and clues she'd given about her future actions.

"Where does the Duke of Montrose's land begin?" Eleanor asked.

Her knowledge of Hearthmere's boundaries must be askew for her to have ventured onto the duke's land. Perhaps the question should be better asked of her steward, but he didn't live at Hearthmere, only came to the house once a month from Edinburgh.

"I'm not certain, Miss Eleanor. Is it important?"

Eleanor shook her head. "No," she said. "The duke employs an interesting shepherd. An exceedingly rude man."

"Old Ned?" The housekeeper's eyes widened.

"Old? I wouldn't call the man old, no."

"Old Ned has been around since I've been here, Miss Eleanor. He's getting on in years but you'll always see him on the glen with his dogs."

Maybe Old Ned had a son who had been acting in his stead today. Someone who needed to be educated in manners. Although she didn't suppose a shepherd interacted with people all that much. From what she'd seen of the man she'd encountered, it would be best for him to stay with sheep.

Still, the duke probably needed to know about the man's rudeness.

The Duke of Montrose's country house—or, as she'd heard it called, the ancestral seat—was not that far from Hearthmere. The duke was rarely in residence, however, preferring to live in Edinburgh. She'd never met the duke. Nor had he ever visited Hearthmere. Or, if he had, it was when she was a child. Perhaps she should ask Mr. Contino if her father had ever sold any of their horses to the duke.

Hamilton, who had several banker friends, once stated that the duke's family had a great deal of interest in the British East India Company with a resulting fortune that grew in size each year.

According to one of the maids who had a cousin who worked there, the duke's home was twice the size of Hearthmere. Yet there wasn't a large staff in residence. Only a handful of people maintained the whole of the property in the duke's absence.

She might have been able to cut down on the staff at Hearthmere if her father hadn't made promises to people who'd worked here for decades. In several situations, more than one generation had served the Craig family. How did you dismiss those people? You couldn't.

She left Mrs. Willett then, wondering if the woman would hurry to her office to write a missive to Eleanor's aunt.

Your niece went riding alone, without the company of a stable boy. If that were not shocking enough, she insisted on removing the saddle from her mare and grooming the animal herself. Not content with that behavior, she entered the house with windblown hair and cheeks reddened from the sun. It is all too obvious, Mrs. Richards, that your niece gives little thought to her appearance.

The housekeeper didn't need to send a letter to Deborah. Her aunt already knew each and every one of Eleanor's flaws. Occasionally she enumerated them, just in case Eleanor had forgotten. Eleanor wasn't nearly as graceful as Daphne, who was always immaculate despite the fact that she'd borne two children. Even her two toddlers were always neat and tidy, unlike the grubby urchin Eleanor had probably been. No doubt her children, when they came, would smell bad, have regrettable diaper accidents, and spit up their food when it was least expected.

Instead of returning to her room since she'd already been seen by the housekeeper and several maids, she began her walk through Hearthmere, a ritual she performed every time she came home. Four years now. Four years of coming back to Scotland, of wishing she never had to leave again, of planning ways she could return. Four years hadn't dampened the wish to live in her native country. Nor had all these years truly eased the loss of her father.

She began at the Clan Hall, the heart of the house. It was as it had always been, cavernous and echoing any footsteps on the stone floor. The arches overhead seemed almost cathedral-like, and in a sense the room was a place of worship. Not to God, but to the legacy of the Craigs. Here they were remembered. Not only her grandfather but his grandfather and scores of men before that. None of them were insignificant even though some names had been lost in the fog of history. They were all Craigs and as such would always be valued and honored.

She stood and walked to the window overlooking the river and pressed her fingers to a pane of wavy glass. Someone had taken the time to gouge their initials into the wood of the sill. When she asked her father why it had not been repaired after all these years, he only smiled.

"I was told that Mary, Queen of Scots, visited here when she was little more than a child."

"And those are her initials?" The writing was so ornate that she couldn't decipher it.

He nodded, his smile never dimming. "That's the tale. Whether or not you believe it is your choice. But no one has ever repaired the damage, just in case it might be true."

There were hundreds of places like that around Hearthmere, where long-dead people had made their mark of some sort or another, where history came alive and her own heritage was too powerful to ever ignore.

Today, however, she was experiencing a sense of sadness that seemed to hover like a cloud over her.

She made her way to the second floor, to a room at the end of the corridor. Pulling out a key from her pocket, she unlocked the door. She and a maid always dusted in here during her annual visit, but otherwise no one was allowed in this room. Her father had lovingly placed all those items of her mother's here. Her dresses hung in the armoire. The vanity was laden with the silver-backed brushes and mirror that had her initials inscribed on them. Bottles of perfume, some of them imported from France, sat in front of the mirror.

This room might be considered a shrine, but it had never been her mother's room and was only a repository for those things she'd liked or valued during her life. Eleanor didn't think her father had come here, but it was a place she often visited, as if becoming familiar with her mother's belongings would help her learn about the woman she'd never known.

Closing the door behind her, she went to the trunk at the end of the bed. Kneeling, she opened it and removed the tray containing her mother's stockings, corset covers, and shifts, putting it aside.

A moment later she pulled out a blue fabric-wrapped parcel. After replacing the tray, she closed the lid of the trunk. Carefully she unwrapped the blue fabric, revealing her mother's wedding dress. To her surprise, not a hint of yellow marred the silk fabric. It was still as brilliantly white as it must have been on the day her parents had married.

This was the dress she would wear to her own wedding.

Her father had once told her that it was better not to spend a lot of time looking back. Yet it was important not to look forward so much that you forgot to live today. He was always so firmly fixed in the day-to-day of his life, in breeding horses and raising her. She was lucky that she had a treasure trove of memories to recall.

She should take his advice. However, her father had never been faced with the prospect of marriage. Nor of knowing that once married she'd probably never be able to live at Hearthmere again. Michael had his own estate and, unfortunately, no love of Scotland. More than once she'd had to endure his lectures on how politically backward her country was.

Her father had been a true Scot and had loved Scotland and Hearthmere. He'd loved the land, too, and every time she rode out, she missed those rides with him. He'd showed her the tree where he'd marked his initials as a child, surprised that the mark was high above their heads now. He would point to a far off and hazy Ben Hagen, saying that they should go there one day and climb to the very top of the mountain.

She had known that she would eventually marry, but she'd always imagined a life in Scotland for herself. She and her husband would come back to Hearthmere often or even live here. The house would be a lodestone for her, a stabilizing influence.

Deborah had settled into life in London with barely a ripple, reacquainting herself with Hamilton, a wealthy widower. Everything had fallen into place for Deborah and even Daphne. Nor was Jeremy discomfited at all. He, too, had made his life in London, with side trips to Edinburgh from time to time to see his friends. She was the only one who hadn't made the transition well, looking back at Scotland as her home.

And now?

Now she had to face the future, whatever it was going to be.

Chapter Six

The next morning, Eleanor occupied herself with another chore, going over the previous year's expenditures.

"Miss Eleanor?"

She looked up from her father's desk to see the housekeeper standing in the middle of the doorway, a curious expression on her face. Putting aside one of the bills she was reading, she asked, "What is it, Mrs. Willett?"

With any luck, the woman didn't want to discuss menus again with her. Or the paucity of salmon this year. Since there wasn't a family to feed, it seemed like a great deal of trouble to worry about her meals. She just wished that the housekeeper would continue on with whatever she did when Eleanor wasn't here. The staff was well fed, and Cook certainly appeared that way. Therefore, someone was doing something right.

"We have a situation, Miss Eleanor. You've been given a present."

"A present? From whom?"

Jeremy was in Edinburgh. Not that he was likely to give her anything. The rest of her family was in London. None of them would be sending her something in Scotland.

"I haven't the slightest idea who could have brought me a present, Mrs. Willett."

"Regardless, Miss Eleanor," the woman said, "it's here. And it's causing quite a commotion in the kitchen. I would appreciate it if you would address the matter at your earliest convenience."

Before she could ask the housekeeper any further questions, Mrs. Willett disappeared from the doorway.

What on earth?

She heard the giggles long before she reached the kitchen. She couldn't imagine what kind of gift she'd been given, especially one that seemed to elicit such amusement.

In the kitchen the maids were excitedly talking, two of them on their knees.

She started to ask a question when something darted out between the legs of the chair and headed for her. It was a large black, tan, and white ball of cotton. It skidded to a stop directly in front of her, aimed for her shoe, and began to chew on her laces.

The puppy was inspiring a great deal of hilarity, even more so after he assaulted her footwear. Eleanor took a step back, but it was no use. The puppy followed her. When she turned to leave the kitchen, he was right there on her heels.

"It's like he knows you're his mistress, Miss Eleanor," one of the maids said.

This was her present? This?

She knew immediately who had gifted her with this rambunctious puppy. There was no mystery whatsoever. Reaching down, she picked up the puppy, tucked it under her arm and left the kitchen without a word.

Once in her bedroom, she put the puppy down and looked around for some way to contain him. He started gnawing on the leg of her vanity, but when she approached him, he stopped chewing long enough to look up at her. His expression was one of utter joy like he'd been transported to puppy heaven.

She picked him up and raised him to eye level.

"You're only going to be here for a little while," she said. "Until I can deliver you back to your benefactor. Until then, I would have you not chew on my furniture, please."

The puppy yipped at her, a tiny little bark that only hinted at what it might become.

How dare he give her a puppy. Who did he think he was?

She really was going to write the duke now. He needed to know that she did not appreciate his shepherd's attitude or actions. The man was a menace and now she would have to find a basket of some sort to put the puppy in so that she could transport him back to his original home.

The puppy was a roly-poly little thing, a bundle of soft fur with teeth. She put him down on the floor and he began biting at her shoes again.

"Stop that."

That didn't seem to work. She simply moved out of range of the puppy's teeth, which might have been successful if he hadn't grabbed the hem of her skirt and held on. When she took a step, the puppy growled and was dragged with her. She bent, retrieved him, and managed to get his teeth off her skirt.

"You have to stop chewing things," she said. Except that now he was gnawing on her fingers. His teeth were exceptionally sharp and when she pulled back her hand and said, "No!" he looked surprised.

No doubt he was like the shepherd—unused to being chastised.

"Until we return you to your proper place, I would appreciate it if you would have some kind of manners."

He barked at her. Not a tiny little yip this time but a full-throated bark. She put him down on the floor, moved to the armoire, and began to change her clothes.

Once dressed for riding, she turned to find the puppy relieving himself in the middle of the two-hundred-year-old chrysanthemum-patterned rug beside the vanity. She screamed, raced to his side, picked him up, and deposited him outside the door before ringing for a maid.

Ann had only been at Hearthmere for two years. She was very young, not more than seventeen Eleanor guessed, with a rangy body and light brown hair frizzing around her face. She was not a pretty girl, but she made up for it with a charming smile she used often. After a while, you didn't notice Ann's looks—you only paid attention to her pleasing character.

Eleanor told her what she needed. The girl nodded, retreating to get the requested articles.

The puppy still sat just outside the open door. Instead of escaping to other parts of the house, he looked like he was waiting to return.

"If you think you're coming back in here, you're mistaken," she said. "You belong in the stable. Or the barn. Not in my bedroom."

He barked at her again.

In a matter of moments, Ann was back with the items Eleanor needed. Plus, she'd found a round basket with a lid suitable for transporting the puppy back to the shepherd.

The sooner done, the sooner over. That's the way all distasteful tasks should be accomplished.

After she finished cleaning the rug alongside the maid—she felt partly responsible for the mess since she'd brought the puppy to her bedroom—Eleanor went to find the puppy and place him in the basket, only to find him asleep in a tight little ball just inside the doorway. When she picked him up, his head lolled sideways. He slitted open his eyes and gave a sleepy yawn, then licked her fingers. Gently she placed him into the basket and put it over her arm, grabbed her divided skirt with the other hand, and made her way down the stairs.

"I wasn't here, Miss Eleanor," the housekeeper said when questioned a few minutes later. "Sally was, however. Would you like to speak with her?"

"I would, thank you."

She remembered Sally from a few years earlier. The girl had been burned in a kitchen accident. The scar on her arm had been a source of embarrassment for the maid. The intervening years had evidently made a difference, because Sally greeted her with no hesitation, even though the scar was still visible.

"Of course I remember him, Miss Eleanor. A handsome man, he was, and him with the little puppy in his arms. That was a sight to see."

"Did he say anything to you, Sally?"

"Oh, yes, miss. Very polite he was. He went on about the pleasant day and asked about my family. I told him as how they live in the Bailthorne Village. My brother's a smith there. Him and my sister's husband."

Evidently, the shepherd had elicited more information from Sally than Eleanor had in all these years.

"Did he say anything about the puppy?"

The girl nodded. "That the little one was a gift. Something to get you over your fear, he was." Sally smiled, no doubt pleased to impart such news. "He said a great many nice things about you, too."

"Did he?"

"Yes, miss. That you were beautiful and had a voice like a mother's lullaby."

"A mother's lullaby?" She felt herself warm.

"Yes, miss."

"But all he said about the puppy was that it was a gift?"

The shepherd was the only person with the temerity to do something like this.

"Did he give you no other information, Sally?"

"No, miss."

Yet he'd taken the time to tell the maid that she had a voice like a mother's lullaby. What, exactly, did that mean?

"Thank you, Sally," Eleanor said, picking up the puppy and heading for the stable.

Maud was skittish, but that might have something to do with the dark clouds on the horizon. Many of the horses at Hearthmere were high-strung and didn't like storms.

She gauged the distance versus the sky and thought that she'd have plenty of time to reach the shepherd, hand over the puppy, and return to the stable before the storm arrived. Or, it might do as storms sometimes did, veer to the east or west and miss them entirely.

The sheep weren't on the road now. Instead, they were contentedly grazing on the slope of the glen. She stopped almost exactly where she had yesterday morning, but the figure on the hill didn't descend. Nor did the dogs.

Finally, tired of waiting, she raised her arm and waved, hoping the shepherd would see her and know that she wanted to speak to him. Otherwise, she would have to take Maud up the hill, which could be dangerous for the mare. Or leave Maud on the road and climb the hill herself.

She raised her arm again. She knew that he'd seen her, but the irritating man didn't come down.

The stable boy had handed the basket up to her once she was mounted. Now she didn't know how to handle the puppy while she dismounted. She was too high to simply drop the basket.

The shepherd had a great deal to answer for. She had a few thoughts about an apt punishment as she tied the reins to the basket handle before wrapping them around the pommel. Once she dismounted she untied the basket.

She would have to climb the hill with the puppy. The least the shepherd could have done was make this easier for her, but of course he knew what she was going to do. He didn't want his gift returned.

That was unfortunate, because she had every intention of doing exactly that. You didn't simply leave a puppy with someone, especially when that person didn't care for dogs. There was a reason for her antipathy, but she wasn't going to share it with him. All she was going to do was hand over the basket, turn, and walk away.

There wasn't any reason to exchange a word with the annoying man.

Chapter Seven

A rumble of thunder had her glancing toward the sky. The storm clouds were approaching a little faster now. If she didn't hurry, the storm was going to be on top of them before she returned Maud to the stable.

The distance to the top of the hill was a little farther than it looked. The puppy kept peeking his head out of the top of the basket and she had to coax him back inside.

"I'm sure you're a very nice puppy," she said, halfway up the hill. "I'm sure you'll be a good companion to someone. It won't be me, however. I don't like dogs, you see."

He only whined in response, which was understandable, especially if you got the gist of what she was saying. She didn't suppose she would like it if someone talked badly about her species. In a way, people did, all the time. Scottish women were sometimes portrayed as fishwives in English newspapers. As if they alone were responsible for every political decision made in Scotland. As if Scottish men were under the thumbs of their wives. Nothing could be further from the truth, but that didn't stop the newspapers from featuring their unflattering cartoons.

Finally she was at the top of the hill, and for just a moment she turned to survey the view. She might choose to be a shepherd if it meant witnessing such beauty every day. The only companions were the sheep. Perhaps after a few hours she would become accustomed to the various sounds they made.

Turning, she looked for the shepherd, but he had disappeared. What kind of game was this idiotic man playing?

The clouds were darkening and growing closer, blown across the sky by a fierce September wind. If she didn't hurry, she and Maud were going to be drenched and that would certainly anger Mr. Contino. As far as he was concerned, the horses came first. If anyone forgot that lesson they were the target of his temper. She wasn't exempt, despite being his employer.

She didn't know the shepherd's name and didn't want to call out, *Shepherd!* Besides, she wasn't sure he would hear her over the sheep's increasingly loud complaints. Did sheep fare well in the rain? How strange that she didn't know. She hadn't made an effort to seek out Hearthmere's flock or even their shepherd.

She pushed her way through the sheep, finding some of them quite willing to give way. Others, like the one that blocked her path, were prepared to be obstinate. Were sheep always difficult to manage?

"What are you about?"

She turned to find that the owner of the voice was an older man wearing a long, dark brown coat, something that reminded her of a monk's habit, but open in the front. He planted his crook in the earth and eyed her with a frown, his wrinkled face bearing witness to years—if not decades—out in the elements.

The dogs at his side were the same ones that had frightened her before. Peter and Paul, unlikely names for vicious beasts.

"Are you Old Ned?" she asked, since he resembled her housekeeper's description.

"Aye, that I am."

She hadn't heard such a thick brogue since her father died, and it took a minute for her mind to translate the words into some semblance of English. She'd let her knowledge of Gaelic fade through the years or she would have asked him a question in that language.

"I'm looking for the other shepherd," she said.

"There is no other but me."

"Of course there is," she said. "The younger man." The handsome one. The annoying one.

"There is no other but me," he repeated.

"That can't be right."

"Aye, it is."

The first raindrops began to fall, large splattering drops that hinted that the clouds would soon release a deluge.

The puppy took that opportunity to pop out of the basket again.

Eleanor put her hand over his head to shield him from the rain and coax him back inside the shelter of the basket.

"I've come to return his puppy to him."

The man glanced around as if looking for someone. "You'll not see anyone but me here."

"He has to be here," she said. "I've come to return his puppy."

"I've no use for a puppy."

Nor was she going to leave the animal with him. The poor thing would likely be trampled beneath the hooves of the suddenly milling sheep. Thunder rumbled overhead and it disturbed them, enough that they were beginning to move of their own accord.

The shepherd began to whistle at his dogs.

"You'll be going, I'm thinking, else you'll be missing your horse next."

He was right. She glanced over her shoulder to find that Maud had started walking down the road. The mare was all for finding the stable on her own.

The rain was falling in earnest now, drenching her in minutes. She made it down the hill and to Maud's side, realizing that she didn't have the shepherd's help this time to mount. Rather than fuss about it, she simply grabbed Maud's reins and began to walk, the whole time rehearsing what she would say to the owner of the puppy when she found him. The puppy himself was curled into a tight ball in the bottom of the basket, sleeping, and sheltered from the worst of the rain.

She hadn't imagined Mr. Contino's ire, but by the time she made it back home she was beyond caring. The rain had stopped by the time she reached Hearthmere, but the storm had already done its worst. Eleanor didn't think she'd ever been as wet as she was right at the moment. Even her undergarments were drenched and she squished when she walked. Her shoes were probably ruined.

Two stable boys rushed out to help her, but they cared more about removing Maud's saddle and rubbing her down than anything else. She didn't even bother explaining to the stable master what had happened as she surrendered Maud's reins.

The puppy, refreshed from his nap, popped up out of the basket, looking around with interest. He whined at her, which meant something, she was sure.

"That's a cute one he is," one of the stable boys said.

She nodded. "And a great deal of trouble."

"If you want, I'll take him off your hands, miss."

The offer took her aback. So, too, did her instantaneous response. "Thank you," she said, "but he's my responsibility now."

She walked out of the stable, bemused. How odd that she'd found it impossible to turn over the puppy to the care of the stable boy. But she didn't know the boy well. Did he have a cruel nature? How would he treat the dog?

Like it or not, she hadn't lied. She was responsible for the puppy, at least until she could find the mysterious shepherd and return him.

How dare the man simply disappear, especially after he'd complicated her life.

The puppy chose that moment to bark at her again. One solitary bark that had her stopping on the path. Placing the basket on the gravel, she opened the top, scooped the puppy out, and let him gambol on the wet grass. She would have to dry him off, but at least he might not have an accident on the rugs.

A little while later Eleanor had changed her clothes and made the puppy a little corral in her bedroom, arranging her hat boxes, trunk, and vanity bench around an area that had been stripped of any carpet. Instead, she had Ann go to the stable for some hay, which she'd liberally sprinkled on the floor. Eleanor reasoned that it would be easier to remove the hay if the puppy soiled it than refinish the floor.

There was only one problem. She had to feed him. It was Ann who gave her that idea.

"Oats, miss. That's what we always fed our dogs."

"Oats?"

Ann nodded. "At least when they're first weaned. This little mite doesn't look to be much older than that. We always gave them a little meat and a few carrots, too, but that can wait until tomorrow."

Eleanor summoned oats from the kitchen, along with a bowl of water for the puppy. After he made swift work of his food, she took the puppy back out to the yard, advice Ann had given her.

"We've had dogs all my life, miss," the girl said.

"While I never have."

Ann looked at her strangely, but Eleanor didn't elaborate. She couldn't tell the story without sounding as if she were asking for pity.

"If you'd like, miss, I could take the puppy and keep him in my room."

"I doubt Mrs. Willett would approve," Eleanor said. "No, I'll keep him here. At least until I can give him back."

Once again she got a quick look from the maid, but didn't explain.

Seated in her reading chair by the window, she watched as the puppy twirled in circles before finally settling down in one spot on the hay. Despite the admonition she'd given herself to feel absolutely nothing for the animal, she got up, went to the bottom drawer of her dresser, and pulled out an old cotton nightgown she'd worn as a young girl. She arranged that in a little mound, then put the sleeping puppy on it. Within seconds he'd settled in again, the deep sigh he gave reassuring her that the nightgown was a bit more comfortable than the hay.

"I have to think of something to call you," she said. "At least until you go back. I can't keep calling you Puppy. Or Dog. Perhaps something to remind me of your owner. Rude. Mr. Disdainful. Handsome Irritant." The puppy sighed again. "Very well, that's not fair, is it? After all, you haven't done anything. Maximillian. That's a very grand sounding name, isn't it? Max for short."

The puppy opened one eye and seemed to shake his head before descending into sleep again.

"No? Not Max?"

How silly she was to think that he disapproved of the name. She tried it out. "Max."

The puppy put one pudgy paw over his eyes.

"All right. Not Max. It should be a Scottish name, though, because you're a Scottish dog. If I'm not mistaken, you're part border collie, and they're supposed to mind Scottish sheep."

The puppy didn't respond.

"Bruce."

The puppy yawned.

"Bruce is a very Scottish name with a great heritage. I think I should call you Bruce."

The puppy yawned again.

"Bruce it is, but only until I find your owner."

Where had the man disappeared to? After the weather cleared she'd return to the glen and have another conversation with the shepherd. Surely he knew who had minded his sheep the day before. Would he refuse to tell her and, if so, why?

With those decisions made, she sat in the reading chair and watched the puppy for a while, telling herself the whole time that all baby animals were charming. No doubt she'd feel the same about lambs and she was sure she didn't like sheep all that much. There was no reason whatsoever to smile about a puppy's antics or feel protective of him.

The shepherd had a great deal to answer for and she would make sure he knew exactly what she thought.

As soon as she found him.

Irritating man.

Chapter Eight

$\mathcal{I}$t was the stable boy who told her about the stranger the next day.

"Mrs. McElwee said that he had a way about him, miss. Gave her a smile, he did, and made her think of her own young and wild days. Her words, miss, not mine." The stable boy had ducked his head down as if that would hide his smile.

"A stranger?"

"Yes, miss. Keeps to himself, though, and hasn't been seen in the village. But Mrs. McElwee saw him walking down the road toward the village."

"Did she?"

Mrs. McElwee had always been the source of information about the area, ever since Eleanor was a little girl. If anything happened around Hearthmere, Mrs. McElwee was sure to know it.

A stranger? Could he have been playing at being a shepherd the other day?

"What else did Mrs. McElwee tell you, Robbie?"

"That he's been staying in the duke's cottage, miss. The one the shepherd uses when he's not with the sheep."

"Has he? Where is this cottage?"

Robbie, thankfully, was filled with information about that, too. Once she mounted, she had the stable boy hand up the basket. Bruce was refusing to stay inside, and popped his head out to see what was happening around him. How could anyone stay angry at that face?

Armed with directions, she set out to find the man.

At least the afternoon was a fair one, with not a hint of clouds in the sky. The wind was little more than a breeze, brushing back the tendrils of hair from her face, making the puppy's ears sit up straight.

Bruce had kept her up the night before. At first she thought something was terribly wrong because of his plaintive whining. She had checked him carefully to ensure that he had no injuries. Finally she decided that the only reason he was crying was that he must miss his mother.

"There is nothing I can do about that," she told him.

When he jumped up on her bed she was startled. However, since his whining stopped, she let him stay. It was a curious sensation, sleeping with an animal. She had never done so before. He was a very warm, soft little bundle of fur who insisted on being right next to her no matter what position she took. She kept waking when he moved.

He had found one of her shoes this morning and had sicced himself on it like it was a bone. When she'd admonished him and taken away the damaged shoe, he hadn't looked the least bit chagrined. He'd only gone after the other one.

She wasn't entirely certain that he was eating properly. She had fed him twice, once last night and then this morning, but was that enough? The puppy hadn't come with any instructions.

No, the shepherd simply must take Bruce back. He must miss his littermates and his mother. Poor thing, to be taken away at such a young age. How young were puppies when they were separated from their families? She didn't know the answer to that question, either.

Maud had a lovely gait at a modest trot. The mare seemed relieved not to have anything to do with the sheep today, too, if the toss of her head was any indication. Riding with the puppy was not as easy as Eleanor had hoped. Maud was evidently not in favor of dogs, either. The puppy, however, was becoming used to his transport in a basket. He sat with his head up, surveying everything he saw. From time to time he would bark at something that captured his attention.

As they reached the crest of a hill, she saw the river before them as well as a cottage sitting like a mushroom on the landscape. Bruce subsided a few minutes later and curled into a sleepy ball at the bottom of the basket. Eleanor kept the cover open so she could keep an eye on the puppy.

There was smoke coming from the chimney, which meant that someone was home.

She really shouldn't be feeling any type of excitement. She was simply returning Bruce, that's all. Besides, the stranger might not be the person she sought after all.

Once at the cottage she moved to the mounting block, leaned over, and put the basket with the sleeping puppy down, then slid off Maud's back. She wrapped the reins around a small post located there, picked up the basket, and made her way down the gravel path to the cottage door.

Her knock on the door was answered but she couldn't understand the words. Was he saying to go away or come in? She pushed down the latch and opened the door slowly.

"Hello?"

The puppy chose that moment to bark. She glanced down to find that he had awakened and was viewing the world with his customary air of expectancy.

Should she take him outside first?

Suddenly she was face-to-face with the shepherd. Or the man who'd pretended to be the shepherd. If anything, he'd grown more handsome since she'd seen him last. His hair was still unruly, however, as if he had thrust his fingers through it. He stood there, attired in clothing not appreciably different from what he'd worn two days ago, but without the blood. There was an ink stain on his sleeve. One hand held the door while the other clutched a sheaf of papers.

"Where are the sheep?" she asked.

"They're being tended to," he said. "Is that what you've come to ask? I didn't see you as someone who loved sheep, Miss Craig."

"I just thought a shepherd tended to his sheep," she said. "Not papers."

"Am I to infer that you think shepherds can't read? Or write?"

That sounded rather priggish, didn't it?

"No, of course not. What you do with your time is not my business. I'm here about something that is my concern, however."

She thrust the basket at him. Bruce sat there, tongue lolling out, looking as happy as any creature she'd ever seen.

When the shepherd didn't reach out to take the basket, she pushed it against his chest.

"How dare you give me a puppy. I don't like dogs."

"You don't like Peter and Paul, but I thought you might feel differently about a puppy."

"You can't simply make choices for people you don't know."

"You're right. I can't. Yet you reminded me of a little boy who felt the same way about dogs until his uncle gave him a puppy one day. The puppy needed a friend and so did the boy."

He could not charm her. She wouldn't allow it. "I don't need a friend."

"Have you so many, then?" he asked with a smile. "Can't you use one more?"

"I don't like dogs," she repeated.

"Neither did the little boy, but he decided, after a while, that perhaps they weren't so bad. The puppy had already decided, you see, that the boy would be his forever."

He put the papers down and took the basket finally, smiling at Bruce and ruffling his ears. "And he was, for many years."

"Are you talking about yourself?"

"I am indeed. This little guy needed a home. I thought you might give him one."

"You made a great many assumptions."

"I agree. I did. Forgive me for that. I simply saw you as a kind person."

"I am a kind person," she said, irritated that he made her sound terrible.

"Who doesn't like dogs."

"Who are you? Don't try to tell me you're a shepherd. I don't believe it."

"Why not?"

She stared at him. "What do you mean, why not?"

"I think I made an adequate shepherd, Miss Craig. I moved the sheep where I was told to move them. I didn't suffer any losses. The dogs obeyed me. Why don't you believe I'm a shepherd?"

"Well, are you?" she asked, frowning at him.

"While I think the occupation is an honorable one, I am not."

"Then who are you?"

"My name is Logan," he said. "Logan McKnight. At the moment I'm a guest of Old Ned."

She took a step back, wishing she knew what to say in response. She should simply leave now while she had the illusion of winning this confrontation.

"Can I offer you some tea, Miss Craig?"

She stared at him. Tea? She should march out of here right this minute and consider herself fortunate not to have to encounter him again.

"Yes," she heard herself saying. "That would be lovely."

Had she lost her mind?

Perhaps she wanted to solve the mystery of who, exactly, he was. He hadn't provided that information. However, it might be considered improper for her to be alone with any man, especially in an isolated cottage. After all, she was engaged to be married.

The thought didn't cause her to gather up her skirt, say something cutting, and leave the cottage. Instead, all she did was step to the side so that Logan could close the door.

They were standing in what looked like the front room, with three doors leading to other rooms, one of them the kitchen. She was surprised at how spacious the cottage was since from the outside it had looked snug and compact.

A set of traps rested in the corner. A bookcase filled with objects rather than books was beside a sagging sofa. The floor was covered with a faded rug that clashed with the flowered curtains. Everything about the cottage was clean but threadbare.

Logan struck her as the kind of person who would not be concerned with furnishings or clothing. However, he was elegant in a way she couldn't explain. The cottage didn't fit him.

"You don't live here, do you?" she asked, her gaze coming back to him.

He hadn't moved, but was still looking at her intently. "Why would you say that?" he asked, retrieving the puppy from the basket.

After opening the cottage door, he stepped outside and deposited the puppy on the ground, where Bruce sniffed the grass, a few rocks, and a thistle or two before finally doing what he was supposed to. Looking up at Logan, he gave a happy little bark, then followed him back into the cottage.

"Please be seated," Logan said, gesturing toward the sofa.

She took the opposite chair instead, since it looked easier to get out of once seated.

He scooped up the puppy and plunked him down in Eleanor's lap.

"I can't . . ." she began, but it was too late; he had already left the room. She and Bruce looked at each other a moment before he yawned once more, circled twice, then made a tight ball of himself and fell asleep.

There was no reason she shouldn't put him down on the carpet. It was worn and faded, but otherwise looked comfortable. He could just as easily fall asleep there as on her lap.

One hand went to his back, her fingers stroking through the puppy's thick fur. He made a sound like a sigh. That was certainly no reason to feel a spike of surprise or even pleasure. She hadn't done anything, merely placed her hand on him, but it was the first time she'd done so with affection.

No, she was not going to feel anything for the animal. She had returned him to his rightful owner, whether he was a shepherd or not. Bruce seemed very contented, however, as if this was the spot he wanted to be above all others.

She sat there for a number of minutes, wondering if Logan was ever coming back. Just when she had decided to put the puppy down on the carpet and seek him out, he entered the room again.

"It's a temperamental stove. I've yet to figure it out," he said, placing a teapot and two cups down on the table in front of her. "There's no tray, either," he added, retreating to the kitchen and returning with a jug of cream and a sugar bowl. Both were chipped, as were the cups.

She didn't suppose it mattered. She'd never taken tea in a chipped cup, but she wasn't about to say that to him. He was acting the host and even though it was obvious he didn't live here, she wouldn't embarrass him by being a rude guest.

"You never answered me," she said. "You don't live here, do you?"

"Nor did you answer me. Why would you say that?"

"The cottage doesn't seem to fit you," she said, feeling a little ridiculous by saying something so odd.

"Doesn't it?"

"No," she said.

She took the cup he'd poured, and added some sugar to it. He excused himself once more and returned with two spoons, one for her and one for himself. His tea was doctored with cream and a good bit of sugar.

It was a strange experience, holding the cup and saucer while Bruce was still on her lap.

"Why not?" he asked. "What about the cottage doesn't seem to fit me, exactly?"

She had the curious thought that he truly wanted to know, that her opinion was important.

After glancing down at the stack of books beside the chair, she answered him. "You would have put your chair beside the window where there's better light," she said. "Instead of in the corner there. Your sofa would be more comfortable and so would this chair. Your china wouldn't have chips."

"I could have fallen on hard times," he said, his smile nowhere in evidence. Instead, there was that curious, intent look in his eyes as if he were studying her. What did he see?

She was too much a coward to ask. She had the feeling he would tell her the truth and she wasn't sure she was ready for that much honesty.

"I hope you like the tea. It's from a small shop in London."

Another piece of the mystery. He lived in London, then, but he was a Scot. That was evident from his speech. What shepherd traveled to London? Or perhaps she was misjudging shepherds as a group. She knew little about sheep and even less about shepherds. She was often annoyed by her aunt's friends who decreed certain things, some of them about her, without any knowledge whatsoever. Here she was, doing the exact same thing.

"It's a blend from India, made to my own specifications. I spent some time there, but not recently."

"Who are you?"

"A friend of the duke's," he said. "Who so kindly allowed me to become someone else for a few days. A shepherd, in this instance."

The tea was excellent and when she said as much, he smiled.

"Why would you want to become someone else? Was being yourself too onerous?"

She was tiptoeing right next to the line between good manners and rudeness. Still, he had opened the door to the current topic of conversation. She had simply walked into that room.

"Yes," he said, surprising her. "Have you heard of the Battle of Magdala?"

She nodded slowly. She'd read reports of it in the newspapers, one of which she read each day. Her father had insisted upon it.

His words still resonated in her memory. *Granted, Eleanor, you may not think that the world impacts your life, but it does in significant ways. It would be wise for you to be aware of it.*

"Mr. Disraeli seemed to think it was a moral victory," she said.

A look of surprise flashed over his face and was gone in an instant.

Normally, she pretended an ignorance she didn't possess, especially around men. With him, however, there was no such restraint. If he'd pretended to be someone else for a few days, so could she. Here, in this little cottage in the Highlands of Scotland, she could be Eleanor Craig, herself.

Chapter Nine

"How did you know about Disraeli?"

"I read at least one newspaper every day," she said. "It's something my father insisted on."

"A wise man, your father."

"Do you really think so? Or are you only saying that because it's something polite to say?"

"Most people don't accuse me of excessive tact, Miss Craig. I normally say exactly what I think, and I have in this instance as well."

"Were you at the Battle of Magdala?"

"I was."

That's all he said. Just two words. She had the impression that if she questioned him further he wouldn't answer.

Still, she felt compelled to say something. "So, you were a soldier."

"Of a sort," he said.

What did that mean? The longer they talked the more confused she became. She had a feeling that he did it on purpose in order to confound her.

The puppy finally woke, stretching, then decided to chew on the fabric of her skirt.

"Stop that, Bruce," she said.

"Bruce?"

She nodded. "It seemed to fit him."

He regarded the puppy for a moment. "You're right. It does."

When Bruce didn't stop chewing she gently put him on the carpet, which meant that he attacked her shoes next.

"See? He already has an affinity for you."

"I'm not prepared to raise a puppy," she said, wishing she had a distraction. Something, anything to get Bruce's attention away from her shoes.

"What happened?" he asked. "Why are you so afraid of dogs?"

He really did have a great deal of effrontery. Nothing stopped him from saying whatever he wished, including asking intrusive questions.

She hadn't intended to tell him, but she heard the story tumbling from her lips.

"I was reading," she said. "I was eight years old and my father was busy with a meeting at the stables. I grabbed one of my favorite books and went into the garden. There's an old tree there that I liked to sit under so that's what I was doing."

Everything about that spring day was stark and memorable. She recalled how the wind blew the hair onto her face. The sun was bright, filtering through the leaves and casting islands of light around her. She was wearing a yellow pinafore with a white apron and she'd already gotten the bottom of her apron soiled. It didn't matter; her father would forgive her such a little sin. In minutes she was occupied with the story she was reading, a tale of a magical prince and a princess in hiding.

Something had disturbed her. A sound, a movement, something that made her look up. There he was, a large brown dog with a black face. He was walking toward her, but something was wrong with his legs. He moved like a spider, not a dog. There was something wrong with his face, too. It looked swollen and he was drooling too much.

"Don't move, Eleanor."

She was so afraid that she didn't even turn to look at her father. The dog approached her slowly, growling, his mouth open and his fangs showing. She knew something was terribly wrong because of his eyes. They looked strange, as if he'd suddenly gone blind.

Any second now the dog was going to reach her.

"Close your eyes, Eleanor," her father said.

Up until this point, she'd been obedient. Anything her father wanted her to do she'd done without complaint. On this sunny afternoon, however, she was too afraid to close her eyes for fear that the dog would jump on her. Her eight-year-old mind told her that if she kept her eyes fixed on him she could will him away.

The gunshot was so loud that it sounded like it had gone through her right ear. The dog's head disappeared in a spray of blood.

Her father gathered her up in his arms, turning her face so she couldn't see the sight. Yet she'd seen enough. Nor had she ever been able to forget it, even after all these years. She could still recall the terrible cold fear that chilled her insides and made her feet and hands feel like ice.

Now she looked down at her intertwined fingers. "I didn't realize until the other day that we've never had dogs at Hearthmere."

He didn't say anything. Nor did he launch into a persuasive lecture on how that experience had nothing to do with the border collies or even Bruce. All he did was place his cup and saucer on the table between them.

"Death is one of those things that makes an indelible impression," he finally said. "I don't think I'll ever forget the sight of my first dead body. It didn't matter that the man was an enemy or that he wanted to kill me. He was dead and all the hope of his life was gone."

"I hardly think that the death of the dog and that of a human being are similar."

"The beings aren't, of course. Death is. Death isn't simply the absence of life. It's a presence of something malevolent. It's an overwhelming force."

She remembered the newspaper accounts of the Battle of Magdala. If he had been there, he'd seen a great many people die.

"That's a terrible thing to have happen to you when you were a child. I still think it's a pity, however, that we judge things so harshly."

When he didn't say anything further, she finished her tea, placed her cup next to his, and sat back.

She would not ask him what he meant. That's exactly what he wanted her to do. Instead, she would simply wait him out. She wasn't at all patient, but she was sometimes stubborn.

"I met an Abyssinian," he said. "An interesting man, someone who offered me water when I was thirsty. He was just like all the men who had fought us earlier. Part of me wanted to judge him like his countrymen, but he hadn't tried to kill me. I saw him as a human being just like me, separate and apart from his nationality. I thanked him for the water and when I would have paid him for it, he shook his head and walked away."

"So I should accept Bruce because he isn't like that rabid dog, is that it?"

"It seems foolish to judge him based on the behavior of a totally different animal. Wouldn't you agree?"

"Why do you care?" she asked. "Why does it matter to you what I think?"

"The easy answer is because you're afraid. I know the emotion well and I would spare you that."

"And the hard answer?"

"I haven't the slightest idea why, other than that you're a fascinating woman."

No one had ever called her fascinating. They didn't refer to her as a woman often, either. She'd felt like a girl for most of her life, unformed, unfinished, and unprepared.

"One with a voice like a mother's lullaby."

He smiled at her and the expression had a glint of mischief to it. "A silly thing to say, wasn't it? However, I wanted to try to describe your voice and that's the first thing I thought of. It makes you think of family and home and good things."

She felt her face warm. No one had ever said anything like that to her, either.

They exchanged a long look. She didn't know what he saw

when he viewed her. Was it a foolish woman, held motionless in time because of an event decades old?

"Is there something inherently wrong with being afraid?" she asked. "Must you banish fear or find some way around it all the time? It seems to me that fear is good in some instances. It keeps you safe. It gives you a warning. It urges you to be wary of your surroundings."

"Fear is not simply a sign of weakness to me. It's an indication that I believe I'm not strong enough for what I must face. Or that I've already lost the battle. Perhaps fear has its place, but it doesn't serve you well when you nourish it for a long time. Or when you hold it close and reinforce it with memory and a reluctance to challenge it. I suspect that you've held on to your fear of dogs to the point that it's almost fossilized. I also think that, given the chance, you wouldn't continue to feel that way. Most of us get in the habit of thinking or acting in a certain way because it's simpler than changing."

She'd never been spoken to in such a way. Not even by her aunt when Deborah was extremely annoyed. Eleanor couldn't decide whether she was hurt or angry or strangely admiring of Logan McKnight's courage for speaking honestly. She had a feeling that he said what he thought to anyone.

She'd never done that. In fact, there were whole days that went by when she realized she hadn't been truly honest to anyone. If she awakened with a headache, she nevertheless told everyone at breakfast that she was feeling fine. If she thought the blood sausage was ghastly, she ate it nonetheless. If her aunt and cousin gushed over a new pattern the seamstress brought and Eleanor thought the dress was a horror, she never said anything. Everything about her life was one white lie after another.

The only time she felt like she was truly herself was here in Scotland.

"You don't know me, Mr. McKnight. You have no idea who I am. You have simply taken a situation and blown it up in your mind to be whatever you wanted it to be. That's hardly fair. Nor is it correct."

"Then you're not afraid of dogs, is that it?"

He was making her choices easy for her. She was trending toward anger, not hurt. Any admiration she might have felt for him minutes earlier was rapidly dissipating.

"It doesn't matter what I am or what I feel. You had no business simply dropping a puppy off at my house."

"You're right," he said. "I didn't. In fact, I took a very great chance that you weren't the kind of person who would cause him any hurt."

Now she was truly annoyed. "Of course I wouldn't."

"Even though you think dogs are the devil's companions?"

"I don't think any such thing. Don't be ridiculous."

"Still, I'm pleased to discover that you seem to be a kind person."

"Of course I am."

"There is no *of course* about it, Miss Craig. The world is filled with people who are not nice or kind. I'm gratified that you aren't one of those, but then, I couldn't imagine you being anything but gentle, sweet, and caring."

He really shouldn't say those things to her. She was about to tell him so when she heard Bruce growl. Looking down, she realized that he'd grabbed the fabric of her skirt between his teeth again and was now playing tug-of-war with it.

Sighing heavily, she bent and extracted the fabric from his mouth.

"You really are in a better position to care for him than I am," she said, standing. "And to do so without any fear, real or imagined."

He didn't stand when she did, which was rudeness in itself.

"Eleanor, I didn't mean to anger you. Or hurt you. My motive was to help."

He shouldn't use her given name, either. It was too personal, almost intimate.

"You assume a great deal, Mr. McKnight. More than you've any right to. As I said, you don't know me."

"Does anyone?"

She stared at him.

"I would bet, Miss Craig, that you keep yourself well insulated from others. Perhaps for fear that they might discern how much of a sham you truly are."

If she'd had something handy and breakable she would have thrown it at him.

"How dare you say something like that. How dare you examine my character and find it so wanting."

"On the contrary, I don't find it wanting at all. You're a fascinating woman. A mystery, I might even say. I believe that you have depths few people realize. Perhaps even you. I would also wager that you're as constrained as any woman I've ever known. You really should allow yourself to be yourself, Eleanor."

"You should thank Providence, Mr. McKnight, that I am constraining myself at this moment. Otherwise, I do believe that I would cosh you on the head with something hard."

"That's a sentiment that's been repeated often in my presence."

"No doubt," she said, heading for the door. Unfortunately, the puppy followed her.

"See? What did I tell you about an affinity? He's already developed an affection for you. Do you have that same effect on all males?"

She glanced at him to find him smiling at her.

If she'd had an umbrella she would've poked him right between the eyes.

She really didn't like this man. She didn't dislike sparring with him, but she did dislike how much she was enjoying it. What a vile creature he was to incite her fury like that and then sit there and smile.

Not just smile, but give her an understanding look as if he knew exactly what she was feeling.

He had as much as called her repressed, some kind of boxed in creature who never revealed her emotions. There were plenty of times when she did so.

He finally stood and followed her to the door. She wished he'd stayed where he was, some distance away.

"Does no one ever talk to you?" he asked, coming to stand much too close.

"Of course people talk to me. What a ridiculous thing to say."

"Not about what a lovely day it is, Eleanor. Or how pretty your hair looks today, but directly to you. Of thoughts and feelings, perhaps. Of ideas, great and small."

Thoughts and feelings? Those were better kept to oneself. Ideas were the province of men. At least, that's what her aunt had always told her.

He bent and picked up the puppy who decided that he would occupy himself bathing McKnight's face with kisses. All he did was smile down at Bruce.

"Reveal yourself, Eleanor. Show the world who you are. Don't hide yourself from anyone, however much you might fear their words."

He really was the most despicable man. Now was the perfect time to bring up Michael, but Michael had no place in this conversation.

What a strange and shocking thought.

No more shocking than what Logan did next. He drew even closer, reached out with one hand and placed it on the back of her neck. Without warning, he bent and kissed her.

It was a sweet, affectionate kiss, holding hints of more. When he pulled back he was still smiling, the puppy curled into the crook of his arm.

She turned, feeling her face flame as she left the cottage. He didn't call after her or try to stop her from leaving. Not one word passed between them, neither explanation nor apology. Or, on her side, a condemnation for the unwelcome kiss.

By the time she reached Maud she was nearly running. She didn't know who she was fleeing: him or herself.

Chapter Ten

$\mathcal{E}$leanor had hoped to get an early start riding the next morning. Unfortunately, one thing or another took precedence, including her aunt's letter. Deborah must have posted it a day after Eleanor had left.

Her aunt giddily explained that she and Michael had set Eleanor's wedding date.

Eleanor read and re-read that sentence before putting the letter down on her father's desk.

Michael had said something about next spring as a wedding date, but nothing firm had been decided. Evidently, Michael and her aunt had chosen a date in May. In addition, he'd given Deborah approval to begin wedding preparations.

How very odd that she hadn't been consulted.

She was so engrossed in her thoughts that she didn't see one of the maids standing in the doorway with her morning tea.

"Miss Eleanor, is something wrong?" Norma asked.

Eleanor shook her head. "Thank you, Norma, I'm fine."

Norma entered the library and placed the tray on the corner of the desk.

"Can I bring you anything else, miss?"

"No, nothing. Thank you, Norma."

What she needed or wanted, Norma couldn't provide. A little respect, perhaps. A little consideration.

When the maid left, Eleanor picked up the letter again, and read it once more.

Deborah and Michael had set a date. She didn't have anything to do with the decision. Nor, did it appear from her aunt's comments, was she going to have much input about the ceremony.

It wasn't the first time Michael's actions had disconcerted her. He was an earl and, as Deborah repeatedly said, given to a certain autocracy of manner.

"He's of the peerage, my dear. You mustn't expect him to act like other people."

Did being an earl mean that he didn't have to consult anyone else? She wasn't a piece of statuary to be moved from the mantel to an occasional table.

Does no one ever talk to you?

Logan's words came back to her. How had he known? She pushed thoughts of him from her mind. The very worst thing she could do now was think about *him*.

He might not be a shepherd, but she didn't know who he was. A friend of the duke's. He could be anyone. A former soldier, except he hadn't claimed to have been in the military. No, the man was an enigma and the sooner she forgot him, the better.

That was easier said than done.

She had thought about the kiss all night. At first she told herself it was a guilty conscience that kept her awake. Then, after she recalled their entire conversation, word for word, she realized it was something far more dangerous. She remembered the glint of laughter in his eyes and his soft smile. Perhaps he had ridiculed her, but it didn't feel that way. Instead it was as if he coaxed her to be herself.

Reveal yourself, Eleanor. Show the world who you are. Don't hide yourself from anyone, however much you might fear their words.

He truly had no right to say such things to her. Yet they were true, weren't they? The letter proved that. Was she a nonentity to her family? Some gray, amorphous creature who occupied a place at the table, who walked through the corridors, who occasionally spoke?

Her father had paid attention to her, but when he died it was as if she'd become invisible. How strange that she only realized that now. Or the fact that people noticed her once more when she'd become engaged to an earl.

She didn't know what to do about the situation, which was why she went to her room, changed to her riding skirt, and headed for the stable.

Only to encounter Mrs. Willett.

She'd forgotten about the inspection of the storerooms, always done when she arrived at Hearthmere for her month. The housekeeper was set for doing that now and Eleanor couldn't think of a justifiable reason to delay. Her foul mood was not an adequate excuse for failing to do her duty.

Therefore, she was three hours past the time she wanted to go riding before she got to the stable. There must've been something in her expression because Mr. Contino didn't say a word to her, merely waved her toward Maud's stall. After the stable boy assisted her in saddling the mare, she was finally away. She deliberately rode in a new direction, unwilling to go near the cottage or accidentally see Logan McKnight.

FRED STEERING STOOD at the open door of the crofter's hut and stared inside. One side of his lip curled slightly and there was a contemptuous look in his eyes.

Strange, how some people instantly disliked certain individuals or situations. What Logan always thought ironic was that the object of their dislike was someone similar to themselves. He'd noticed that plump women were critical about other plump women. Cutthroat politicians identified that trait in their contemporaries. In this case, Fred was sneering at the obvious poverty in the cottage. The man had grown up in one of the poorest parts of London and had educated himself through a series of happy accidents, namely that he'd nearly been run over by the Duke of Montrose's carriage. The result was that the duke himself had taken on the care of young Mr. Steering.

Logan had hired him as his secretary and he'd been well pleased with the young man's ambition, knowledge of people, and common sense.

Logan sat there watching, his finger in a book, taking note of where Fred's eyes lit. He examined the small kitchen, the wooden dowel where Old Ned hung his coat. The sofa sagged. The chair next to it, where Logan sat, was surprisingly comfortable. Ned had built it himself and had carved wolves and other animals on the arms and back. No sheep, however.

"Sir?" Fred said, finally seeing him. "Are you ready to leave?"

"I am. And you, as usual, are right on time." He motioned to his valise and the briefcase where he'd kept those papers that he needed to read in the past two weeks.

"Yes, sir."

"I take it you've brought me more work," he said, glancing at the leather case under Fred's arm.

"Yes, sir, Mr. Disraeli has some documents that he would like you to look over and give him some input on. Some things to do with Scottish law, sir."

"Immediately, I take it?"

Fred nodded.

At least he'd been able to get away for a while. The respite had allowed him some time to think, to examine the path his life was taking. Like Fred, he'd been guided by the Duke of Montrose. Now he was a member of Parliament, duly elected and expected to serve.

He'd often had the thought that life wasn't predestined like some religions believed as much as the result of an ongoing battle. Maybe angels were on one side and Fate on the other. The angels decreed that a man be kind. Fate gave him an enormous inheritance. The result was a benefactor lauded by society for his generosity.

In his case he thought that the angels might have given him the ability to talk someone into anything. In turn, Fate decreed that he should believe wholeheartedly in Scotland. Therefore, he was an evangelist of sorts destined to clash with his peers in Parliament on an ongoing basis.

He'd taken his nationality for granted until he'd gone to London. There, it had been pointed out to him, at every possible turn, that he was slightly less acceptable than an Englishman. While he'd always thought being a Scot gave him an advantage, it was all too obvious that some Englishmen—including a few of his fellow members of Parliament—didn't feel the same. Disraeli had been cunning enough to have figured out his irritation. The man didn't hesitate to take advantage of it on an ongoing basis. Therefore, he asked Logan for a Scottish point of view on any proposed legislation remotely involving Scotland.

When he stood, Bruce, who'd been sleeping next to the chair, stretched and yawned.

Fred stared. "You have a dog, sir."

"Actually, he's more of a puppy at the moment, Fred."

"Are you taking him to London?"

"No," he said. "We're going to take him home."

He hoped Eleanor would understand. She'd named the puppy, which was a sign that she didn't dislike him as much as she said. Plus, Bruce needed a home. Perhaps raising the puppy would help her overcome her fear of dogs. If nothing else, Bruce would create a bond between Logan and Eleanor Craig.

He didn't want to forget her, an unusual reaction since it had never happened to him before. He hadn't the time for relationships of any sort, let alone one with a woman living in Scotland. Perhaps they could begin a correspondence, one with her castigating him and him teasing her.

Eleanor Craig interested him.

She seemed entirely without artifice or vanity. She hadn't worn a hat. Therefore, she didn't have any concerns about deepening the shade of her complexion. Her riding habit, altered to allow her to ride astride, was old, and he doubted it was in fashion. She hadn't seemed to care whether her thick brunette hair had come loose from its bun. Nor did she fiddle. She didn't look for a mirror or constantly press her hands against her clothing, face, or hair. She didn't simper. Yet Miss Eleanor Craig was not apathetic by any means. She almost vibrated with emotion, especially when challenged. Her blue eyes had flashed at him, her anger not difficult to interpret.

Bruce would serve as a bond between them. If not, then a wall. One way or another he wasn't going to let Eleanor Craig slip out of his life.

WHEN ELEANOR RETURNED to the house, it was in time to see a carriage pulling out of the drive and heading toward the road. She sat and watched it for a minute, wondering who could have visited Hearthmere.

It was Mrs. Willett who answered the mystery.

"You've had a visitor, Miss Eleanor."

"A visitor?"

"Yes, miss. He seemed surprised that you weren't in and wished to leave you a note."

"Did he?"

Mrs. Willett nodded. "I let him use the library for a moment." The housekeeper approached her, holding out an envelope of her own stationery. "I've sent the puppy to the stable."

"The puppy? Bruce?"

"Yes, miss," Mrs. Willett said, her mouth pursed into a moue of irritation. "He desecrated the carpet."

Eleanor didn't respond to the housekeeper. When she tore open the envelope there was only a single sheet of paper. The handwriting was bold and masculine.

> *Bruce cried most of the night and I think he missed you. I've brought him back because he needs a home and I think you need him.*
>
> *Let me know how he goes on and how you do as well.*

Then the aggravating man left his address in London.

She looked at the housekeeper. "Did he say nothing else?"

"No, Miss Eleanor."

At least he didn't comment on her voice this time.

She calmly folded the letter, tucked it into her pocket, and, before she could change her mind, headed for the stable. Like it or not, Bruce was her responsibility and she couldn't turn over the care of him to someone else. Besides, there were a number of very large cats in the stable. He might well become their target.

She would retrieve the puppy and set about duplicating the conditions she had the other night. Once he was settled, she would make sure to write Mr. McKnight and let him know exactly what she thought.

He was an idiot if he believed he could get away with making decisions that impacted her. Who did he think he was?

She stopped on the path. Why was she so intent on correcting a stranger when she was allowing Michael to do the same thing?

For the second time, Logan's words came back to her. *Reveal yourself, Eleanor. Show the world who you are. Don't hide yourself from anyone, however much you might fear their words.*

Perhaps she should begin to show the world who she was, exactly, beginning with the annoying Logan McKnight.

Chapter Eleven

$\mathscr{F}$ive days had passed out of her precious fortnight of freedom. Five days that slipped by too fast. Eleanor hadn't done half of what she'd wanted to accomplish and the week was almost done.

She was out walking Bruce when Mrs. Willett approached her, an oilskin packet beneath her arm.

"The papers are here, Miss Eleanor. Where would you like me to put them?"

"The papers?"

"Yes, miss. The newspapers from Edinburgh and London."

"I thought we'd had those discontinued after my uncle died."

"No, Miss Eleanor. They've been coming every week just as they always have."

"Who reads them?"

The question wasn't an embarrassing one, but the housekeeper's face reddened all the same.

"The staff if they've time after their duties are finished. I've done so myself."

No doubt she gave them to Mr. Contino, as well.

"Thank you, Mrs. Willett," she said. "If you'll put them in the library I'll look them over later."

"Yes, Miss Eleanor."

If no one had read the papers Eleanor would have stopped them. Over the past five years she'd culled what she could in order to ensure that Hearthmere could support itself.

She took one of the London papers and went to sit on the bench beneath a sprawling oak. She and her father had often sat here in the evening. Bruce bounded up to sit beside her, making her smile. She held the length of rope with the loop at the end that she'd gotten from the stable. Surprisingly, however, the puppy didn't need to be coaxed to come with her. He followed at her heels wherever she went. Nor did he run away once they'd gotten to the lawn. Instead, he went off to do his business and then returned to her, sitting at her feet and looking up at her as if he expected praise.

She'd given it to him, despite the fact that she knew she was probably spoiling him. Could you really be spoiled when you were so young and away from the rest of your family? She reached out her hand, and scooted him close to her, smiling again when he insisted on licking her fingers.

"You've already been fed, you silly thing," she said. "And I know you ate everything because I watched you eat." Bruce had inhaled his meal of minced beef and chopped carrots.

She didn't know anything about dogs, other than that they were scary. Puppies, however, were a different matter. Bruce was a round little ball of fur with four legs and a tail that looked like it might become as bushy as the rest of him. When he barked it was a sound much larger than his size. Perhaps he had to grow into his bark.

They sat together as she read. Parliament was being stirred up by a firebrand. The reporter didn't name names, other than referring to the MP as a tireless advocate for Scotland. The reporter was decidedly English and held Michael's opinion about Scottish politics while she silently cheered for the firebrand. It was time Scotland had a champion or two.

Bruce gave up licking her fingers for chewing the end of her belt. She couldn't help but wonder what her father would say about Bruce. He had tried to talk her out of her fear of dogs but she'd learned, early on, that rational discourse wasn't a match for emotion. You really couldn't talk someone out of what they were feeling.

She'd known that at eight years old.

No place in London gave her the feeling of freedom she was experiencing right at the moment. No one was insisting that she attend some event or another. She wasn't being questioned by her aunt or cousins. She wasn't obligated to be here or there. Her schedule was her own, not subject to anyone's dictates.

What a pity she wouldn't be able to live here all her life.

Why did she have to marry? Who had decreed that all single women were not fulfilled unless they had a husband? Who were the people who ridiculed spinsters? Were their lives so perfect that they could afford to make fun of someone else? Why was a man not considered strange if he remained unmarried?

"You've gotten to a certain age, Eleanor. You're expected to marry." Her aunt's words.

Was that why she was marrying Michael? Not because of any undying love or attraction, but because she'd grown weary of hearing the same lecture?

Even her cousin had added her thoughts. "A woman has to marry, Eleanor," Daphne said. "If she doesn't, people look at her odd. They think there's something wrong with her. You don't want people to look at you like that, do you?"

She didn't know if Daphne meant to be unkind. Her cousin was a creature of vibrant emotions. At least, that's what her aunt had said, explaining, "Daphne is a bright butterfly in life."

Eleanor could only suppose that she was a slug in comparison. Some pale creature who slid through life without being noticed by anyone.

That was fine with her. She would let Daphne and Aunt Deborah make dramatic pronouncements and weep at any provocation. Eleanor didn't possess the temperament to be histrionic and found that sort of person exceedingly tiresome to be around.

She preferred to experience life in manageable bites rather than consider it a feast to devour before it disappeared.

Yet if she didn't marry, what would she do with her life? The answer had always been in the back of her mind. Live at Hearthmere.

Yet the die was cast, the Rubicon crossed, the marriage offer accepted. She was going to be wed, if only to continue basking in her family's approval.

Family is everything.

The entire family was aflutter with the thought that she was going to be made a countess. A title wouldn't change her. She wasn't going to alter her character simply because she'd gotten married. If she said such a thing her aunt would give her another speech. Her cousin would toss her head and say that she didn't appreciate her good fortune.

According to Daphne, Michael's courtship, such as it was, was an accident. He couldn't truly have chosen her, Eleanor, over other girls that season. Or perhaps he had done so because Daphne had already married.

Daphne was a natural beauty, according to one suitor. The stars in the sky, the sun, or nature itself had nothing on Daphne when she smiled at him. Another suitor had penned a song, one that detailed all the ways Daphne made the world a better place simply by being in it.

Daphne's white-blond hair was so pale a shade that, by candlelight, it looked like a halo around her head. Her eyes, like her mother's, were bluish green, a shade likened often enough to ocean waves that the compliment sounded trite and mundane. She was tall and willowy, exceedingly graceful, an excellent dancer, and, according to Aunt Deborah, a sparkling conversationalist.

In comparison, Eleanor's hair was brown. It was simply brown with no redeeming features like red or gold highlights. Her eyes were blue, but not a remarkable shade of blue. She had her father's eyes. Her eyelashes were long and curled of their own accord, not requiring any torturous devices to make them do so. Her hair, too, curled on its own, a little too much from time to time.

She didn't have Grecian features or a delicate classical beauty. She was just herself with a chin that was perhaps a little too stubborn and a high forehead that required she wear her hair in a fashion to compensate. Her nose was just a nose, but her cheekbones were rather high, giving her an intriguing appearance when she turned just so.

Her teeth were good, white and straight. Even Daphne's were not as straight as hers. Her voice was, perhaps, not as breathy as her cousin's. She didn't want to force people to lean forward in order to hear her. Plus, it seemed rather ridiculous to pretend to be so fragile, especially after coming off the dance floor. If a woman was really that delicate she would have fainted during a waltz.

She detested dancing and no amount of teaching would make her more competent at it. Last year she'd had a dancing master who came to the house, parading her through the upstairs ballroom while pretending to hear a nonexistent orchestra.

"I can do wonders, madame," he had finally announced to her aunt, "if the student wishes to avail themselves of my talents. Unfortunately, your niece has no such wish. She has announced on several different occasions that she thinks dancing is ridiculous. Ridiculous, madame. How is anyone to contend with that kind of attitude?"

Her aunt, however, had prevailed upon Monsieur Lejeune to return. That's one of the things Eleanor had to look forward to when she went back to London. The man had garlic breath and clammy hands. Beyond that, he had a love of dance that she was doomed never to share.

Fortunately, Michael felt the same way. Therefore, she doubted they would dance all that often in the future.

Her aunt, enlivened by the thought that Eleanor was going to be a countess, was determined to do what she could to expand Eleanor's talents.

"You are to be a countess, my dear girl. A countess! I had thought that you might marry a tradesman or perhaps someone Hamilton brought home for you to meet, but this? This is the opportunity of a lifetime. You must present your best side at all times."

She and her aunt had, ever since coming to London, ignored each other for the most part. The difference between then and now in terms of how Deborah treated her was disconcerting.

Every time the wedding was mentioned her aunt smiled brightly at her.

So she was treated to dance lessons, comportment lessons—which concentrated on her walk, how to sit, stand, and move—lessons on etiquette, including being quizzed on how to address everyone from the Queen on down, and generally being shaped into Deborah's idea of a countess.

She caught Hamilton's look occasionally and knew that while he commiserated, there would be no rescue from that quarter.

No, she was going to have to save herself, but she didn't know how. Perhaps letting Deborah handle all the arrangements for the wedding was one way. At least she wouldn't have to be involved with all of that. Her aunt was nothing if not determined. Look at what she had accomplished in her life. She'd gone from being a poor but proud London woman to marrying a Scottish poet. Her second husband was a fabulously wealthy soap magnate and her current home was a mansion in the loveliest part of London. Those feats were not accidental. Deborah Craig Richards was a woman with an iron will.

Eleanor would have to return to London shortly even though she didn't want to go.

Only two weeks. The first week was nearly over. Time had flown by and part of that should be laid at the feet of a certain Scot by the name of Logan McKnight. She really should write the man, if nothing else, and tell him how she didn't appreciate his bringing Bruce back to her. Except . . . she looked down at the puppy, now playing with a leaf. Except that he was the sweetest thing. He'd been a joy to have around for the past few days.

Oh, bother. The man still needed a dressing down. What a pity that she wasn't going to deliver it.

Chapter Twelve

"Tell her to get rid of the bloody dog, Mother."

"Such language, Jeremy. We don't talk that way in this house."

"Sorry, Mother. But she's been a stubborn idiot about that dog. She stopped the carriage and insisted on returning to Hearthmere just because I told her I didn't want to travel with him all the way to London. She took her own carriage here. We were a damn odd caravan. We lost sight of them several times, whenever she insisted on letting the cur out to wander on the side of the road."

"How very odd. Eleanor doesn't like dogs."

"Something happened in Scotland, then. She likes this one."

Eleanor glanced down at Bruce in her arms. He licked her chin. She stroked his ears in response.

She really should make her presence known instead of lurking in the butler's pantry. She hadn't meant to listen. She'd been on her way to the kitchen door.

They'd only been back in London for two days. Her aunt hadn't said anything about Bruce. Eleanor had been very careful to take him to the small backyard every few hours, so he hadn't had any accidents. She didn't make a fuss out of asking for minced beef and vegetables for him. She'd been more than willing to share her meals with him if the cook had refused. She hadn't. Instead, she'd petted the puppy, telling Eleanor that he reminded her of a dog she'd had as a girl.

All she had to do to keep Jeremy happy and mitigate any future problems with her aunt was to announce that she had every intention of getting rid of Bruce. After all, she had Logan McKnight's address. It would be easy enough to call on him and give Bruce back.

Except that she wasn't sure she wanted to relinquish the puppy.

Most of her life she'd been alone, a feeling she had even when surrounded by people. Although her uncle, aunt, and cousins had moved to Hearthmere, she'd never felt part of their family. She hadn't considered Daphne or Jeremy to be her siblings. Nor did they treat her as if she was their younger sister. She was simply Eleanor, someone to ignore if possible and barely tolerate if not.

Bruce was a companion she hadn't even known she needed. Logan was right. The puppy did seem to have an affinity for her. Plus, she had a growing affection for him.

He still ate as though he was starving, which meant that she sometimes fed him at noon in addition to mornings and evenings. It didn't seem possible, but he'd grown in the past dozen days. His paws were just as large, but he seemed longer and something was happening to his tail. It was growing increasingly fluffy.

"What are you going to do about it?" Jeremy asked now.

"As long as the dog's not a problem I don't see that there's anything I need to do about it," her aunt answered.

"I don't want a dog in the house," he said.

"That really isn't your concern. This isn't your house. When you have your own establishment you can dictate the rules."

Eleanor could just imagine Jeremy's expression at that comment. Her cousin had completed his education, but had not yet settled into an occupation. Her aunt's husband had offered Jeremy at least three separate positions in one of his companies, but Jeremy was still "mulling over his options." However, he had not yet moved out of his stepfather's house and was supported in all ways by Hamilton Richards.

She might have considered him spoiled, but for one thing. Her aunt was not overly maternal to her son. When she spoke to him—or about him—she did so in a distracted, almost offhand manner.

Daphne, however, was a different matter. Daphne might be married, with her own establishment, but she was often here. It wasn't a rare sight to see Daphne taking tea with her mother or even being here for breakfast. As far as Deborah was concerned, Daphne was a perfect being. From the very beginning of her season Deborah believed that her daughter's ethereal beauty would capture a title. For that reason Deborah spent a fortune on new clothes, a dancing master, even a French teacher to make Daphne seem more polished and cosmopolitan, the perfect wife for a duke or an earl.

As a child Eleanor had often imagined what her mother might've been like if she hadn't died in childbirth. A common tragedy, she'd been told when she was old enough to get the correct answer as to why she didn't have a mother. She'd told herself that it was foolish to wish for something she'd never had, especially since she was lucky enough to have warm and tender memories of her father. As a little girl she'd often perched on top of his shoulders as they walked from the house to the stable complex. Her first memories of him were punctuated by his laughter. People liked Archie Craig.

In that way her Uncle William had been like his older brother. He'd been a gentle man, one with a soft voice and a retiring manner. She often found it difficult to believe that he had attracted the lively Deborah.

Hamilton Richards seemed more her aunt's type of partner. His voice was loud, his character boisterous. He commanded rather than asked. She couldn't imagine Hamilton ever pleading for anything, even Deborah's hand in marriage. Their union had been a surprise to everyone; they'd only been back in London a matter of months before her aunt announced the upcoming nuptials.

Her cousins had been ecstatic to move into the mammoth townhouse in a fashionable square. As for Eleanor, she hadn't cared. She'd trailed along, almost as an afterthought. It was only at Hearthmere that she felt she belonged.

"She's fixated on that dog, Mother. It nearly bit me the other day."

Bruce did no such thing. Jeremy was exaggerating again.

She really needed to step out and announce herself. Bruce had not, thankfully, found anything to bark at, although Jeremy wasn't one of his favorite people. When Jeremy had returned from Edinburgh, the puppy had greeted him by lifting his leg and relieving himself on Jeremy's shoe. She'd been so startled that she hadn't apologized to her cousin. Then, the look on his face had been so amusing that she'd burst into laughter. He'd been angry ever since.

"But you won't do that again, will you?" she whispered to Bruce. He licked her chin again in agreement.

She'd made the decision to take a Hearthmere carriage to London because she hadn't wanted to spend all that time with Jeremy sulking or glowering at her. She hadn't sent Liam home yet. The driver had expressed a wish to see a bit of London, so both he and the carriage would remain here for a little while. Thankfully, Hamilton hadn't objected.

Eleanor backed out of the butler's pantry, nodding to several of the maids who knew quite well that she'd been eavesdropping. The servants in London had a rigid hierarchy and considered themselves better than most people, including their employers. She had the feeling, however, that they occasionally commiserated with her. Aunt Deborah could be fearsome in her expectations. When any one of the servants failed to meet her standards, she didn't hesitate to dress them down wherever she found them. Consequently, the entire household was privy to her irritation.

Now Eleanor slipped out the side door to the back of the house, past the square of lawn, and into the alley. Only then did she put Bruce down on the ground, making sure that his lead was secure.

She'd heard Hamilton say once that he'd purchased the property because of the park. A short distance away from the back door was a wrought iron gate. She lifted the latch and entered, Bruce following eagerly.

This area of Queen's Park was secluded and, for the most part, private. Because Queen's Park had no statuary, lakes, or buildings—unlike Kensington Gardens or Hyde Park—it was rarely crowded. People chose other places to walk or ride. Eleanor preferred the magnificent, fully grown trees and wide gravel paths here.

Even in the midst of a sunny day, the canopy of branches overhead shaded the area. When it was drizzling it was still pleasant, the leaves sheltering her and creating almost an intimate and shadowed space.

Yesterday was the first time she'd brought the puppy here, but Bruce already seemed to anticipate the outing. Queen's Park had always been a respite from her London life and it looked like Bruce felt the same.

After consulting her watch, she found her favorite iron bench and sat, allowing the lead to play out a little. In less than an hour she was meeting with Michael. He'd asked to call on her today, the visit their first since Eleanor had returned from Scotland.

She and Bruce went through their training. She had a few pieces of liver one of the maids had slipped her earlier wrapped in a handkerchief in her pocket. In Scotland Norma had told her how important it was for dogs to be trained. Having no prior experience she'd taken the maid's word for it and had learned what she needed to teach him.

When he sat, she praised him and gave him a piece of liver. Standing, she walked to the other side of the path, watching as he obeyed the command to stay. The one she thought was most important, however, was a command for him to come to her. Otherwise, she'd never be able to let him off his lead.

She dropped the lead, took four steps away, and said, "Come."

He came to sit in front of her, a fluffy ball of fur with large paws and a strange-looking tail. She could swear he smiled at her when she bent down and gave him another piece of liver.

They practiced for another fifteen minutes. When the liver was gone they walked down the wide road for another few minutes, Bruce investigating the grass, the gravel, and the falling leaves. Finally, when there was no more time to spare, she led him back through the gate.

Bruce seemed as reluctant as she to head to the townhouse. She reassured him that they'd return later, just before it got dark. For now she had to talk to her fiancé.

Chapter Thirteen

The tea tray had been delivered along with an assortment of pastries. Michael was late, but then, Michael was often late. Eleanor had learned to factor in an extra quarter hour whenever he was expected somewhere.

The only time she'd said something to him about his punctuality, his eyes got that hooded look as if his lids were half closed. He stared at something in the distance and kept his silence longer than was comfortable, giving her the feeling that she'd overstepped. His next comment proved it.

"If I'm late, Eleanor, it's for an excellent reason. You will simply have to accept that."

Sometimes when she asked a question, Michael wouldn't deign to answer. At other times, he would change the subject. It had only taken her a few occasions to learn that it was better to wait until Michael wanted to divulge something than to ask him about it.

Her aunt had added her own coaching. "He's an earl, Eleanor. You can't expect him to be like other men."

Why not? He was human, like other men. What kind of training had Michael received from birth to believe that he was somehow superior to others?

Deborah, in her way, was like Michael. She, too, did not like being questioned, especially when it was a topic about which she knew. Aunt Deborah counted social functions, dress, comportment, and even marriage among her areas of expertise.

Eleanor did not mind ceding some of the details of her wedding to her aunt. After all, Deborah had more experience in those matters. However, she was adamant about one issue. She'd brought her mother's wedding dress, still wrapped in the blue fabric that had protected it for years, with her back to London. She wouldn't budge on that; she was going to wear her mother's dress.

She glanced down at Bruce, sleeping in the little nest she'd made for him out of a cast-off blanket. He was already a favorite among the staff. More than one maid had come to her and asked permission to offer him a bit of a treat. At the rate they were going Bruce would not only grow, he would get fat. Perhaps it would be wiser for her to say no, but it was the first time she'd ever talked to some of the staff.

When they had moved into Hamilton's home, she'd tried to establish some type of rapport with the servants, only to be chastised by her aunt.

"One does not socialize with the staff, Eleanor," she said after finding her in the kitchen chatting with a new maid. The poor girl was barely more than a child and had seemed miserable. Surely a kind word was not out of the question?

After that episode, however, she'd kept her conversation with the servants to *please* and *thank you*. Yet because of Bruce, a few of the maids started sharing tales of their own dogs with her.

Had Logan known that Bruce would be a link to other people? No, it wouldn't do to think of Logan right now, especially when she was waiting for Michael. Was Logan punctual? She had a feeling that he was. How very odd that she was guessing at a stranger's behavior. She didn't know him. Yet their short conversation was one of the most honest she'd ever had.

Riding away from the cottage that day she'd felt two uncomfortable emotions. First, she missed her father with a surge of grief so powerful it was as if he had just died. If he'd been alive, she would've gone to him and told him about the strange shepherd who wasn't a shepherd. The second emotion was another type of grief, perhaps. She kept looking down at the empty basket, missing Bruce.

Had Logan known that she would miss Bruce? Was that why he'd brought the puppy back?

She was, perhaps, giving too much weight to a chance encounter. Or perhaps Logan McKnight had been wiser than she'd given him credit for being.

Perhaps she should write him to say that she appreciated the gift of Bruce, after all. That would be the polite thing to do. Or even call upon him since he lived here in London. She didn't have her own maid, but Aunt Deborah was beginning to interview candidates for the post. Evidently, a countess must have a lady's maid. Until someone was hired she could surely borrow one of the upstairs maids to accompany her to Logan's lodgings. That way, the visit wouldn't be considered shocking. Merely two Scottish neighbors calling on each other. That's all.

"You're looking well," Michael said from the doorway. "That color flatters you, Eleanor."

She stood, clasping her hands together.

"Thank you," she said, wondering if she should tell him the blue dress was new, then decided against it. "You're looking well, too," she added, before sitting again.

Michael was an exceedingly handsome man, blessed with a smile that lit up his blue eyes and made him seem even more charming. His black hair was thick and often tumbled down on his brow. His features were perfect as if God himself had arranged each one to fit in his aristocratic face. He was tall and broad-shouldered, possessed of a grace demonstrated in any of his activities, from walking to dancing to simply standing, allowing the rest of the world to look their fill.

If she were viewing him dispassionately, she wouldn't be able to find anything about him to criticize.

He could be kind. Witness the time he'd asked Jenny Woolsey

to dance after she'd been sitting along the wall for nearly an hour. Since he didn't enjoy dancing himself, it had been a nice gesture. When Eleanor had been distraught over the treatment of a draft horse, Michael had intervened.

If he was sometimes autocratic, perhaps it was an adequate counterbalance to his perfection.

When he'd first made an appearance at a dance, she'd been impressed by his charm. He'd greeted numerous people by name, was complimentary to the young women he met, and seemed to sincerely like those men who came up to him.

When he'd initially asked her to dance, she'd been stunned. Michael Herridge was asking *her* to dance? Of course she said yes, only to catch the looks of several of the girls with whom she shared her season. It was the first time in her life that she'd ever incited jealousy in anyone, and she had to admit it was a heady experience.

Their conversation was somewhat muted by her awe of him. She couldn't remember what they'd talked about at first. Not horses, certainly, even though she knew more about them than anything else. Certainly not the breeding program at Hearthmere. In addition, she'd been given strict instructions by her aunt not to discuss politics. Men, Deborah claimed, were put off by a woman who espoused a political viewpoint. Any political viewpoint.

From that night on, Michael made a point of singling her out, and she'd been flattered by the attention and a little bemused. Her aunt was overjoyed and heaped praise on her—something that had never happened before.

When Michael told her that he'd already spoken to Hamilton and her aunt and that he would very much like her hand in marriage, she'd been dumbstruck. It hadn't occurred to her until later that it meant she'd be the Countess of Wescott.

Jenny pulled her aside and asked her what she'd done to attract—and catch—Michael.

"I don't know," Eleanor said honestly. "I just danced with him."

"I saw you two talking a great deal."

Michael was actually the one who talked. She had just listened about his plans for Abermarle, his position in the House of Lords, or his mother.

When news of their engagement filtered through society, she'd been alternatively viewed with irritation or surprise. She understood why. She wasn't one of the season's beauties. She didn't have a sparkling laugh. Nor was she exceptionally witty. If she was able to talk about the subjects that interested her she might have seemed a great deal more captivating.

As it was, she was simply *the Scot*, the woman who'd convinced the Earl of Wescott to marry her. No one could understand why Michael had picked her. Nor could she.

They hadn't fallen in love. Such things were not expected in a society marriage. It was fortunate if both parties liked and respected each other, but even that wasn't necessary. A girl with enough attractiveness and a good family was expected to find a marriageable male from a good family and with an income substantial enough to support her and any future children. That was the way of the world.

For the great blessing of becoming a countess and carrying Michael's name she would be amiable, bear him children, and not shame him in any way. That, too, was expected.

They attended events as a couple now. Because they were engaged they didn't dance or even converse as much. When they did talk the conversations were mostly one-sided. As long as she listened, didn't interrupt, or ask questions they did very well together.

He was still charming and she was still bemused.

"I've missed you," he said. "It seemed to be a very long two weeks."

She cleared her throat. "I understand that you and my aunt have come to a decision as to a wedding date," she said.

"We have. Does that not meet with your approval?"

She poured him a cup of tea, fixing it the way he liked before handing it to him.

"Could you not have waited until I returned? I would have liked to be consulted."

"Your aunt led me to believe that she had your approval in making arrangements."

"It's my wedding day, Michael. Not hers."

"Is this what traveling to Scotland does to you, Eleanor? Makes you bold and difficult?"

She looked at him. She'd thought about her words and moderated her tone of voice, yet he still considered her comments bold and difficult?

"Is the date not convenient to you, Eleanor?"

"It's fine."

"Just fine? I was hoping that you would think the date too far away. That you might be a little more eager to be a bride."

"Of course I am," she said, hoping that sounded agreeable enough.

For long minutes they didn't speak. When Michael resumed their conversation it was to tell her of improvements he was making to his London house.

"I have to prepare for a wife, after all," he said, smiling at her.

He truly did have the most charming smile, but the expression disappeared a moment later.

"What is that?" he asked, looking down at the floor.

"Bruce. My puppy."

"What's he doing in the parlor? He should be left outside."

"He's been very well behaved."

"Take him out of here, Eleanor."

She looked at him. "Why?"

"Why? Because I told you to."

"He hasn't done anything, Michael. He hasn't even barked since you arrived. I'd prefer that he stay where he is."

"And I prefer that you take him out of here." His look was direct and strangely uncomfortable.

"Do you not like dogs, Michael?"

"The question isn't my likes or dislikes, Eleanor, but why you've become defiant. Is that what going to Scotland does to you?"

He was, perhaps, right to be surprised at her behavior. She'd never questioned anything he said before today.

"Men don't want to be around disagreeable females," her aunt had told her.

Was she considered disagreeable simply because she objected to his order about Bruce?

"I insist, Eleanor." He had that narrowed-eyed look that warned her he wasn't pleased.

Bending down, she slipped the lead around Bruce's neck before standing. Michael stood, too.

"I have to leave."

She was probably supposed to plead with him to stay. Or apologize for offending him. She did neither.

When he bent and kissed her cheek she forced a smile to her face.

"Defiant women aren't very feminine, Eleanor."

Her aunt would have been proud of her. She kept her smile in place as she walked Michael to the door, waiting until he got into his carriage. When he gave her a wave, she returned it, then took Bruce upstairs to her room, closed the door, and sighed in relief.

Chapter Fourteen

Ever since leaving Scotland, Logan had been inundated with paperwork and intensive reading for Disraeli. He had so many projects that he hadn't made time to stop in Edinburgh and see his sister and her family.

After everyone in his office left for the day and before he readied himself for the political dinner that evening, he spent several moments composing a letter to Janet, explaining why he hadn't visited.

Janet would understand. Janet always understood. Dylan would be a little less forgiving. His brother-in-law was protective of his wife, which was just the way Logan wanted it. In addition, Dylan had few family members of his own. Therefore, he counted Logan's appearance as even more important.

The bad thing about ambition was that you occasionally associated with people who had the same upward trajectory. Benjamin Disraeli had been named Prime Minister only a few months earlier and had already accomplished a great deal. He'd succeeded in passing several key pieces of legislation that amended the Scottish legal system, expanded the Post Office, and ended public executions.

According to the Prime Minister, one of his greatest achievements was the defeat of Tewodros II. Logan knew all about the Battle of Magdala. He'd been asked to accompany Robert Napier's forces to report firsthand to the Prime Minister.

Next time, however, he was going to demur when the man suggested that he observe a military expedition. Abyssinia had been educational, but grueling. He'd learned a great deal about himself, military strategy, and how to ride and command an elephant. He'd also learned how to kill his fellow man and be a witness to wholesale brutality.

The battle had been a bloodbath: thousands of men armed with nothing but spears being decimated by hundreds of Englishmen and Indian infantry equipped with the latest rifles. The Abyssinians hadn't stood a chance against their firepower yet they'd kept coming, sent to their deaths by their emperor.

Logan wouldn't have been fit company for Janet and her family straight after Abyssinia. It had been better for him to wait, but he was planning on seeing them all soon.

His niece and nephew were delightful children. Jennifer and Alex were bright and perceptive and with enough will and personality to remind Logan of him and his sister growing up. He and Janet had been close ever since their parents died and they'd been taken in by a relative.

Luckily, the rest of their childhood had been blessed. They'd been given affection, attention, and were surrounded by the knowledge that they were important for their own sakes, not simply because of who their parents had been.

Alexander was having a birthday in a month, and Logan penned a note to his secretary to remind him of the event a week ahead. He would do everything in his power to arrange time away from his work to travel to Edinburgh. In the meantime, hopefully his letter would mollify Dylan and his sister.

When he was done writing them, he picked up another sheet of stationery. Fred normally handled his correspondence, but not his personal communications. Logan would never turn over this particular task to his secretary.

After some trial and error he finally worded the letter to his satisfaction. Perhaps it would take some time for her to respond. Or perhaps she never would.

He leaned back in his chair, thinking of Eleanor. He saw her face, the dawning smile when she looked down at Bruce. Her loneliness had struck him then, a thought that was both immediate and surprising. It had been the primary reason he'd brought Bruce back to her. Would she deny it or would she, with defiant honesty, admit it and throw the question back at him?

Because of the press of his work he didn't have time to be lonely. A partially honest answer, but not the whole of it. The truth, both difficult and newly born, was that there were moments, especially in the middle of the night, when his isolation gnawed at him.

He'd never been lonely before Abyssinia. He'd never questioned himself as much as he did now, either. Perhaps one had something to do with the other.

The time in Scotland had been a respite. He'd needed those weeks to recuperate. Yet he'd still felt unlike himself when he returned to his offices. Some of that could be laid at the feet of Eleanor Craig. She'd been in his mind constantly, ever since leaving Scotland.

Would she be surprised to hear from him? In addition to maintaining a connection with her, he genuinely wanted to know about Bruce. The fact that she'd named the puppy was a good indication that she felt something for him.

If Bruce proved true to his parentage, he'd be a medium-sized dog with superior intelligence and a sense of loyalty as well as protectiveness.

Perhaps when he went to Edinburgh he could make a side trip to Hearthmere, just to see how the two of them were getting along. The idea of seeing her again was intriguing. The give-and-take of their conversation had made him feel alive in a way that startled him. He wasn't given to impulsive gestures, yet that's exactly how he'd acted around Eleanor.

Before he sealed the envelope, he added a few sentences to his letter, then re-read his words:

Dear Miss Craig,

I hope this letter finds you in good health and spirits. I hope, as well, that Bruce is heeding your instructions.

I realize that my actions in bringing Bruce back to you might have struck you as arbitrary. I can assure you that they were anything but that. I sincerely believe that Bruce is better served in your household than anywhere. He needs a home, as do we all. I think that you can provide an excellent one for him.

You have been in my thoughts a great deal ever since I returned to London. I have replayed our meetings many times. I can say with honesty that I have never enjoyed a conversation with another woman as much as I have with you.

I will be in Scotland shortly and would like to see you once again. Please let me know your thoughts on this matter.

He signed the letter, declining to use his title, preferring to address her simply.

Would she agree to see him or would she wish him to perdition? Either was entirely possible. Until he heard from her he'd occupy himself with the tasks at hand, answering Mr. Disraeli's inquiries, getting through the reams of paperwork he needed to read and/or sign, and attending all the various functions Fred had already placed on his calendar.

Logan had a raft of questions about Eleanor Craig and none of them could be answered by anyone but her. She wasn't married. Nor was she right out of the classroom. He guessed that she was in her mid-twenties. Why was Miss Craig on the shelf? What would she say to him if he had the temerity to ask her that question?

He liked a mystery, as long as there was a chance of solving it. Would she let him get close enough to do so?

If the dinner tonight proved to be as boring as most of those dinners were, he'd occupy himself with thoughts of Eleanor. A dangerous pastime, perhaps, but an enjoyable one.

Eleanor wanted to escape tonight's dinner. Two things stopped her. First, her aunt's announcement that the guest was a Scot. Second, Michael had been invited to attend and had accepted the invitation. She certainly couldn't fail to appear when her fiancé was here.

Consequently, she dressed with the help of her aunt's maid, who lent her skills in taming Eleanor's hair. The style was extremely flattering. She stared at herself in the vanity mirror. She looked well rested. Her eyes were clear. Her cheeks were slightly flushed. Even her hair was cooperating, curling exactly where Barbara wanted it to curl.

The blue evening gown was new, a present from her aunt and uncle to celebrate her engagement. The silk exactly matched the shade of her eyes. Tonight she almost looked like a countess. In time, perhaps, the gold of her earrings would be replaced by diamonds. Did a countess wear a tiara? She sincerely hoped not. She couldn't imagine anything more terrible than having even more pins in her hair, or trying to balance something heavy on her head throughout dinner. She wished there was someone she knew who might answer that foolish question without a bit of derision.

Michael's mother was alive, but she was quite elderly. She'd borne him late in life and was now being cared for by a series of protective nurses. Eleanor had only met her once, and the poor woman had to be reminded of her name three times. She was not going to be a source of information or comfort in her marriage.

Michael had already informed her that his mother's care would be her responsibility. Or at least ensuring that there was adequate staff on hand to always look out for the elderly woman. Evidently, he considered that task beneath him.

No doubt it was that way in most marriages: the wife was responsible for the family's well-being. How strange that she'd never considered such a thing. However, she'd never really thought about marriage. As a child, playing with her dolls, she'd fantasized a romance, a wedding, but nothing beyond that. She had never once considered what living with a husband might be like.

How strange that the woman in the mirror didn't look panicked.

"There, Miss Eleanor. What do you think?"

"I think it's beautiful, Barbara. Thank you."

The maid nodded once in response.

"You look lovely, miss."

That was a surprise. Normally Barbara never unbent long enough to say anything complimentary. Or perhaps she had misjudged the woman. Barbara had been with Deborah ever since Edinburgh. The maid had taken to London and evinced no homesickness or yearning for Scotland. In fact Eleanor had often heard Barbara complaining about *Auld Reekie*, the nickname for Edinburgh. She had other criticisms of their native land. Some were justifiable. The winters in Scotland were cold, making it feel like you were chilled down to your bones. Even in the summer there were cool breezes hinting of winter.

What about the sunsets, however? Or the dancing northern lights in the winter? Or the kindness of almost every Scot you met? What about Edinburgh being a city of learning, history, and culture? Or the advances that Scots offered the world? Barbara never spoke about those things and the omissions were glaring.

Eleanor could be as critical of London. Sometimes the smoke hung low in the sky like an ever-present fog. The air was so thick that you could taste it. It was necessary to hold a handkerchief over your nose and mouth when running from the door to the carriage.

There were times when it felt like the entire world had come to London. The streets were congested and even walking from your carriage to one of the shops was difficult.

What good did it do to complain? It didn't make your circumstances easier. Calling to mind all the difficulties only seemed to make the situation worse.

Tonight she would greet their guest and be as hospitable as possible. From what her aunt had said, he was an up-and-coming politician. A bit of a rabble-rouser, known for his staunch defense of Scottish politics and his friendship with the Prime Minister, Mr. Disraeli.

With any luck he wouldn't clash with Michael, who'd not been shy about discussing the "Scottish problem." Her fiancé made no secret of his opinion about bringing Scotland more closely under the control of England. There were too many people, according to Michael, who had thoughts of Scottish independence, even in this modern day. They needed to be choked off, brought to heel, and admonished.

Eleanor thanked Barbara once again and watched as the woman left the room. Once the maid was gone, she scooted the bench back and looked at Bruce. Thankfully, the puppy had been asleep the whole time the maid was there.

He woke, stretching before coming to her and licking her fingers. Her slippers were next to receive attention, but she tucked her feet beneath her gown.

"You can't eat my shoes tonight," she said. "And you must promise me to be on your best behavior. You have to stay here while I go downstairs. No barking. Understand?"

He grabbed the hem of her dress as an answer and tried to chew on it before she removed it from his mouth, replacing it with his rope toy.

Mary, one of the maids from Scotland, had been her accomplice in sneaking Bruce in and out of the house for the past few days. She would come and get the puppy in an hour or so and make sure he went out on the lawn. If she knew Mary, she'd also spend some time playing with Bruce.

Eleanor looked around the room for anything Bruce could eat that he wasn't supposed to eat, sprayed perfume behind both ears, gave herself one more glance in the pier glass, and opened her bedroom door.

She could hear the voices and immediately wanted to turn, re-enter her bedroom, and close the door. She'd much rather have Bruce as her companion than any of the people downstairs.

TONIGHT'S DINNER WAS one of those indeterminable political events that were a necessity, unfortunately. Logan's host was a wealthy industrialist, known for his generosity in making political contributions. Therefore, it would be a good idea to make his acquaintance. Plus, according to Fred—who always did exemplary research prior to one of these dinners—the family had ties to Scotland.

Logan couldn't afford to ignore any connection to his home country, especially in light of certain legislation that he was fighting to pass.

At times like these, he wished he was married. It might be easier to attend one of these dinners if he had a companion, someone to take the attention away from him for a little while. It would also be nice to have a wife with whom he could commiserate when the evening was over. Someone who would understand how much he detested being on display.

Hamilton Richards's home didn't surprise him. He'd seen a half dozen of these mansions in London, all occupied by wealthy men who believed that their fortunes gave them a right to have more say in politics. Money was a great leveler and he'd seen it used on more than one occasion.

Perhaps he was supposed to be impressed by the richness of the furnishings, the soaring ceilings and the chandeliers from France. He'd seen it all before. He'd grown up surrounded by wealth and privilege, but his uncle had done what he could to ensure that Logan's connections weren't common knowledge. Most people— and it was a fact of life that Logan had come to understand—were insular. They really didn't see farther than their own lives. They had little curiosity about others, which had suited him. Such an attitude had made it possible for him to be elected to Parliament.

He met Hamilton Richards and his wife, Deborah, complimented them on their home, and thanked them for the invitation. Mrs. Richards was a beautiful woman of mature years with blond hair, distinctive eyes, and a manner that immediately put Logan on alert. He'd seen that sharp-eyed gaze before. Deborah was not the retiring sort. Wrinkles radiated outward from the corners of her eyes, but the lines above her mouth were more telling. She pursed her lips a lot, no doubt in dissatisfaction.

Hamilton was slightly shorter than his wife, with a head of

white hair, prominent mutton chops, and bushy eyebrows. He looked a little like Father Christmas transplanted to this fashionable house.

Next was an introduction to Daphne Baker, Deborah's grown daughter, and her husband, Thomas. Both husband and wife were exceptionally attractive. Daphne was the image of her mother twenty years earlier complete with a low, seductive voice. The look she gave him held a hint of flirtation, almost as if she were daring him to reciprocate.

He'd gotten those looks before and he'd always wisely declined.

The next guest was a surprise. He'd met Michael Herridge before, knew that the Earl of Wescott had no qualms about his disapproval of certain legislation that would benefit Scotland.

Evidently, Richards wanted sparks to fly this evening. If that was the case, the man was going to be disappointed. Logan was an expert at determining when a battle was worth fighting. This one wasn't.

He would endure the dinner and be a grateful guest. He would compliment his host and hostess, be as amenable as possible, and leave without entering into any arguments, however much Herridge chose to bait him.

At least that's what he told himself.

Chapter Fifteen

$\mathcal{E}$leanor's feet would not move.

She tried, but her feet were frozen on the step. The townhouse had a large foyer, the black-and-white squares dramatic beneath the massive brass-and-crystal chandelier. The staircase curved up and around, the banister a work of art in metal and wood. One hand gripped it tightly and she hoped she could keep herself from falling.

Would she hurt herself badly if she fainted from this height?

She'd only come close to fainting once in her life and that was during her first season. Aunt Deborah had insisted on her corset being pulled an inch tighter than it normally was and she hadn't been able to breathe correctly the whole night.

One of her hands fluttered to her chest. No, she was breathing well. Yet her heart felt as if it stopped and started not once but several times. During all of it, she'd been unable to move her feet.

She couldn't move. Her feet would not work.

He was staring at her.

Logan McKnight was staring at her.

She tried, she really did, to look away, but his gaze pinned her there, feet immobile, breathing fast, heart erratic.

What was Logan McKnight doing here? Was he the member of Parliament who was a rabble-rouser? She could almost imagine it of him. He would question everyone the same way he had her, no doubt.

He'd kissed her. He'd kissed her and she hadn't run screaming from the cottage. Nor had she slapped him. She hadn't said a
word to him, merely left. That's all she'd done.

What was he going to say? She could just imagine the collective
reaction if he divulged that she'd called upon him without a maid.
Even worse, she'd taken tea with him, sitting for nearly half an
hour alone in a cottage with him.

She should take him aside, as soon as possible, and plead with
him to remain silent. It was entirely possible that he wouldn't
agree, just to be contrary.

What was she going to do?

"And my fiancée," Michael was saying.

Now Logan would say something like, *"I've already met Miss
Craig before. In fact, we have had an intimate conversation, the two of
us. I ended up kissing her."*

"Miss Eleanor Craig," Michael finished.

Suddenly her feet were freed from that invisible grip. She descended the rest of the steps, her gaze on her footing, not the man
she was about to confront. Finally, she stood in front of him.

She said something, words that she had uttered hundreds of
times before, thankfully. They were instinctive, effortless cour-
tesy extended to a stranger. None of the words she spoke meant
anything to her. Nor did they divulge a hint of what she was
feeling.

He bowed slightly, then looked back at Michael.

Thankfully, he didn't say anything about having met her before. Blessedly, he didn't go into the details of their conversation.

"It's a pleasure, Miss Craig," he said.

Had his voice always been that low, sounding of Scotland? Or
had she previously been so annoyed by what he'd said that she
hadn't paid any attention to how he'd spoken?

He wasn't as handsome as Michael, but there was something
about him that was different from the other men in the room. A
sense of power, perhaps, that even Hamilton didn't possess. Or
perhaps it was determination. You immediately got the impression

that this was a man who said what he meant, meant what he said, and was determined to achieve whatever he set out to do.

He suddenly terrified her, but not in a way that made any sense.

She knew, with a strange and unwelcome certainty, that he might lure her to do unspeakable acts, to ruin herself, to say the most outlandish things. He might even say to her, *"Eleanor, let yourself be free. Be as you are in Scotland. Let me see that woman again."*

She felt feverish. Her cheeks had to be red. How odd that her hands and feet were cold.

He turned from her to answer a question someone had asked him. She felt immediately released as if she'd sprung back into the London Eleanor, silent and utterly proper.

She moved closer to Michael.

"You're looking lovely," Michael said. "I approve of your new gown."

She didn't bother asking how he realized it was new. Michael kept a tally on the oddest things. He noticed when she had new earrings. Or when she'd nearly worn through a favorite pair of shoes. Details were important to him, but sometimes she wondered if he saw the minutiae but never the larger picture.

He knew what she wore to social events, but never understood how much she detested them.

Her cousin was coming closer, advancing in that way of hers that looked like she was gliding, as if her feet didn't quite touch the floor. Despite the fact that she had given birth to two children—both of them darling creatures—Daphne was as slender as when she was a debutante.

Her complexion was pale and flawless. Her blond hair was always arranged in an elaborate style flattering her oval face. Her blue-green eyes, a rare shade Eleanor had never seen in anyone other than Deborah, were her most arresting feature.

She exuded something that only recently had Eleanor identified as confidence. Did all attractive people have it?

Perhaps it was knowledge that they'd been better served by nature than the rest of humanity. Perhaps, every morning, after looking in the mirror, they were reassured as to their worth. Eleanor didn't know, because she didn't possess such confidence. The closest she came to feeling it was the time she spent in Scotland, where she was surrounded by things she loved and memories of a father who loved her. Was the confidence beautiful people felt provided by the people around them instead of their physical appearance? Was it the adoration of others that fed their self-esteem?

Another question for which she had no answer.

Daphne spoke, words Eleanor couldn't hear. No doubt something along the lines of asking him to escort her into dinner. Just as easy as that, Logan was gone, offering his arm to her cousin, turning and leaving Eleanor without another word spoken. It felt as if he should have said something.

"I'll keep your secret. I won't tell anyone that I stole a kiss from you and you didn't protest."

He didn't say anything at all.

How surprising to feel disappointed.

HE DIDN'T UNDERSTAND how the hell Eleanor Craig was here in London, in this house. Let alone that she was engaged to be married, to a man who elicited only contempt from him. Herridge was a poseur, someone who spouted all the right words, but rarely followed through with his promises. Nor did Herridge know what the hell he was talking about half the time. He understood only about a tenth of the topics of his frequent lectures. The only saving grace was that the man was easily bored. He took up his position in the House of Lords periodically, but not as often as he should have. As far as Logan was concerned, the fewer times he attended Parliament, the better.

That was the man Eleanor was going to marry?

He couldn't decide if he was angrier about the omission of her engagement or the fact that she was going to marry Herridge. The man was a puffed-up idiot. She wasn't. Unless he'd totally misjudged her.

". . . in Parliament?"

He realized that he hadn't been paying attention to his companion's question. No doubt Mrs. Baker was not used to being ignored. She was a beauty with white-blond hair and piercing green eyes. In certain parts of the world she would probably be worshiped as an idol come to life. Here in London she'd no doubt been feted as the toast of the season.

Seen beside Eleanor, however, she was a gaslight next to a candle. He'd never liked the glare of a gas lamp, preferring candlelight where feasible.

To HER DISMAY, Eleanor was seated next to Logan.

"You two will have a great deal to discuss, both being from Scotland," her aunt said sotto voce as she passed Eleanor.

Evidently, her aunt had forgotten that she'd lived in Scotland for the past two decades, given birth to two half-Scottish children, and raised them there.

Of course, Eleanor couldn't say anything of the sort, so she sat, prayed that Logan would direct his attention to anyone but her, and hoped that the rest of this evening would not prove to be interminable like most of the social events she had been commanded to attend.

She hadn't wanted a season, but she'd known there was little chance that she could escape one. Daphne had been the toast of London a few years earlier. Aunt Deborah was hoping that Eleanor could make some kind of mark, if only to continue the family reputation. Unfortunately, that first year Eleanor fell short. The nightly ritual of having to explain everything to her aunt had been tiresome. When they attended the same function she was relieved, on one hand. It meant she wouldn't have to recount who was there, what they wore, and who said what. On the other hand, it meant that Aunt Deborah gave her a narrow-eyed glance most of the night.

Just as she was right now.

Aunt Deborah was probably going to be disappointed in her tonight, too.

Eleanor was, frankly, at a loss when it came to social functions. She didn't, despite the fact that she had diligently practiced, have the ability to laugh in that tinkling way some women possessed. Her laugh came out as a guffaw which had the effect of startling her companion.

She was bored when talking about the weather or other acceptable topics at the dinner table such as traffic in London, the erection of the newest statue, or the play currently being performed.

What she wanted to talk about would shock all the guests. Women did not discuss breeding in any form and definitely not when it came to horses.

To Eleanor's left was Logan. To her right was Daphne, and she sat across the table from Michael. The seating arrangement was commonplace. Nothing out of the ordinary, except for their guest. He was most definitely not the normal kind of visitor.

She took Logan's presence to mean that Hamilton was becoming more involved in politics. Was he going to contribute more? Or did he simply see himself as an elder statesman, someone who could give younger men advice on how to run the country?

Logan leaned closer to her. His sleeve brushed her wrist, making it tingle. What would she do if he actually put his hand on top of hers? Everyone would look. Not only would behavior like that be unacceptable, but it would cause everyone to speculate.

Thankfully, he didn't touch her.

"What are you doing here?" he asked in a soft voice as he concentrated on his soup. "You're supposed to be in Scotland."

"I'd much rather be in Scotland." A comment she couldn't make.

"I live here," she said, hearing the dull tone of her own voice. There was no excitement in it. Why should there be? She was merely stating a fact. "Most of the time."

"I wrote you," he said. "Just tonight, as a matter of fact."

Another surprise. She glanced at him and then quickly away.

"What did you say?"

"I inquired about Bruce, of course."

"Of course."

"How is he?"

She smiled, an easy expression when thinking of the puppy. "He's upstairs, in my room, happily chewing on a toy."

"I take it he's well, then."

She nodded. "Very well. And growing. You should see the change in him."

"I'd like that."

When she glanced at him it was to find him smiling at her, his eyes twinkling with mischief. "I doubt anyone would understand if you took me to your room."

She shook her head.

She mustn't look at him. Instead, she should concentrate on Michael, now in conversation with Daphne's husband. Thomas was obsequious to a fault, almost servile. Even Daphne didn't grovel as much.

Don't look at Logan. Don't look at him. Look away. Focus instead on the soup bowl placed in front of you, or the pattern of the china. The soup was a creamy bisque. Deborah's cook was extremely talented. Every meal Eleanor had eaten in London had been excellent. *Think about that instead of Logan McKnight, for the love of all that's holy.*

The rest of dinner was blessedly uneventful.

Her cousin was amusing, charming, and utterly delightful—words she'd heard Michael use once to describe Daphne. Jeremy, on the other hand, was somewhat sullen, but that didn't surprise her, either. He liked to be the center of attention and when there was a large group, like tonight, he faded into the background. He didn't have a title, a fortune, a position in politics, or a company that he was running single-handedly.

As far as Logan was concerned, he was the perfect guest. He deflected those questions he didn't choose to answer with a smile or a quip. He didn't discuss legislation, but she had a feeling that it was going to be a subject of much discussion when the gentlemen left the table.

Once dinner was over, the women would go into the drawing room and the men into Hamilton's study, where they would avail themselves of the facilities, smoke cigars, drink brandy, and talk politics.

"You didn't tell me you were engaged," Logan said in a low voice.

She glanced around surreptitiously, wondering if anyone had overheard. Everyone was concentrating on their fish course. Everyone but her aunt, who was seated at the foot of the table and looking over everything with an eye to any imperfections.

"No."

"No, you aren't? Or no, you didn't say?"

"Must you discuss this now?" she whispered. "You didn't tell me you were a member of Parliament, either. You let me think you were a shepherd, of all things."

"I almost confessed that day in the cottage. I was afraid, however, that you would be so impressed that you would turn into every other female I've met."

She stared at him. "What kind of female would that be?"

Perhaps her voice was a bit louder than she intended, because Thomas, Daphne, and Hamilton glanced at her.

Logan, however, only smiled.

Had he done that on purpose? She had the idea that he was goading her deliberately and that it was some kind of payment for not telling him she was engaged.

Annoying man.

"I understand you've recently returned from Abyssinia," Hamilton said.

She sensed Logan's instantaneous reaction. How foolish. Yet she knew, somehow, that he was wishing that the conversation would take a more comfortable turn.

"Yes," he said. Just that and no more.

The terseness of his response would have been a signal to anyone not to continue that line of questioning, but Hamilton had never been intuitive or even mildly aware.

"I understand the campaign was a success. Good thing we beat the barbarians back."

Logan put down his fork and sat back in his chair.

She didn't know how she knew, but the next words out of Logan's mouth would not be suitable for the dinner table. He was going to spear Hamilton with a few well-chosen words. Or he was going to regale the entire table with details too ghastly even for nightmares.

"I've recently returned from Scotland," she said brightly, holding up her glass of wine. "Have you recently traveled to Scotland, Mr. McKnight?"

He looked at her for a long moment. Perhaps he could read the pleading in her eyes. Or maybe rational thought broke through the fog of his anger.

"Indeed I have, Miss Craig. I was taking a sabbatical in the Highlands."

"Truly?"

She gripped her wineglass too tightly, wondering if she'd made a terrible mistake by mentioning Scotland. Was he about to divulge everything, including their kiss? Daphne looked entirely too interested in their conversation and Michael was frowning.

"It's a backward country," Michael said.

Eleanor nearly closed her eyes and moaned aloud. The very last thing she needed was for Michael to toss hot coals onto a dry bale of hay.

Logan leaned forward, addressing Michael. "I'm sorry you feel that way."

Evidently, he could be a politician after all.

"Of course Scotland isn't a backward country, Michael," she said. "In fact, I would be willing to wager that we've given the world more inventions and discoveries, not to mention advances in medicine and science, than England or the rest of the Commonwealth."

Michael looked surprised at her comment, as did the rest of the people at the table. The only person who was smiling was Logan.

As she sat back, allowing a servant to replace her fish course, she realized that Logan had done it to her again.

Chapter Sixteen

*Un*fortunately, the end of dinner didn't mean the end of the evening. The gentlemen did adjourn, leaving Aunt Deborah, Daphne, and Eleanor to go to the drawing room. As usual, Daphne played the piano. Her cousin was accomplished in a great many things. She could paint as well, and several of her landscapes adorned the walls of the townhouse. She also sang beautifully and had often entertained guests.

Eleanor could stumble through a selection of tunes, but she couldn't sing. Nor did she recite poetry with any great skill. Her talents were those things that had no place in the drawing room. She could ride like the wind, since she'd been on horseback nearly before she could walk. She could run a household, and make bread, scones, and a selection of biscuits whose recipes she'd learned from Hearthmere's cook. In addition, she was a prodigious reader, having educated herself by beginning at the first bookshelf in Hearthmere's library and continuing on. She was currently at the *P* section and was determined to finish the entirety of the library one day.

None of those skills seemed to have a place in the life she led right now. Nor would they in her future.

The gentlemen were, no doubt, involved in interesting discussions while she was pacing the drawing room.

What a pity that she couldn't participate in those conversations, but she was not supposed to know anything about what went on at Parliament. She would wager that she was as well informed as any man, with the exception of Logan perhaps. Yet because she was a woman, she was expected to only want to discuss house-keeping matters or fashion. The only exceptions to those topics were children and sometimes a man's peccadilloes.

Michael was never a subject during the all-female sessions in the drawing room. Nor, she suspected, would Logan ever be. There was something about both men that prevented them from being an object of gentle teasing. In Michael's case it was his title. With Logan it was the way he carried himself, as if he and the world had come to an agreement of sorts. It had already taken his measure and not found him wanting.

Thomas, however, was an endless source of ridicule, the comments initiated by his wife. Daphne had a razor-like wit and didn't hesitate to use it on anyone. Nor was Hamilton exempt. Despite the fact that he'd welcomed Deborah's family and was exceedingly generous to all of them, he was regularly lampooned by both women for one thing or another.

Eleanor was certain that she was the subject of ridicule the minute she was away from her aunt and cousin.

It was much harder, on the whole, to find things about each person to celebrate than it was to discover flaws or failings. Just as it was easier to be sad about a circumstance than it was to force yourself to look for something good in every situation.

She was standing in front of the fire, still cold although autumn had begun chilling the air. Daphne was at the piano while Deborah sat at the window in her favorite chair. The room was the most popular public room in the townhouse and decorated in shades of blue and green. It was a lovely room if a bit blowsy with all the flower patterns on the upholstery and occasional pillows. It flattered her aunt and cousin's coloring, leading Eleanor to believe that's why these particular shades had been chosen. She doubted that Hamilton had any input into the new decorations.

"Michael looked exceptionally handsome this evening," her aunt said.

Eleanor nodded.

"You will be a very attractive countess," Deborah added. "His equal in appearance."

Her aunt had been fulsome in her compliments ever since Michael had spoken to Hamilton. Eleanor wished she had as much confidence as Deborah did.

"If I am, it's all due to you," Eleanor said. "And your training. Although I'm not feeling up to being a countess."

"What do you mean?" Daphne said, hitting a discordant note on the piano. "What a ridiculous comment, Eleanor. You had better feel up to being a countess. From the moment you're married you'll be the Countess of Wescott in any function you attend. The honor of the family will be yours to uphold."

Eleanor stared at her cousin. She'd rarely heard Daphne so passionate.

"Not to mention all the duties you'll be expected to perform. You're to oversee the annual spring fair. You're to preside over the inspection of the servants once a month. You must ensure that the grounds of Abermarle are immaculate at all times, the perfect home for Michael. You are to meet with the head of the church which is on the grounds of Abermarle. There are a great many functions that require your presence. For example, the Wescott School for Girls. You are their sponsor. As such, you must address them at the beginning of term and award academic prizes at the end of every school year."

"How do you know all of that?" Eleanor asked, amazed.

Daphne stood and walked away from the piano, heading for the sofa near her mother.

"All you have to do is ask a few questions, Eleanor. Talk to people who know his mother, ask what she did. It's very simple."

Except that she'd never considered investigating her duties with the battle planning of a general. She'd obviously underestimated her cousin. Nor had she ever considered that Daphne had once set her cap for Michael.

Michael had been a bachelor for some time. That was one of the first things she learned about him, along with the notion that he was unattainable. The longer she thought about it, the more sense it made. Of course Daphne would have set her sights on an earl. Perhaps that's why she'd been so out of sorts ever since the engagement had been announced. Did she think that the life facing Eleanor should have rightfully been hers?

More than once before tonight, Daphne had made some kind of disparaging comment about Eleanor's ability to take on the role of countess with equanimity.

"You'll have to learn how to address everyone and heaven forbid if you make a mistake. No one forgets something as important as that."

According to Daphne, the peerage was a coven of gorgons, dragon-headed and spouting fire, eating those who dared to mingle among them. Since she didn't want to embarrass her family or herself, Eleanor had been determined to learn everything she needed to learn. Yet secretly she doubted that everything would be as dire as Daphne predicted.

Instead, Eleanor suspected that her life was going to be remarkably similar to how she was living now. Her residence would be lovely, large, stately, and impressive. The servants would be numerous, except that they would call her Your Ladyship. She'd have different stationery and perhaps more people would wish to call on her. Otherwise, she would be doing exactly what she was doing now, waiting on Michael, questioning her life, and wishing she was in Scotland.

LOGAN COULDN'T GET past the fact that Eleanor was engaged to be married. She'd conveniently left that information out of their conversation. Not only was she engaged, but she was going to be Michael Herridge's wife.

The man was an ass.

Worse, he was an arrogant, autocratic ass. Logan hadn't liked him from the minute he'd met the man during one of his uncle's social events. Thankfully, they didn't have the occasion to meet all that often.

Herridge had a reputation of being a womanizer. Rumor had him with a selection of mistresses, most of them former actresses. Logan honestly didn't care about the man's morals—at least, he hadn't until he'd been faced with the fact that Herridge was Eleanor's fiancé.

He'd been surprised, and not in a good way, by the change in her. Except for that one comment about Scotland, she'd been subdued and silent during dinner.

What had happened to the woman he'd met in Scotland?

That woman was nowhere in evidence tonight. The disappointment he felt was tangible. He wanted to talk to her, to figure out what had changed so drastically in such a short time.

Fear had something to do with it. He noticed her glance around the table beneath her lashes, as if afraid that someone might have overheard his remark. Was she treated badly?

Why was she living in London and not Scotland? Why wasn't she home at Hearthmere? All this evening had provided him was another mystery, but this one annoyed him. He wanted to understand all the facts. Right at the moment, all he had was conjecture.

"You were instrumental in helping Disraeli with the voting act," his host said, passing him a snifter of brandy. Logan took it and nodded.

"It seemed a good step. We're not there, completely, but it's more than where we were. A million new voters were added to the rolls."

"What do you mean, first step?" Herridge asked. "What the hell do you want? For everyone in the Commonwealth to be able to vote?"

"Why not?" Logan asked. "If a government is going to have any control over your life, shouldn't you be able to choose it?"

"Next you'll be saying that women should be able to vote."

"There is already some talk about that," Logan said. "Don't be surprised if it happens down the road."

"Are you insane?"

Logan sipped from the snifter. Like everything tonight, the brandy was the best money could buy.

"I'm not saying it will happen next year or the year after that, but it's inevitable."

Logan couldn't decide who looked more disturbed by that information: his host, Herridge, or the other two men.

"I've known a great many women who were as well versed in matters as were men. Some perhaps more so. Why should they be denied the vote simply because they are women?"

"Don't be a fool, man. Because they're women, that's why. Everything is emotion to them. They have no ability to reason."

From what Logan had seen, Eleanor Craig wasn't overemotional, had the ability to discern a problem and its solution, and was the most determined woman he'd ever met. Of course, that was the woman in Scotland, not her pale shadow here.

Perhaps he should hold Herridge responsible for the change. That decision ratcheted up his dislike of the man. Herridge should stick to his actresses and leave Scottish women alone.

"You're wrong," Logan said. "But if that's your opinion of women, I pity the females in your life, including your fiancée."

Herridge took a few steps toward him and was restrained only by Richards grabbing his arm. The older man said something to the earl, but the words were so low that Logan couldn't hear.

As for Logan, he was tired of being polite. He only had a certain tolerance for arrogance and stupidity, and he'd reached his for tonight. He placed the almost full snifter on the sideboard, then turned to his host and said, "If you'll pardon me, I think I should leave. I see no good coming from any further discussion."

"Perhaps that would be for the best," Richards said.

If Richards had wanted to influence him in some way, the evening had been an abysmal failure.

Logan opened the door of the study with a feeling of relief.

*B*EFORE *E*LEANOR *COULD* comment on Daphne's revelations, they were interrupted by the men returning. She hadn't expected them so soon and it was evident that something had happened. Hamilton looked distressed, enough that Deborah stood and went to her husband's side. Michael's face was splotched with color. Jeremy looked less bored than usual. Even Thomas, usually the most amenable of men, wore an expression she'd never seen. There were twin lines above his narrowed eyes and his mouth was pursed as if he was holding back words that weren't acceptable for mixed company.

Only Logan appeared calm, wearing a half smile which made her suspect he was responsible for the other men's anger.

"I must take my leave, Mrs. Richards," Logan said, coming to stand in front of Deborah. "Thank you for a delicious dinner and for your hospitality."

He glanced at Eleanor. "If you would walk me to the door, Miss Craig, I would be appreciative."

What was he doing? Everyone looked as surprised as she felt. Such a request was out of the ordinary. She should refuse, but that would probably only make the situation worse, or she could simply do as he asked.

She nodded, preceded him out of the drawing room, down the hall, and to the foyer.

Once at the door, she turned to him. "You shouldn't have asked me to walk you out."

"Why not?"

"It's not done."

"Now you sound like Fred."

"Who's Fred?"

"My secretary. My campaign advisor. My calendar watcher. My mother, in a great many ways."

She folded her arms and stared at him. "He certainly wouldn't have been happy with you tonight."

He smiled at her, that smile that had the ability to wipe the thoughts from her mind. He really shouldn't have that effect on her. Her fiancé was in the drawing room. The majordomo was lurking somewhere. Any moment now he'd pop around the corner.

"What happened in there?"

Logan smiled. "Meet me tomorrow and I'll tell you."

"What?"

"Meet me tomorrow," he repeated. "I'd like to talk to you without so many eager ears about."

"I can't."

"You can."

"I shouldn't."

"Perhaps you're right," he said. "But I'd like to see Bruce again. Could you arrange that?"

"I walk him three times a day in Queen's Park," she said, opening the door and standing aside.

"I'll be there."

She watched as he descended the steps and signaled to his driver. Only then did she close the door, knowing that she had to turn and go back to the drawing room. She glanced up at the steps longingly, wishing she could retreat to her room now. First, however, she'd have to make whatever excuses she could to her relatives and Michael.

It was obvious that she was the topic of conversation when she returned to the drawing room. Everyone stopped talking at her appearance.

Michael was standing there with Daphne and Thomas. Deborah was seated next to Hamilton, whose face was flushed. His white muttonchops were still quivering with outrage.

What had Logan said to them?

"What was that all about, Eleanor?" Daphne asked.

Eleanor hated it when Daphne assumed that superior attitude, as if she was somehow the arbiter of everything that was right, proper, and just. Especially when Eleanor was without a valid explanation.

"I don't know," she said.

"Why did McKnight want to talk with you?" Michael asked,

his face expressionless. She'd learned to gauge his mood by the look in his eyes, however, and right now he was irritated.

"I don't know," she said again, wishing she wasn't being forced to lie.

The truth would be too difficult to explain at the moment. The time for doing that was when she and Logan had first encountered each other tonight. She should have said something to the effect of, "Oh, yes, I remember you, Mr. McKnight. We met in Scotland."

Instead, they'd pretended not to know each other.

"What did he talk about?"

She didn't lie easily, but she found herself doing so now. "He expressed an interest in Hearthmere's horses."

He stared at her for one long uncomfortable moment before nodding.

"You shouldn't have agreed to accompany him to the door, Eleanor," her aunt said. "He was wrong for singling you out. You compounded the issue by agreeing."

"It won't happen again," she said, wondering if that was enough groveling for everyone.

It was a curious feeling being a pariah. She felt as though they were all looking at her out of the corners of their eyes and waiting for her to do something else shocking.

Michael was still annoyed. That was obvious from the way he said his farewells with barely a word to her while thanking her aunt and Hamilton fulsomely for the evening.

It was a distinctly unpleasant experience being frozen out. She would never mention Logan McKnight again. Nor would she let anyone know that she had every intention of meeting him in the morning.

Chapter Seventeen

Eleanor was up before the rest of the household, so she was able to take Bruce out, then grab a quick breakfast before dressing. She and Bruce slipped out of the house via the servants' stairs, heading for Queen's Park.

It was early, too early to expect Logan to be there. That's what she told herself when she entered the wrought iron gate and closed it behind her. They walked a little farther than their normal route, heading for a more populated area. They only encountered one couple walking arm in arm and two men on horseback.

The day was a brisk one, with an icy tinge to the breeze. She'd only worn a shawl this morning, but she didn't return to the house for her coat. The cold was all she smelled. Gone was the lingering scent of late-blooming flowers or even the dust stirred up by the horses.

Bruce investigated an insect, caught a twig, and barked at the wind stirring up falling leaves.

She found a bench alongside one of the paths, sat, and went through Bruce's training. He didn't seem ready to listen, but the lure of the liver finally convinced him to demonstrate what he'd learned.

An hour passed and there wasn't a sign of Logan. She was foolish to be disappointed and even sillier to be here at all. Her nose felt as if it would be permanently cold, and her fingers were getting numb.

She'd told Logan about Queen's Park only because it was

important that they meet. She needed to ensure he knew two things, namely that she was engaged to be married. He shouldn't single her out in any way should they happen to meet in the future.

Second, she wanted his word that he wouldn't say anything about what had happened in Scotland. She didn't want to have to explain her momentary lapse in judgment to anyone. Besides, she already had more than enough complications in her life.

One of them was trying to chew on the toe of her shoe right now.

She pulled back her foot and tried to interest Bruce in a twig instead.

Bruce was no longer a fluffy little ball of fur. The shape of his face was changing. His nose was elongating and he was acquiring an impressive amount of very sharp teeth. In a matter of months he would be nearly the size of Peter and Paul, the dogs that had guarded the sheep. Even now he had some behaviors that confused her until she realized that one of his parents must have been a herding dog. He would sometimes circle her as if trying to move her in a certain direction.

If Logan had shown up she was going to ask him about Bruce's parents. He didn't look exactly like Peter or Paul, but she suspected that he was still part border collie.

She stood, calling out to Bruce, and gently tugging on the end of the lead.

"We might as well leave, Bruce."

When the puppy returned to her side, she bent down and petted him from his pointy ears to his fluffy tail.

"It's silly to be disappointed, isn't it?"

Michael was her fiancé. She should keep that thought uppermost in her mind. Anything she felt for Logan McKnight, be it curiosity or compassion, should be squashed immediately. As should the memory of his kiss.

Up until then Michael was the only man who had ever kissed her. He'd done so almost like a brand, as if to say, "There, you're mine."

Logan's kiss, on the other hand, had been light and quick, almost teasing.

She'd spent entirely too much time last night thinking about him, putting everything she'd learned about Logan into place, like he was a puzzle she was solving.

Bruce strained on the lead.

"We'll come back, I promise," she said. "You can investigate whatever you're interested in later."

It was no use. He was pulling and he never did that. Even worse, he twisted his head back and forth. She didn't realize what he was doing until the lead completely slipped off. In a flash Bruce was running.

"Come back!"

She grabbed her skirt with both hands, grateful that she'd worn one of her older dresses this morning. She hadn't needed more than two petticoats with it. Nor did it require a bustle.

She made it across the road and saw Bruce jumping up excitedly on Logan's pant legs. She stopped where she was, watching as he bent and corrected the puppy.

"Down. Sit."

To her amazement Bruce did exactly that. But his tail still wagged so fiercely that it shook his entire body.

A minute later Logan looked over to see her. "You need to stop him from doing that. One of these days he'll be capable of knocking someone down."

Emotions flooded her. Gratitude that Bruce hadn't run away. Confusion that Logan was criticizing her. Joy that he was here and guilt because of feeling that.

"You're right," she finally said. "But he's doing very well with other commands." She listed everything that he could do.

Logan bent and scratched the puppy's ears. "Then you're a smart boy, aren't you? Do you want to learn some things your mother can do?"

She watched as Logan led the way back to the bench where

she'd been sitting. Once there, he waited until she again sat before joining her.

"Who are his parents?" she asked. "I suspect one of his parents is a border collie, but what about the other?"

He smiled. "No one knows," he said. "You're right. His mother is a champion herder, but let's just say she went far afield. Bruce is the only one of the litter who looks like his mother. The others must take after their father. They're coal black with white-and-black faces."

When Bruce tried to climb his trousers, Logan gently pushed the puppy back down to the grass.

"This is a hand command," he said, flattening his hand and showing the palm to Bruce. "He'll learn this first. Then you'll add the word to it. *Down*, in this case."

He ran through a series of commands she was determined to memorize. One by one they practiced them with Bruce. Not surprisingly he was quick to learn, earning praise from both of them.

"Later on," Logan said, "all you'll have to do is whistle to get him to obey."

"I can't whistle."

"Of course you can. Everyone can whistle."

"I can't."

"Have you ever tried?" he asked.

"Of course I have." When he looked dubious she repeated, "I have."

"Whistle for me."

"What?"

"Try to whistle."

"How ridiculous, Logan. I'm not going to try to whistle."

"You never know if you can or can't do something until you try, Eleanor. Who knows, you might be an expert at whistling. People would come from all around just to hear you."

How silly he was being and how foolish she was for smiling at him.

"I honestly never thought of giving him commands by whistling."

"It's how a shepherd controls his border collies from far away. A whistle travels farther than a man's voice."

"You know a great deal about being a shepherd without being a shepherd."

"I've known Old Ned since I was a boy," he admitted. "I learned everything from him."

"Including how to train a dog?"

"That, too."

For the next quarter hour he showed her and then Bruce various commands, including go left, go right, go far, and stop. To her surprise Bruce picked up the last two with little difficulty, but the first two needed practice.

"You'll need to train him every day. It's not something you can just do once or twice. Consistency is the key."

"Do I really need a dog that's trained to herd sheep?"

"Those commands can come in handy at any time. Besides, a well-trained dog is a better companion. Something else you need to consider. Bruce comes from a long line of working dogs. He'll need a job."

"I don't have any sheep he can guard," she said.

"Then his job will be to protect you."

She looked down at the puppy, now rolling on his back in the grass. Even though he seemed to be growing larger every day, it was still difficult to think of him as a guard dog.

"You knew that when you gave him to me, didn't you? Did you think I needed a protector?"

"Honestly? I wasn't thinking of that. All I knew was that he needed someone to love him and I thought you could do with a little companionship as well."

"Do you go around giving puppies to strangers all the time?"

"It's the first time I've ever done it. And probably the last. Unless, of course, I meet another beautiful woman on the road in Scotland."

He really had to stop saying things like that. She wasn't beautiful, especially compared to Deborah or Daphne. She was simply herself.

"Now, about whistling," he said. "All you have to do is wet your lips, then make sure your mouth is pursed a certain way."

He demonstrated, whistling one note.

She did as he instructed, making a moue of her mouth.

"Breathe through your lips."

She did, making the tiniest sound, nothing close to his whistle, however. Still, he seemed pleased, smiling at her.

A man's smile had never had that effect on her, but his did. It was as if his happiness incited hers, which was ridiculous. Her emotions weren't tied to his. Nor did he have the ability to alter her mood. Or shouldn't.

"Do it again," he said.

He startled her by placing both his hands on either side of her mouth and pressing her lips together even more.

"There. Try a whistle again."

This time, the sound was stronger.

He dropped his hands. "There, you have it. All you have to do is practice for a bit and you'll be able to do more than one note."

He was too close. His eyes were direct, almost as if he was talking to her in his gaze. His look told her that he wanted to do much more than teach her how to whistle.

Reason enough for her to pull back, but she didn't.

"You'll have to practice your whistle as well as Bruce's training."

"He's a great deal of trouble, you know."

The puppy was a bother in many ways, but he was also a joy, which surprised her. She truly hadn't realized how lonely she was in London. Bruce was a bit of Scotland by her side. He demanded her attention and it was surprisingly gratifying to care for him.

"I imagine he's taking you away from all your fittings for your trousseau," he said.

There it was, the mention of her engagement. How strange that he'd brought it up this way.

Bruce jumped up on the bench, the first time he'd done so, wedging his way between the two of them. Once he was satisfied that his favorite people were near, he settled down, making himself a nest on the fabric of Eleanor's skirt.

She smiled down at him, petting him as he sighed into sleep. There were times when he almost reduced her to tears because he was so sweet and defenseless.

"You've always struck me as a woman of intelligence."

She glanced at him.

"I can't understand, however, why you would agree to marry Herridge. The man's an idiot."

"I don't think that's a fair assessment. You and he may have differing opinions on certain matters, but it doesn't mean that he's an idiot."

"Very well, he's an ass."

Anyone else would offer an apology for that particular word, claiming that it slipped out unintentionally. Knowing Logan as she was beginning to, she knew it was deliberate. She also knew that he wasn't going to apologize.

"Why did you agree to marry him?"

No one had ever asked her that question before. She looked at him and then away, concentrating on the line of oaks stretching out before her.

"Everyone has to marry."

"Do they?"

She glanced at him again. "Don't tell me that you've never given a thought to marriage."

"It isn't something that's important. At least, not yet."

"When? When you're old and doddering?"

His smile was quick, amusement mirrored in his eyes. "Perhaps not that far away. But it hasn't been something I've given a lot of thought to."

"Perhaps you should. No doubt you have a great many women interested in you. After all, you're probably a catch. You're a member of Parliament. You have some intellect. You have all your limbs."

"What about my sterling character, my ethics, my morals?"

"No doubt those all play a part," she said.

"What was it about Herridge that made you say yes? I doubt it was his sterling character, ethics, or morals. Was it his title?"

"No," she said, looking down at Bruce adrift in dreams. Was he herding sheep? Or just running through the grass? "If anything, his title was a detriment."

Logan's expression wasn't difficult to read.

"I know you don't believe me, but it's the truth. Oh, everyone in my family is overjoyed, but the prospect of being a countess is rather frightening."

Why on earth had she told him that?

He looked at her the way Bruce did sometimes with his head tilted slightly, an expression in his eyes that made her think he was waiting to be convinced.

She shook her head. She really didn't want to continue this conversation. It was too personal.

"What happened last night?" she asked.

"Last night?"

She frowned at him. He knew perfectly well what she meant.

"Did Michael insult Scotland? Or did Hamilton demand to know about Abyssinia?"

He smiled. "Neither. We were discussing women, as I recall. How emotional they were and how lacking in sense."

"Do you feel that way?"

"It wasn't me. That was your future husband."

Now was the perfect opportunity to tell him that he mustn't single her out in any way. Doing so would further irritate Michael, and although she was certain that irritating Michael would please Logan to no end, it would only cause her problems.

When she said as much to him, he didn't say anything for a moment.

Finally, he said, "I'm going to make it my life's work never to see you again, Eleanor."

She met his eyes before looking away. Why would he say something like that? He hadn't seemed like the kind of person who would deliberately hurt someone else.

"Why?" she couldn't help but ask. Even as she did she knew it was foolish. She was tiptoeing too close to something forbidden. Instead, she should welcome his words, proof that one of them was sensible.

"Why?" He sat back, regarding the canopy of branches above them. "Because you're a temptation. You make me want to say things that I shouldn't. Or do things that are unwise. You intrigue me and irritate me and a half-dozen other emotions. It would be infinitely better if I forgot you."

"Oh."

She didn't know whether to be pleased at his words or horrified. He wasn't sensible after all.

Neither was she.

"I'm surprised that you don't clash with Herridge, but you don't, do you? He doesn't see you as you truly are, does he? You're an entirely different person in London, Eleanor, than the woman I met in Scotland. What's happened to you?"

"You can be the most obnoxious man."

He grinned at her. "There she is. That's the woman I've been missing."

She frowned at him. She really shouldn't be here. Nor, if she was honest with herself, should she be enjoying herself so much.

She could almost hear her aunt's voice, disembodied and sounding too censorious. *Eleanor, what do you think you're doing? Michael wouldn't be happy if he saw you now. Do you want to jeopardize your engagement?*

They really should go back to addressing each other properly, not as Logan and Eleanor. Yet as long as they were alone—another impropriety—did it matter?

Her aunt would say yes. So would her cousin.

So would all of society.

How very strange that she didn't seem to care.

"Why are you so different here? In Scotland you were animated, interesting, and a fascinating woman."

"And I'm not now?" she asked, her face warming.

"You're still fascinating, but not for the same reasons. I'm confused. There's Scottish Eleanor and then there's London Eleanor. What happens, you cross the border and you change?"

She didn't know how to answer him. "I don't feel like myself here," she finally said. "I never have."

"You're suffering from the same disease I've seen in other fellow Scots. You feel inferior to the English."

"Do I?" She regarded him with amazement. "I don't think I do, no."

"Then why are you so different?"

She thought about it for a moment. She knew who she was at home. Eleanor Craig of Hearthmere. Here she was simply Eleanor Craig, transplanted Scot. Of no importance, actually.

When she said that to him, he smiled. "You do feel inferior or you wouldn't say that you're of no importance. You're just as good as any English woman, Eleanor, and perhaps better than most. You're a Scot."

"I shall take care to remind myself of that every morning," she said.

How odd that it was so easy to smile at him. Or feel a rush of pleasure when he smiled back.

Chapter Eighteen

$\mathcal{H}$e stood, and just when she thought he was going to walk away, he turned and extended one hand to her. She put her hand in his, marveling at the warmth of his palm, and stood.

"You're freezing," he said.

"I'm a little cold," she agreed.

"You should return to the house right now."

She nodded. She really should, for more than one reason.

Her conscience made her step away slightly as Bruce jumped up and off the bench. She reached for the lead, saying, "He'll run away."

"No, he won't," Logan said. "Besides, he needs to learn to remain at your side."

"Who's being trained, me or Bruce?"

Logan smiled. "Both of you. Next time you come, be sure and bring some treats for him. There are those who believe that punishment is the best trainer, but I'm not one of them."

She reached into the pocket of her skirt with her free hand and pulled out her handkerchief.

"Liver," she said, showing him. "One of the maids told me that anything that smells strong will work. I detest liver myself, but Bruce seems to love it."

"Wise girl. And wise you for listening to her."

The warmth she felt wasn't wise at all.

She loved hearing his voice because it brought back Scotland to her. Her cousins didn't sound Scottish and that was due to her aunt's constant correction.

Instead of returning to the house, they walked together, hand in hand, for a few moments. She should have pulled her hand free, but she left it in his. For warmth only, although that excuse sounded feeble.

"Are you really going to try to avoid me for the rest of your life?"

"Our paths hadn't crossed before, Eleanor. I doubt they'll cross again. London is big enough. After last night I'm sure your family wouldn't relish our association. Besides, I got the impression that you would rather I hadn't appeared."

"I was afraid you were going to say something about meeting me in Scotland. I hadn't acted very proper with you."

How odd that she found it so easy to be honest with him.

He placed her hand on his arm and together they walked to the road, keeping to the side of it. She glanced behind them and he was right. Bruce was on their heels. Still, she didn't feel all that comfortable letting him roam free.

"If it makes you feel better you can put the lead on him."

She did just that, and when she joined him again she didn't put her hand on his arm. Instead, they walked close together. Anyone looking at them would think that they were a couple. A man and his wife, perhaps, or a woman and her fiancé. They might even be relatives, but she doubted anyone would guess at what they were: nearly strangers but oddly friends.

"Tell me about Eleanor Craig," he said. "Pretend that we've never met. What would you want me to know about you?"

She glanced at him. "Why? You don't want to see me again."

"Very well. I'll begin, shall I?" He hesitated for a moment, and she was certain he wasn't going to speak further, but then he surprised her. "I didn't want to be in Abyssinia. I didn't want to die in a battle that few people knew about and even fewer would care about."

"Isn't that the definition of courage? To be afraid and yet carry on?"

"I'm not a hero. I was trying, most of the time, to figure out how not to die."

"I think anyone would feel the same, don't you? Or do you ask more of yourself than most people would? Do you have to be better than anyone else?"

"Yes."

Surprised, she glanced at him again. "Why?"

He shrugged. "Perhaps it was the way I was raised. I have an obligation to the family name. I'm expected to be better than average."

She didn't know what to say to that.

"Perhaps it's because my parents are dead."

"So are mine," she said.

"Any brothers or sisters?" he asked.

She shook her head.

"I have a sister who's married and lives in Edinburgh with her husband and two children."

He shouldn't divulge any more about himself. She didn't want a connection to him. She didn't want to feel compassion or even curiosity. All of those would be dangerous emotions to have around Logan McKnight. She already felt closer to him than she should.

She should have remained silent. She shouldn't have offered any information about herself, but she found herself talking.

"I was born at Hearthmere," she said. "My mother died three days after my birth. My father raised me, at least until I was eleven. When he died, my uncle and his family came to live with me."

She didn't think her uncle had been very prosperous in Edinburgh. The terms of her father's will were that her uncle and his family could live at Hearthmere until Eleanor turned eighteen. At that time it would be her decision whether her uncle's family remained.

That decision, however, had been taken away from her. At the age of seventeen her uncle had died. Deborah lost no time in returning to London, taking her two children and Eleanor with her.

She told Logan an abbreviated version of her history. When she was done, he only shook his head.

"What does that mean?" she asked. "Are you disgusted? Annoyed? Disbelieving? I don't know what it means when you just shake your head like that. That's why we have words, Logan. Or should I just whistle to you?"

His laugh startled her.

"I understand why you became London Eleanor, but I think I prefer the Scottish version better."

She frowned at him. He reached over and hugged her, surprising her again. He really shouldn't touch her and he most definitely shouldn't hug her.

"We shouldn't be here together," she said.

He nodded. "I shouldn't be so close to you now."

"No, you shouldn't. Are you really going to try to avoid me?"

"I'd be a fool not to."

She didn't want him to disappear, which was a bit of idiocy on her part. He had no role in her life. He was right; her family wouldn't understand their relationship. She wasn't entirely certain she understood.

He lured her as no one else ever had. He tempted her to do things she'd never thought of doing. She wanted him to kiss her again except this time she didn't want a quick, teasing kiss. This kiss should be slower, softer, longer. She would remember it for the rest of her life. Or perhaps she would recall her own daring, walking with Logan in a shadowed wood.

She placed one hand against his jacket, close to his heart. She really shouldn't touch him any more than he should reach out and place his hand at the small of her back, gently guiding her forward. They were almost embracing, the pose of a couple ready to kiss.

If they were in Scotland she wouldn't feel a frisson of alarm. They weren't in Scotland, however, but in a public park in London. Anyone could see them. Anyone would remark about their closeness and the fact that neither one of them drew away.

She should recall that she was engaged.

Yet nothing mattered but looking into Logan's eyes, keeping his gaze as he placed his other arm around her, fully embracing her.

She didn't say a word of protest as he bent his head. Nor did she move away when he kissed her, his arms pulling her even closer. For a matter of seconds, perhaps minutes, she lost her sense of self, the apartness she'd felt for years.

Her hands grabbed his jacket, holding on as her knees nearly buckled. Her heartbeat escalated; her breathing grew tight. Blood heated and pounded as her skin warmed. She wanted to be closer, for this feeling to continue, to never end. He was no longer a stranger or quite a friend. Instead, he was more than that. She couldn't explain it to anyone, even as the kiss ended and he stepped back.

She, too, stepped away, her gaze on the ground and not on him. How could she possibly meet his eyes? She should be ashamed of her actions instead of hungering for something that lay just beyond her knowledge. She'd heard of passion before as well as desire. Some of the books in Hearthmere's library had not been geared toward history, politics, religion, or animal husbandry. Some had been poetry where lovers extolled the virtues of being with their heart's desire. Or novels where women longed for knights or gave their hearts to men of strength and courage.

This association was different, less noble, and perhaps more earthy. She wanted him to touch her bare skin, to follow through with all the sensations his kiss promised. She wanted to know what lovemaking was like when her senses were involved as well as her mind. When he tempted her and challenged her and made her laugh.

The world would not understand why she stood there, one hand still on his arm, the other clutching the fabric of her skirt. Nor would society comprehend how difficult it was to take another step away from him, letting her hand fall. Glancing down at Bruce, she made a show of ensuring that his lead was in place. Would Logan see that her hands trembled?

She couldn't think of a word to say to excuse her behavior. Perhaps it would be wiser to accuse him, to excoriate him for his actions. After all, he was the one who had initiated the kiss. She hadn't stepped away, however. Nor had she run away as she had in Scotland. Even now, she wanted to kiss him again.

If the world knew her thoughts, she'd be chastised and shamed. Thankfully, no one would ever know.

All she had to do now was turn and walk away, encouraging Bruce to stay at her side. That's all. All she had to do was lift her foot and put it down a few inches away, and begin her departure.

She wanted to remain with him, and wasn't that a telling confession? She wanted to ask him about his childhood, about his thoughts for the future. She wanted to know about his sister and her children, how he came to know Old Ned. What he had learned about sheep, about Parliament. What were his greatest wishes? What did he want to achieve as a member of Parliament? Who did he emulate? Who was his mentor? A variety of questions espousing a curiosity that she'd never felt before for any man.

Everything about him interested her.

She finally managed to turn and walk a few steps away. He didn't say anything when she stopped, her back to him. She was a fool to expect him to urge her to stay.

They had both acted irrationally and despite their better selves. She glanced at him over her shoulder to find that he was watching her.

"I . . ." Her words ground to a halt. What did she say to him? How could she possibly explain herself? He was too entrancing, too interesting, too compelling. She should never be alone with him again. Nor should she ever have another thing to do with him.

"I have meetings tomorrow," he said in that voice she already loved so well. "But I'll be here the day after."

Now she should tell him that he was wiser earlier when he said he was going to avoid her. She should remind him of that statement and tell him that it was the safest and best course. Instead, all she did was nod just once before turning back.

Heading for the gate was the hardest thing she'd done in a very long time.

Chapter Nineteen

The day Logan was due back at the park, Eleanor took extra care with her appearance. She wore one of her newer dresses, a rich dark green that reminded her of spring in Scotland. Unfortunately, due to the weather, she had to cover it up with her plain black cloak, but the hem peeped out. If the wind wasn't so forceful in the park she'd unbutton it to reveal the dress.

In addition, she asked Barbara for help with her hair. If the woman thought it was odd that Eleanor needed her services midmorning, perhaps she would believe that Eleanor was preparing herself for the life of a countess, to be as attractive as possible at every moment of every day.

An hour later she left the house with Bruce on his new leather lead. This one was longer to accommodate his training. In the last day and a half she'd also practiced whistling not only when she'd taken Bruce to Queen's Park, but also in the privacy of her bedchamber. No one knocked on the door to ask what that odd sound was, so evidently the original builders of the house had made the walls thick enough that she wasn't overheard.

Once through the wrought iron gate she found herself walking rapidly, then made herself slow down. It wouldn't do to look too eager.

She'd gone most of her life without knowing Logan. What did it matter that she hadn't seen him for a day and a half? Someone

didn't come into your life that quickly and make themselves in-
dispensable. Yet it was as if a spot that hadn't been there before
had suddenly appeared and he'd slipped into it easily. So easily
that when he wasn't there the space felt like an enormous cavern.

She wanted to hear his voice again. She wanted to know about
his day. What kind of meetings had taken his time? Perhaps he
wouldn't tell her, considering it confidential knowledge that she
had no right to know.

No doubt he was such a source of fascination for her because
he was unabashedly Scottish. Or because he reminded her of
Hearthmere. Or simply because he'd expressed an interest in her.

The proper thing to do would be to tell him that she couldn't
see him again. Kissing him had been wrong, even though she
hadn't been able to forget either of his kisses.

She was engaged to be married.

Today she would tell Logan that he'd been wiser than she in
wanting to forget her. She would tell him that it would be wrong
for him to come to Queen's Park again. Both of them needed to
remember the proprieties. They'd already crossed the boundary,
but they could retreat behind it once more.

Don't come here again. Forget me. I won't meet you. Such easy sentences and all she had to do was say one of them. Say it and ignore
the sadness when she did.

They walked some distance to the bench where she and Logan
had sat.

He wasn't there and the first thing she felt was disappointment.
The second emotion was a sense of relief. She wouldn't have to
say anything to him. He'd already decided that it would be better
not to appear.

How odd that the hurt felt like a living thing now, pushing
against her chest. She felt like crying, except that she never cried
in public.

Instead, she would fall back on her behavior of the past five
years. She would bury everything and hide her emotions from

everyone. She'd be silent and well behaved, mute and not betray-
ing, by word or action, anything she felt.

Bruce grabbed a twig from somewhere and was happily gnawing on it.

"Put that down," she said.

He ignored her.

She grabbed it and tossed it a few feet away. "You don't eat
twigs," she said. "They're not good for you."

He tried to eat her fingers, instead, until she told him no in a
loud voice. He gave up her fingers for her hem and was chewing
enthusiastically on it before he gave it up to attack another twig.
He brought it to her as a token of affection and it snagged the
fabric of her skirt.

"Oh, dear, I'm going to get a lecture about that, Bruce. But thank
you, all the same."

"Why a lecture?"

Her heart lurched. He was here. He had come. The day was
suddenly brighter, the morning sun streaming through the trees
a promise of the rest of the day.

"I didn't think you were coming," she said, giving him the truth.

"I wasn't going to."

"Then why are you here?"

"Because I'm an idiot."

Before she could question him further he added, "This isn't
wise, Eleanor. I told myself that at least a hundred times, but here
I am."

Bruce whimpered and wiggled, retaining his lesson not to
jump up on Logan's trousers. He did, however, lick his fingers
when Logan bent to pet him.

"So, should I welcome you or send you away?" she asked as he
sat beside her, Bruce jumping up to join them.

She knew which would be proper, but that didn't seem to matter.

He didn't answer, which was just as well. They could both pretend that this meeting wasn't improper.

"Tell me about your family."

"My family?" When he nodded, she thought for a moment. "I only have my aunt and two cousins left," she said. "Hamilton is my aunt's second husband. I never know what to call him. He's not strictly my uncle. My aunt's first husband and I were related. Deborah and I are related by law, I suppose."

He settled back against the bench, petting Bruce.

"My cousin Daphne is married," she said. "Although she doesn't seem like it. She's always there, back at my aunt's house like she never left. She's either taking tea with my aunt or eating a meal with us. Or they're off shopping together."

"You don't go with them?" he asked.

She shook her head. "I'm a lamentable shopper," she confessed. "I have no style of my own, you see. I can't look at something and say whether or not it would flatter me. Most things don't, I've found. I prefer plain colors rather than patterns and definitely not stripes."

"Why not stripes?"

She glanced over at him. "You can't possibly care."

"On the contrary," he said. "What is it about stripes that you object to, exactly?"

She considered the matter. "They don't make any sense. You have stripes going up and down on the skirt, but on the bodice they're often perpendicular."

"Does everything need to make sense to you, Eleanor?" he asked with a smile.

She nodded. "I think it does, in some elemental way. A great many things in London don't make sense."

"The exact sentiments of a Scot."

She looked up at the sky visible through the awning of branches. Autumn was upon them and all those abundant, luxurious leaves were falling to the ground. Bruce jumped off the bench to attack a few and roll around on the others.

"I'd rather be in Scotland. Anywhere in Scotland, but mostly home, at Hearthmere. Or on Maud, where I could ride for hours and not see anyone." She looked over at him. "Except for sheep, of course. And a shepherd or two."

"Herridge doesn't care for Scotland."

"No," she said, agreeing.

"Will you be able to return once you're married?"

The truth was there, stark and incapable of being hidden. "No. Probably not."

They sat silent for long moments. At least he didn't say anything else about Michael. She didn't want to think about her fiancé now. There was time enough to mull over her marriage later.

These moments, however long, stolen and improper, didn't fit into her future.

"How did your meetings go?"

"Two went well. The third was abysmal. All in all, it wasn't a complete loss of a day. Of course, I didn't get to see you."

"I missed you." Should she say that? Probably not. She shouldn't be as honest with Logan as she was. Nor should she even think of him as Logan. The proper way to address him was Mr. McKnight. However, they'd skirted propriety from the beginning, hadn't they?

He didn't respond to her comment. He was so much wiser than she.

"Is it anything you can talk about? Or were those meetings secret?"

"I think one of them might be best avoided as a topic of conversation. It dealt with party politics and that is first boring and second down to egos, I'm afraid. The other issues were closer to home, things like the Scottish border and tariffs. Not at all fascinating, but always necessary."

He could make even the most mundane subject interesting. Talking to him about legislation brought the personages she'd only read about to life. Most of the time he didn't identify people by name, but by characteristics of their personality. She grew to suspect that one man was Mr. Disraeli, simply because he seemed to have a literary bent and way of looking at things. Plus, Logan indicated that he had a contentious relationship with a prior Prime Minister.

The more Logan talked, the more fascinated she became, see-ing life as a member of Parliament in a totally new way. She saw Logan differently, too. Someone might consider him brusque and demanding, but those character traits served him well in politics.

"Do you like standing for election?" she asked.

"Do I like it? It's more difficult than being granted a seat in the House of Lords along with a title. But then, we get more work done and what we do matters more."

"No doubt Michael feels the same," she said with a smile.

"Do you talk to him about politics?"

She shook her head. "It's not an approved subject. I'm not to bother my female head about it. I'm to concentrate on things like clothes and hats and gloves."

"Not shoes? Not stockings?"

Warmth was traveling up to her face. Her cheeks felt hot.

"You know quite well you're not supposed to mention stock-ings to me. Next you'll be discussing unmentionables."

"I should very much like to talk about unmentionables with you," he said. "I have often wondered why a woman wears as many undergarments as she does. Could you not dispense with your shift? After all, you have on pantaloons and a corset, do you not?"

She'd never imagined a conversation like this with anyone, let alone Logan.

"You have to wear a shift. Otherwise, the corset would chafe. It's very uncomfortable even over a shift."

"Why wear it? Is it because you don't think the human body is attractive enough and you have to squeeze it into some semblance of what society decrees?"

She truly should change the subject immediately. Yet she had the curious compulsion to answer him.

"Someone decided that a tiny waist was feminine. Therefore, every morning most women are laced into their corset."

"Most women? Are you?"

"Logan, I can't answer that."

"Why not? We've always been honest with each other. Is there a place beyond which we can't be honest?"

"There are subjects that we should not discuss. My corset is one of those."

She wore a corset, but she slipped it on by fastening the front busk since she didn't have her own maid. It wasn't unduly uncomfortable, because she could always adjust it if she wished. Daphne, however, insisted on her corset being pulled tight every morning. Probably because she wanted to prove that she still had a girlish figure even after giving birth twice. Deborah was the same. Sometimes at breakfast her aunt looked pale enough to faint.

None of which Eleanor was going to divulge to Logan.

Even the thought of talking about such things made her feel flushed. Yet one day, in the not too distant future, she would be a wife. A man was going to have the right to do more than speak intimately about her undergarments.

She was going to have to welcome Michael into her bed. He was going to initiate her into lovemaking. It was Michael's head that was going to be next to hers on the pillow. Michael was going to touch her naked body.

She didn't want to think about her wedding night, about being in her nightgown in front of Michael. The thought was excruciatingly embarrassing. He would, no doubt, expect her to remain silent and acquiescent through the entire process.

Because she'd been around horses all her life, she had a good idea of what her wedding night entailed. She could almost envision the moment, her sitting on the edge of the marital bed, clad in a new silk nightgown, hands clasped together nervously while her new husband approached her.

Would he say something to her like this? *You're about to bed an earl. I've picked you out of all the other women who were pursuing me. You should demonstrate your gratitude, Eleanor.*

She'd thought about her wedding night before, but it had never struck her as forcefully as it did now. Michael would know everything about her. Michael would know her intimately.

"What is it, Eleanor?"

"I just realized something," she said, picking her way through the words. "I just realized something I should have always known. It's like when you take a walk every day and you never notice a certain house on the corner. Or a certain lamppost or something that was there all along. All of a sudden, for no reason it becomes obvious to you. You see it for the first time when it's always been there."

He reached out and grabbed her hand, holding it between his hands.

"What's always been there?"

"Oh, Logan, I can't tell you. It's like one of those secret meetings of yours."

She really should draw her hand away but she kept it in his, taking unexpected comfort from his touch.

"Eleanor, you can always talk to me."

She stared down at Bruce attacking a leaf. "No, I can't. You've already said that you shouldn't be here. That you shouldn't have come. One day you won't. It's not fair to become a friend, Logan, and then take that friendship away."

"Is that what I am, a friend?"

She glanced at him and then off into the distance.

"Yes," she finally said. "You're my friend, but you're more than that. I don't know what to call you." She looked at him. "Is there a word for it?"

He met her gaze. "We're treading on dangerous ground, Eleanor."

She nodded, well aware of that.

"You're a conundrum, Eleanor Craig. You represent a temptation, one that I should avoid."

She didn't know what to say.

"A wiser man would've sent you a note, something along the

lines of 'The press of business requires me to stay in my office this morning. Regrettably, I will be unable to visit with you again.'"

"You've evidently penned that note in your mind to know its contents so well. Why didn't you send it?"

"As I said, you're a temptation."

"I didn't make you kiss me," she said, annoyed. "I haven't done anything out of the ordinary. I've simply been myself. A great many people consider me to be excessively boring."

"Then they're even more foolish than I am."

A flush seemed to envelop her entire body.

"I would be in a great deal of trouble if anyone knew we were meeting," she said. "No one would understand. They would ask what I could possibly find to discuss with a member of Parliament. A firebrand like you."

"You've been reading the newspapers."

She nodded. "I have. I read about you in Scotland, only I didn't know it was you. You're featured prominently and often. Is it true that you're Mr. Disraeli's pet?"

He laughed, startling her. "You mustn't read Anderson's column. He's a hack and has no love for me. Or liking, for that matter."

She did. She had a great deal of liking for Logan McKnight. The fact that it might be growing into more was suddenly frightening.

Eleanor abruptly stood. "I should return," she said. She didn't want to leave him, which was why she needed to, as quickly as she could.

She hesitated for a moment, holding on to Bruce's lead. She needed to say something, but no words came to mind. At least any that were safe, innocuous, and proper.

All she did was force a smile to her face. She turned, grabbing her skirt with one hand and Bruce's lead with the other, and nearly raced from the park.

Chapter Twenty

When Eleanor went to the park the next day with Bruce, she told herself not to be disappointed if Logan didn't appear.

He wasn't there in the morning. She occupied herself with training Bruce and walking farther than they normally went. Part of the time he was off the lead, but he always stayed beside her.

If someone had given her a puppy when she was a child, she wouldn't have grown up with a fear of dogs. She couldn't imagine ever being afraid of Bruce, not when he was so protective of her.

He growled at a squirrel who ran across the grass and then up a tree trunk. He barked at a shower of leaves. More than once the fur on his back stood straight up when someone rode past. Horses didn't seem to bother him, but carriages did, and he didn't hesitate to make his disapproval known.

After his training session he jumped up on the bench, turned in a circle, and settled in for a nap. She sat beside him, absorbing the scenery around her. Here in Queen's Park it was quiet, the cacophony of London seemingly miles away. This was the one place in the city she'd always felt at peace.

Now it would never be the same.

"I'm an idiot, Bruce."

He slitted open one eye and looked at her, flicked his tongue out, then fell back to sleep.

"I'm silly to miss him."

He only sighed in response.

She smiled and watched the leaves falling around her. Soon they'd all be gone and there would only be stark branches against a gray sky.

There wasn't much of a breeze today so she loosened the scarf around her neck. Her cloak kept her warm. Fortunately, Bruce didn't seem to mind the cold. All that fur must insulate him well.

When he woke the two of them went back to the townhouse. After lunch they would come back as they usually did. In time, perhaps, she'd forget that Logan had once been here.

A fitting occupied most of her afternoon. If her aunt hadn't been in the room Eleanor would have asked a series of questions of the seamstress. Mrs. Fournier had once lived in Paris and was very knowledgeable about a variety of subjects. In the past they'd had many fascinating conversations. Since Aunt Deborah was present, however, Eleanor remained mute. Deborah did not approve of speaking to tradesmen.

After the fittings, Eleanor took Bruce back to the park, feeling foolish as she sat on her usual bench and practiced whistling. He was an exceptionally smart puppy—retaining those lessons that Logan had begun earlier.

"Eleanor."

At first she thought it was wishful thinking. She'd wanted him to appear so fervently that she imagined him saying her name.

"Eleanor."

She turned and there he was. Not a figment of her imagination, but real.

Bruce ran to him, greeting him by wiggling, then trying to chew on Logan's shoe.

They didn't speak even after he came and sat down beside her.

So many questions crowded into her mind, but the most important one was this: *Why have you returned?* She didn't want to ask it and was almost afraid to hear his response. He might tell her that it was the last time he'd be here. There would be no more conversations between them. No more mutual interest.

She sat silent and still. When he reached over and grabbed her gloved hand she didn't say anything. Nor did she pull free.

When Bruce began barking at the swirling leaves, they turned and looked at each other, both smiling. It was such a perfect moment that she knew she'd always remember it and the day.

They never discussed the foolishness of each of them being there after that. Neither one of them mentioned that they should follow rules prescribed by other people. Not once did Logan tell her that he was going to try to forget her. Nor did she ever tell him to stay away.

Each day was like a cherished jewel, something set aside in a box that marked it as special. A ruby, perhaps, or a diamond sparkling with light. The autumn was fading into winter but she didn't notice the chill. The mornings were often foggy and dreary. Sometimes the afternoons were miserable with an icy drizzle. She never noted the weather at all, only the time. An hour here, an hour and a half at the most, until she was due back. Ninety minutes of freedom that she treasured.

At night she thought of things she wanted to tell him. In the morning she could barely wait until her aunt was occupied with other tasks to escape to the park. Logan came mostly in the afternoons, but sometimes in the mornings. She told herself to never anticipate him, yet she couldn't help herself.

Most of the time they were alone. Only occasionally did a carriage come by or someone on horseback. They were far enough away from the center of the park that few people strayed there. Bruce was the only witness to their meetings.

Society would not understand the two of them being alone in such a secluded location. Ostensibly, it was to train Bruce or to reinforce the commands he'd already learned. In actuality, that only took a small amount of the time they spent together. Mostly, they talked. She told him about Hearthmere and her memories of growing up a happy child, believing that the world was a wondrous place and everything in it almost magical.

He countered with his own memories of a childhood that seemed almost as enchanted despite being an orphan.

They were Scots in an English world and there was a difference, one sometimes of language, certainly of accent and upbringing. A Scot wasn't dour, per se, but he did look upon the world in a slightly different way than an Englishman. An Englishman was confident of his superiority, even if the attitude wasn't warranted. A Scot was almost imbued with a sense of fatalism, knowing that he would probably be outnumbered in any battle. Knowing, too, that he might lose, but that he was going to fight as hard as he could for as long as he could. Logan was the epitome of that type of thinking. She only hoped that she would be as courageous if ever in a conflict.

She told him of Hearthmere's extensive library and her father's plans to create the greatest racing stable in all of Scotland, if not the world. They talked of horses and sometimes sheep, occasionally dogs, and once in a while politics.

He seemed surprised at her knowledge of Parliament.

"It's not difficult to discover what's going on if you read the newspaper."

"Don't believe everything you read there, Eleanor. They lie a great deal about politicians. Or politicians lie a great deal. Either is true."

She studied him. "Do you lie, Logan?"

To her surprise he answered her easily. "I'm guilty of the sin of omission," he said. "I would much rather not say something than be pushed into a lie. But I would be lying to you if I told you that I always speak the truth. There are times when I don't. I like to think it's because circumstances decree it."

"Do they?"

"Yes, most of the time. When the Prime Minister asks my opinion about something and it's either a personal question or something about which I simply don't care, I will try to answer in a way that pleases him. I think it's something we all do. Don't you?"

"I don't think I can tell you that I've always told the truth, and doesn't that sound terrible?"

"I think it sounds human. I've never met a perfect person. If you know of one, please introduce us. It might be an interesting meeting."

She certainly wasn't perfect. Witness the fact that she would much rather be with Logan in the park with her dog than at any society gathering.

At those dinners, balls, or other functions, she was not, thankfully, required to say much, merely respond with a smile or one or two words. Michael seemed to approve of her silence, as did her aunt and Hamilton. Once again she was Eleanor the meek, Eleanor the unassuming. Eleanor, who was always just a shadow, a quiet little mouse of a woman.

Only with Logan was she herself.

For two weeks he met her each day, even on Sundays when the rest of the family was at home. It was commonplace for her to take Bruce to the park, however, so no one remarked when she continued to do so. Her aunt even commended her for ensuring that the puppy wasn't a bother.

Bruce wasn't allowed outside of Eleanor's room unless she was with him. He'd gotten used to his lead and obeyed all his commands. Even Hamilton was impressed. One morning when he'd come across them as they were leaving for the park, he'd even petted Bruce and complimented her on his behavior.

Her visits to the park made the rest of her days brighter.

Logan sometimes left before she did, returning to his carriage parked down the road. She always felt a surge of disappointment when she watched him walk away, wondering if one day he would change his mind and stop coming.

She didn't know what she would do then.

When she returned to the townhouse with Bruce she always grabbed a little snack for him and a cup of tea for herself, taking them to her bedroom. On this particular day, however, she was greeted by the sight of her aunt sitting at the enormous oak table.

Her aunt never sat in the kitchen. Her aunt was rarely in the kitchen, since she always met with the housekeeper and the cook in the small sitting room off her bedroom.

None of the maids were in the room, which was strange, but understandable since her aunt was here. Even the cook had absented herself. Eleanor couldn't help but wonder where she'd gone.

The kitchen was large, painted white, and had two wide windows facing east that allowed sunlight to flood into the room. A selection of vegetables was sitting at one end of the table, alongside a cutting board and two wicked-looking knives.

Had Deborah banished everyone in the act of preparing for dinner?

Bruce wisely moved to sit behind her.

Eleanor didn't know whether to address her aunt directly or simply stand there like a penitent. There wasn't any doubt in her mind that Deborah had been waiting for her to return from the park. Or that she hadn't wanted a witness to this meeting.

That meant only one thing. She knew about Logan.

"I've been waiting for you, Eleanor."

"Have you?" she asked.

"I've been made privy to something shocking."

She remained silent.

"You might say that it's proof you're deceptive in nature."

She'd never lied about meeting Logan, but she'd never discussed it, either.

Her aunt reached into her pocket and withdrew a letter that she waved in the air.

"Logan McKnight wrote you, Eleanor. Your housekeeper forwarded the letter. What do you have to say to that?"

"You have no right to open my mail."

"I have every right. You live here, under my roof. It's not Scotland, Eleanor, when you were able to dictate our lives."

Confused, she stared at her aunt. "What do you mean, dictate your lives? I did no such thing."

"Of course you did," Deborah said, her laughter holding a

brittle edge. "We all felt it, every day. I couldn't paint a room without your approval. I couldn't buy new furniture without your okay. I couldn't lift a finger to change anything about that ghastly barn of a house. I wouldn't be surprised if stress about it all drove William to his death."

Eleanor didn't understand. She never said a word to any member of her family about what they could or couldn't do.

"You should never have inherited Hearthmere. Leaving it to you was idiotic."

Her aunt could say anything she wanted about her, but Eleanor wasn't going to allow her father to be impugned.

"Hearthmere wasn't entailed, Aunt Deborah. My father had every right to leave it to anyone he wished."

"It should have been to his brother," Deborah said. "And in turn, to Jeremy. He wouldn't have to spend so much time trying to find his way in the world if your father had done what was right."

Jeremy would've been a terrible steward for Hearthmere. He would've drained the estate dry and been uncaring about the staff or the horses. The idea of Jeremy managing Hearthmere was ludicrous, but Deborah evidently believed that justice had not been done for her son.

Eleanor held out her hand. "May I have my letter?"

For a moment she didn't think Deborah was going to surrender it to her. Finally, she did so, throwing it across the table.

Eleanor grabbed it and without reading put it into her pocket.

"You're engaged to an earl, a peer. Your life will substantially change for the better, but you're not the only one whose life will be altered. Have you not considered that?" Despite her reddened cheeks, Deborah's voice was calm.

When Eleanor didn't speak, her aunt continued. "Hamilton's business ventures will be enhanced once people know that he's related to the Earl of Wescott. Your cousin will have avenues open to him. The relationship will even help Daphne and her husband.

Are you so selfish that you would choose this relationship over your family?"

"It isn't a relationship, Aunt Deborah. Logan and I are friends."

"Of course it's more than that. A member of Parliament sent a letter to an engaged woman. It's a physical representation of a scandal. Do you think that other people aren't interested in what Logan McKnight does? Have you not seen the articles about him in the newspaper?"

Eleanor nodded.

"If anyone gets wind of this, Eleanor, your engagement is over."

"There's nothing for anyone to hear. We're only friends."

"Will Michael think that?"

She doubted it. Michael would think the worst.

"Your fiancé doesn't like Mr. McKnight. He made that point abundantly clear to Hamilton."

"Are you going to tell Michael about the letter?"

"Of course not. I, for one, do not want anything to damage your engagement. I wish I could say you felt the same."

Eleanor didn't respond. What could she say?

"Do you feel something for this man?"

When she didn't speak her aunt continued. "If you do, I urge you to rid yourself of your feelings. You have a perfectly acceptable relationship with Michael."

She must have had some reaction to her aunt's words because Deborah stood and walked toward her.

"Don't be so foolish to think that you must marry for love. I did that once and look how terrible it turned out."

"My uncle?"

"Of course your uncle. It's difficult to remain blissfully in love if you don't have two coins to rub together. The man could never manage money. Not that he had any. Don't be a fool. Marry for money. Marry for prestige. Marry for a title. You'll be a countess, for the love of God." She sent Eleanor a withering look. "Marry for the sake of your family."

Eleanor doubted if there was anything in the letter that hinted at a scandal. Meeting Logan in the park, however, was different. She'd never heard Deborah scream, but it was not beyond the realm of possibility if her aunt learned about that.

Eleanor didn't say another word as she turned and left the room, hoping Deborah wouldn't call her back. She didn't, leaving Eleanor to wonder what was going to happen now. She entered her bedroom, closing the door behind her. Bruce immediately jumped up on the end of her bed, curled into a ball, and sighed deeply.

She pulled the letter out of her pocket and read it, hearing Logan's voice in the words he'd written. Just as she'd thought, there was nothing untoward about the letter, nothing hinting that they'd kissed.

A wiser woman would send word to Logan that she couldn't meet him anymore. She had his address. She could easily dispatch a footman to his residence or send her own driver there.

When she said as much to Bruce, he looked interested for a few minutes before directing his attention to his paws.

Her father would have counseled her on honor. He would have said what he'd said so many times: a man is defined by his word. Was it any different with women? It shouldn't be. She'd agreed to marry Michael. She'd given her word.

Her future loomed in front of her like an enormous wall. She couldn't see over it or around it. Nor could she tunnel beneath it. It was simply there and she had to accept that it was too late to change anything.

Chapter Twenty-One

The next morning Eleanor woke early, made Bruce's food, and took the bowl to the small yard in the back of the house. After he finished eating, she grabbed a Chelsea bun from the kitchen and ate it as she took Bruce to the park.

The whole time she was wondering if Deborah had told Hamilton about the letter. Eleanor fervently hoped her aunt wouldn't say anything to Daphne. Her cousin wasn't known for her ability to keep a secret.

She had no doubt about Hamilton's reaction. He hadn't quit complaining about Logan since the dinner party. According to Hamilton, Logan had been excessively rude, impolite to Michael, and inconsiderate of other viewpoints. She hadn't defended Logan, but it had been difficult to remain silent.

Surprisingly, Logan was already at the park, sitting on the bench beneath the giant oak where they met most often. He sat with one arm along the back of the bench, staring off into the distance. The canopy of branches, barer every day, heralded the oncoming winter. Only intrepid walkers showed up in the cold. She'd always come to the park in all seasons. It had been the one place she could escape her aunt. Now Queen's Park was not simply a refuge. It was where she and Logan talked and spent time together.

Time seemed to be accelerating, her wedding looming larger each day. Deborah and Daphne were busier than ever planning the ceremony, the parties before and after, and every conceivable celebration of Eleanor's ascent to countess.

She approached Logan slowly, not wanting to disturb his reverie. Bruce, however, had other ideas, racing to the bench, jumping on it and then on Logan. At first he laughed, and then he corrected Bruce in that calm voice of his.

"Down, boy. Don't get so excited that you forget your manners. You're going to be a countess's dog. You mustn't forget that."

She tried to push back the spear of pain his comment caused and greeted him.

"I think he grows at night. When I wake in the morning I half expect him to be another few inches taller."

"Pretty soon he'll be the same size as his mother."

They were talking as if they were strangers again, not two people who'd met every day for weeks, exchanging thoughts and experiences, being direct and honest in a way she'd never experienced with another person.

Had something happened?

She came and sat on the bench, making room for Bruce to sit between them. She carefully gathered her skirt to one side, put her feet together and then her hands, staring at the profusion of leaves blowing across the grass. London never felt as cold as Scotland in the winter. However, she was a Highlander and had grown up tolerating Scottish weather.

Perhaps they could talk about the seasons. Or she could ask about Mr. Disraeli. Or perhaps she should simply remain silent. Yet she'd never been meek and reserved with Logan. She was not going to begin now.

She turned her head to look at him. He was watching her, his eyes giving nothing away.

"Why are you here so early?"

"Because I had a curious need to see you," he said.

Bruce chose that moment to jump off the bench and attack some errant leaves blowing across the path.

"Why?"

"Damned if I know. I think it has something to do with setting the mood for my day. I find that everything goes better when I'm able to share a little of it with you. Those days when I can't be here I find myself resenting the press of my business, the same work that used to thrill me, that fascinated me so much that I gave it my life."

"Don't say things like that, Logan. I never know how to respond."

"But don't you understand, dear girl? You don't have to say anything at all."

He hadn't kissed her after that first day. They had taken care to be proper and cautious around each other but that thrumming awareness was always there, at least on her part.

Now he was saying he felt it, too.

"This is the very last place I should be yet I find myself unable to stay away."

She should say something, anything, but not one word came to mind. She should stand and leave. Or the best thing would be to say goodbye to him. Their paths had unexpectedly crossed, but he'd been right from the first. London was large enough that they wouldn't necessarily see each other again.

Her marriage would happen and his career would prosper. Perhaps one day she'd read that he'd married. Or that he'd been elected to an even more important position. Perhaps he'd see the announcement of her first child. Their futures were planned by circumstances and people around them.

"What do you want me to say, Logan?"

"Nothing. You might as well offer an apology for dawn or sunset. You are yourself. I have somehow become attuned to Eleanor Craig to the point that you're important to me. To my days. To my dreams."

He studied her, an intense regard that had her wanting to squirm. It was like he had never seen her before or wanted to imprint the sight of her in his mind.

"Should I tell you to run away, Eleanor? That way you would be safe."

"I've always felt safe with you," she said.

"Ah, but if I told you what I wanted to do, it would frighten you. Perhaps you should escape like the devil himself was on your heels."

Her stomach felt like it was bobbing up and down. Her hands were shaking and her feet felt strangely cold. Nothing was right on this beautiful morning. Yet everything was. He was saying things he shouldn't say, but she didn't silence him. She didn't lean over and press her fingers against his lips. She didn't demand that he stop speaking. Nor did she monitor her own words.

"I doubt you could do anything that would scare me, Logan. I know you to be a gentleman."

"Ah, but you don't know my baser self, Eleanor. Or what I'm capable of doing. I want to take you back to Scotland. I want to keep you in my bed for a month or so."

She could feel her cheeks warm even in the cold air.

He smiled. "Do you know how wide your eyes are? You're shocked, I can tell. But you're too well mannered to get up and run. Perhaps I should urge you to."

"If I'm shocked it doesn't mean I'm frightened," she said. "Nothing you could say would make me fear you."

He stretched out his hand and she put hers in it. "I never want you to be afraid of me, Eleanor."

"How could I be?" She smiled back at him. "Besides, I'm a Scot. I can ride any horse at Hearthmere, even the stallion that worries Mr. Contino. A Highland storm doesn't scare me and I've walked through a blizzard."

If she was really fearless she would tell him that if he abducted her she would go willingly, to Scotland or anywhere he chose. Let him show her what passion was. She already knew desire. Every time they met she fought back the urge to kiss him. Every day she wanted to walk into his embrace, stroke his arms, or wind her hands around his neck.

She needed to touch him with a desperation that was almost physical.

She dreamed of him, passionate dreams that had her waking breathless in the middle of the night. The longing she felt dissipated so slowly that sometimes she and Bruce crept down the back stairs before dawn, standing on the lawn to let the cold night chill her skin.

Perhaps she and Logan were reaping what they sowed. The attraction had been there from the beginning. They should have fought it. Or, if that wasn't possible, they should have been strong enough to stop meeting, knowing that each day would only strengthen the yearning.

She stood and walked some distance away, Bruce following. She hadn't trained him today so he probably thought this was some new lesson.

The crunch of leaves was a warning. Logan's arms encircled her and she leaned back against him, closing her eyes.

Please let me remember this moment. Please don't let me forget this.

"Eleanor."

Kiss me. Could she say that? Could she be brave enough to demand that of him?

This odyssey was ending. She felt rather than knew it. How could it continue? It was only good fortune that people were unaware of these meetings in the park. They'd been lucky, but she was a fool to think that they could escape detection forever.

She turned in his arms, put her hands flat on his chest, and met his eyes.

"These moments make the rest of my day bearable. I sometimes find myself awake at night, wishing I could push the hours forward until I see you again."

She shouldn't be saying these things, but how could she keep silent? This was Logan and the words belonged to him. Yet even as she spoke she felt the burden of her conscience. Nothing could come of this. They didn't have a future together.

"Eleanor."

How softly he said her name. How beautiful it sounded when he said it.

She leaned close and rested her forehead against his chest, wishing that circumstances were different. She'd beg him to take her away. They would be lovers and friends not just for a short time, but the rest of their lives.

His arms tightened around her, his chin resting on her head. She was content to stay this way forever, uncaring about a passing carriage or a horseback rider. Let the world stare. Let them whisper among themselves. *Who are they? Why are they embracing in public? What is their story?*

Perhaps they would think that she and Logan were star-crossed lovers, except that they'd only kissed. She'd imagined more and perhaps he had as well.

She pulled back a little, her courage bright and formidable. "Kiss me."

"Eleanor."

His honor was holding them both at bay. She didn't want him to be honorable. She wanted him to tuck his decency into his pocket for a few minutes. Ignore the training of a lifetime, give her what she needed.

"Kiss me."

She didn't need to urge him a third time.

The world disappeared and there was only Logan. Logan, steady and firm, pushing back reality and gifting her with bliss. She held on to him as her head spun, as her blood warmed, and sparks of sensation traveled outward from deep inside.

His lips were firm but soft. His breath was heated. When he tilted his head slightly, her mouth opened beneath his. She'd never known a kiss like this, intrusive yet welcoming, sensual and familiar.

Bruce barked, the sound bringing her back to sanity. Logan stepped back first, keeping his hands on her upper arms to steady her.

The puppy circled them, no doubt because he wanted his liver treats and they were lax in their training. She bent, retrieved the end of his lead, but instead of giving him a command, she turned and headed toward the gate.

She glanced back once to find Logan watching her. She wanted to return to his side and beg him to spirit her away. Or kiss her again until she forgot everything but him.

Instead, she left the park, knowing that the day of reckoning had finally come. They couldn't meet like this again.

Chapter Twenty-Two

Logan finished packing the papers into his valise before returning to his desk. He'd already dismissed Fred for the night, sending his driver to take his secretary home.

This final task was the one he dreaded the most. He needed to write Eleanor.

Tomorrow morning he'd be on his way to Edinburgh. His nephew's birthday would be in a few days, and that was one of the reasons he was going. The other was to call on his uncle.

Both visits were necessary, and timely as well.

Tomorrow, before he left, he was due to give a speech on taxing units and he couldn't think of a damn thing to say. The words wouldn't come. He always wrote his own speeches. Sometimes he conferred with Fred if his secretary had done additional research. Mostly, however, what he said was what he thought. Unfortunately, he was unable to think about anything but Eleanor.

His conscience was screaming at him to do the honorable thing. The time had finally come. No, he should have done this weeks ago but he wanted to keep seeing her. He needed to see her.

Perhaps with a little practice he wouldn't recall the sight of her face. If he concentrated, he would forget what it had been like to kiss her. He could banish the sound of her laughter given enough hours. Gradually, he'd be able to erase her from his thoughts. Finally she'd become only a fond and distant memory.

Except that he was certain he was lying to himself.

She couldn't marry Herridge. She couldn't be anyone's fiancée. She couldn't become some other man's wife.

He should tell her about his uncle. Would she break off her engagement if she learned about his family? If she did he'd forever wonder if she wanted him for himself or for another reason.

He would miss her, more than was wise.

He'd told her things he'd never divulged to another person. He wanted to explain himself, to have Eleanor know him in a basic, elemental way. He wanted her to be so in tune with his thoughts that she could understand what he was thinking. He wanted to be open and direct, holding nothing back. In the past he'd always withheld something of himself, feeling that it was important to maintain his privacy. All that had gone to hell with Eleanor and it shocked him.

Soon she'd be a bride. He might even be invited to her wedding. He would be expected to sit and watch her repeat her vows to a man he detested.

He stared at the blank sheet of stationery for long moments before he finally picked up the pen.

THAT EVENING ELEANOR spent an hour preparing for a function she and Michael were attending. In addition, Aunt Deborah and Hamilton would be sharing their carriage. Jeremy was off doing whatever Jeremy did during the week, a little gentlemanly gambling with his stepfather's money or carousing with his friends.

Or perhaps Jeremy led a secret life, not unlike she had recently.

After dinner they were all herded into a drawing room that was enlarged by opening up a second room. There they listened to a succession of women playing the piano. Their hostess introduced a woman with an Italian name who was evidently famous for her operatic voice. For a quarter hour Eleanor managed to sit and pretend an interest in a tale of spurned love in Italian, but the aria was simply a backdrop to her own emotions.

The past few weeks had been the most enjoyable she'd ever spent in London, yet at the same time she'd felt a series of emotions.

Some guilt, of course, that she was meeting Logan in secret. Confusion, that she could be so attuned to one man even as she was pulling away from another. Her conscience vied with her wish to be with Logan all the time. Perhaps that's why she was angry, because she knew it could never happen.

When the entertainment was blessedly over the guests milled around the room, talking. She sat against the wall, listening as two older women made a game of guessing which husband was faithful to his wife and which wife had strayed. Eleanor was surprised at the venom of their comments, then wondered if she would be a target for their speculation after her wedding.

The rest of the evening was as hideous as most social events. When they arrived back at the townhouse she waited until her aunt had left the carriage to address Hamilton, then asked him to go on ahead so that she could speak to Michael.

"What is it, Eleanor?" Michael asked once they were alone in the carriage.

"Will you be a faithful husband, Michael?"

"What kind of question is that, Eleanor?"

His tone was annoyed, but she noticed that he didn't answer her.

"Am I not allowed to ask?"

"I don't like what has happened to you, Eleanor, ever since you returned from Scotland."

The veneer of London Eleanor was fading through constant use, and soon only the real Eleanor would be visible.

That wouldn't please him, would it?

"You've been different ever since your visit to Hearthmere. It's a good thing those visits won't happen again."

She wasn't surprised by his words. Nor was she startled by his tone of voice. Michael had become more and more autocratic the longer they'd been engaged. What would he be like as a husband?

"I'll leave you here," he said. "I'm not coming in."

Nor did he say anything further.

A footman helped her exit the carriage. Once on the pavement she turned back to the open door and said her farewells.

"You will not ask me questions of this nature again, Eleanor. I will not be harangued. Not now. Not ever. Is that understood?"

She nodded, then turned and mounted the steps.

At the door the majordomo handed her a letter. She instantly recognized the handwriting. Just as quickly she knew what it was.

She didn't join her aunt and Hamilton in the drawing room. Instead, she walked upstairs, thanking the maid for watching Bruce in her absence.

"I took him out, Miss Eleanor, and he was a good boy."

He greeted her with a hundred kisses, sniffing her feet, her hands, and anywhere there was a different smell about her.

She readied herself for bed, and once she'd donned her nightgown and pulled down the covers, she sat on the edge of the mattress, the letter in her hands.

For nearly a quarter hour she sat there holding the letter, refusing to open it. If she didn't open it she wouldn't read his words. If she didn't read his words it wouldn't be real. He would be in the park tomorrow with his smile, his laughter, and that beautiful voice of his.

Bruce began to snore from the end of the bed.

Finally, she opened the letter, taking care not to damage her name written in Logan's distinctive hand.

She told herself that she'd be able to bear whatever he'd written. She'd survived the loss of her father and being taken from Scotland. She would live through this, too.

My dearest Eleanor,

I want so much for you. Happiness and joy, laughter and purpose, friends, and to be surrounded by those who love you. Your life will be a rich tapestry of experiences and moments, none of which I will share.

We met at the wrong time, you and I.

Yet I will never forget you, even as I counsel myself that I should. I must. I will forever wonder about Eleanor of Scotland,

*the woman with laughter in her eyes who looks on the world
with quiet wisdom. I will see the rain and wonder if it falls on
you, witness a sunset and question whether you see it, too.*

*I will never be quite as lonely as I was before meeting you
because I know you're in the world.*

I will not be back to Queen's Park. I will not see you again.

Logan

She carefully folded the paper, placed it beneath her pillow,
then thought better of it and tucked it into the Bible on her bedside table. She got beneath the covers, rearranged her pillow, and
slid her feet around a sleeping Bruce.

Only then did she cry.

Chapter Twenty-Three

𝓔leanor began to avoid Queen's Park. Instead, every day she took a well-worn path near the lake and over to Hyde Park. The distance was greater, of course, but at least she didn't have to be reminded of Logan's absence.

She saw his name in the newspaper nearly every day. Someone was always writing about him, either complimentarily or scurrilously. She wanted to trim the complimentary articles and keep them safe somewhere and deface the scurrilous ones. What did they know about his character? How could they possibly judge him so harshly?

She missed him and thought that Bruce did, too, because he always pulled her toward the wrought iron gates. She would always correct him and tell him that they were going on an adventure of sorts.

Bruce was the only bright spot in her day. Somehow, Logan had known that he would prove to be a great companion.

One morning about two weeks after receiving Logan's letter, she was coming in from the park, hoping to make it up the back stairs and to her room before anyone saw the two of them. Unfortunately, Daphne called out to her from the small Ladies Parlor adjacent to the back hallway.

Reluctantly, Eleanor entered the room, Bruce following.

Daphne did as Daphne always did, gave her a sweeping inspection that ended with a curl of her lip.

"Have you no sense of decorum, cousin? You have leaves on the bottom of your skirt and your hair is a disaster."

Eleanor didn't respond. Doing so would only make her more of a target for Daphne's withering criticism.

"What if the earl sees you in such a state?"

That's how her entire family referred to Michael—the earl. As if she might somehow forget his rank.

"I do not doubt that he would regret his offer immediately," Daphne added.

Eleanor blew out a breath. Perhaps she would never, even if she practiced every day, attain the degree of sophistication that Daphne effortlessly demonstrated. Yet she'd never be as rude as Daphne, or behave as badly to a member of her family.

Her father had taught her that family was everything.

Not to Daphne.

She knew quite well that Daphne's comments were a result of jealousy. Like it or not, Eleanor was engaged to an earl—a man who would always rank higher than Thomas in the hierarchy of London society. No doubt Daphne thought that such a thing was basically unfair, especially since she was so much prettier and more accomplished than Eleanor.

What her cousin didn't understand was that Michael's rank or status or even his title didn't matter to her. This whole countess business was beginning to be a chore more than anything else. She would much rather have been a simple missus without all the pomp and circumstance she was having to learn.

"I'm going to my room."

"The earl's here," Daphne said. "He's been waiting for you."

"Why?"

"Perhaps you should ask him, Eleanor."

"Why aren't you with him?"

Daphne never lost an opportunity to ingratiate herself with Michael. The fact that she wasn't entertaining him was curious.

"He's not in the mood for company."

That was not good news.

Eleanor should change, fix her hair or wash her face, if nothing else. Yet there was a chance that, if Michael had been waiting for a substantial time, he might grow annoyed at a further delay. Instead of going upstairs, she turned and led Bruce into the small parlor Michael preferred.

Had Michael learned of Logan's letter? Worse, had he somehow learned of their meetings in Queen's Park?

Her aunt's style of decorating was to choose a color, then use it to excess in that particular room. There was a Green Parlor where you felt as if you were walking into a spring bower. The dining room was yellow, such a bright shade that her eyes always had to adjust. A bluish green was the predominant color in the main drawing room and a pleasant shade of peach for the hallways on the second floor.

This room was gray, a masculine color, which was probably why Michael preferred it. The sofa and chairs were upholstered in a patterned silk that matched the walls and curtains. The only spots of color were the lush emerald ferns hanging in the window, supported by gray ropes from the ceiling.

Michael was sitting in one of the chairs in front of the fireplace, a heavily carved wooden box on the table beside him. Although his face was expressionless, she could tell he was angry. It showed in the flatness of his eyes and his stillness. He didn't move, even when she entered the room. He didn't stand or greet her. She was invisible to him, which meant that she would have to begin this meeting with an apology.

"Forgive me, I didn't know you were going to be here today."

He inclined his head slightly, but didn't respond.

She came and sat on the adjoining chair, Bruce at her feet. She should have taken him upstairs, but she didn't want Michael to have to wait any longer.

The maids loved Bruce and went out of their way to pet him or slip him some treat during the day. Aunt Deborah and Hamilton were noncommittal about the puppy. Michael, however, always demanded that she put the dog up somewhere, saying that dogs belonged in a kennel, not a parlor.

To her surprise he didn't immediately tell her to remove Bruce. Instead, he handed her the wooden box.

"Inside is the ancestral bridal ring worn by all the Herridge wives. It will be placed on your finger during the wedding ceremony."

She opened the lid cautiously. There, on a small silk pillow, was a ring at least an inch and a half wide, decorated with a selection of amethysts, emeralds, rubies, and diamonds. A large black stone in the middle had been engraved with the Wescott crest.

It was the most horribly gaudy thing she'd ever seen. All she could think was that she'd have to wear gloves constantly.

"I need to make sure it will fit you."

He took the box, plucked the ring from its pillow, and grabbed her hand.

Bruce growled at him.

Michael drew back, frowning.

"Don't be afraid. He won't bite you," she said, although she wasn't entirely certain of that. Bruce rarely growled except at leaves and squirrels. Granted, the puppy was showing signs of being a large dog, but he was gentle and sweet, not fearsome.

"I'm not afraid," Michael said. "Get rid of him."

She stood. "I'll take him to my room."

"No, get rid of him."

"I beg your pardon?"

"I've put up with this situation long enough. Get rid of him, Eleanor. If you want, I'll do it. Have a maid take him to my carriage."

She stared at him. "What do you mean, you'll do it?"

"Exactly that. He's a nuisance and needs to be dispatched."

"Dispatched?"

He just looked at her.

She bent down and picked up Bruce. He was growing so large that it wasn't as easy to do as it had been a month earlier.

"I'm not asking, Eleanor. I've given you a direct order. I don't expect you to disobey me. Not now and not when we're married."

Did Deborah have that kind of marriage? Not from what she'd observed in Scotland. Her Uncle William had been a kind and generous man. Deborah sometimes seemed to be the stronger person in that marriage. Nor was Deborah's marriage to Hamilton that sort of relationship. Thomas adored Daphne and nearly worshipped her.

Her marriage with Michael would be different. She'd be little more than a servant in his eyes.

"Do you understand?" he asked, his voice holding an edge of coldness.

"Yes," she said. "I understand."

"You'll get rid of the animal, then?"

When she didn't respond he said, "I insist upon it."

"Is this the way our marriage is to be, Michael? You issuing orders and me obeying them without question? Am I never to have an opinion?"

"This new rebellion of yours is not attractive."

"Why did you ask me to be your wife, Michael?"

He frowned at her. Quite an impressive scowl at that. She was probably supposed to be quelled into silence by his look.

"What kind of question is that?"

A rational one. An explainable one. A commonsensical one. A normal one.

"Please," she said. "Allow me a little curiosity on this one matter. I would truly like to know."

She forced herself to face him, to meet his gaze and endure his study of her.

"You were biddable, Eleanor. Of all the women I'd met you were the most manageable."

It wasn't her looks, then, or her personality—although she doubted if he'd had a chance to learn who she truly was before asking her to be his wife. Not her possession of a lovely home in Scotland. Nor the fact that she was related to Hamilton Richards.

Michael had selected her from all the other women because she barely spoke in his presence, because she listened to him rather than demand he do the same.

She'd been a ghost of a woman, easily manipulated and ordered about. A timid, frail wisp of a creature who would never dare stand up for herself or espouse her own thoughts and beliefs. The woman he'd met during her season had been that person, a London persona she donned because she had to, because it was necessary in order to survive in this world she disliked so much. That wasn't who she truly was, however.

Logan was the only person who knew the real Eleanor.

"Your aunt assured me you would be a dutiful wife. I don't know what happened to you in the past weeks, Eleanor, but I don't like the change."

Michael's words made so much sense. Of course that's why he'd chosen her. What would he say if she told him that it had all been a lie, that the woman he'd known was dying a little each day?

She had her answer and it didn't solve anything. Instead, it made the situation even worse.

She fell back on old habits, arranging her face into a calm facade, a half smile curving her lips. She willed her gaze to show nothing of her thoughts. Not her anger. Not her fear. Nothing.

"I want you to get rid of him. Do you understand?"

"I understand."

The cloud on her horizon, the storm cloud of her marriage, was growing closer and looking even more thunderous. Yet a half-dozen people were expecting to be blessed by that union. Every member of her family was overjoyed that they would soon be related to a peer. Michael's earldom would spread its influence and that's all they noticed. They wouldn't, after all, pay the price. She was the only one who would do so and it was becoming all too obvious that this marriage would be very costly indeed.

"And you agree?"

Of course she didn't. What he was demanding of her was unkind at the least and barbarism at the worst. What did he expect her to do, simply abandon Bruce within the city? Take him to the park, remove his lead, and bid him go fend for himself? Did he expect her to drown him in the Thames? Or take him to the worst part of the city and allow him to be tortured by gangs of ruthless children? Or, perhaps, give him to someone—like Michael—who would kill the puppy without a thought?

Was it possible to hate someone temporarily? She doubted if hate could be borrowed and then be put back wherever that emotion lived when it wasn't used.

What would happen if she allowed herself to hate Michael about this situation? She suspected that the hate would bleed over into other circumstances. Even worse, she suspected that the man who was to be her husband could also be her enemy.

She and Logan had talked about lies one day. She'd admitted that she hadn't always told the truth. Now she lied to Michael while meeting his eyes. She nodded and said, "Yes, I agree."

He smiled, finally satisfied and generous in his despotism.

Chapter Twenty-Four

Her driver, Liam, was still in London. Eleanor hadn't sent him back to Hearthmere since he was enjoying his visit to the city. The next morning she sent him to Logan's home with a note and a request that he keep this errand to himself. It wouldn't do for the Richardses' household to know that she was communicating with Logan. Liam had only grinned at her and promised.

"If he's home, wait for a reply. If he isn't, then leave the note."

Knowing how long Logan's workday was, she honestly didn't expect to get an answer as quickly as she did. Her note had been direct and short.

I have a problem and you're the only one who can help. May I call on you at noon?

Within an hour he'd answered with one word. *Yes.* That was all. He hadn't inquired as to the nature of her problem or why she thought he would be able to help. Just yes, that was all.

When she was moved or touched she allowed herself to cry, but that wasn't very often. Today, however, no doubt because she'd not slept the night before, she found that one simple word had the ability to reduce her to tears.

What she was about to do would probably be labeled as foolish by any number of people. Looking at the situation from the out-side, she would probably agree. Her actions wouldn't be deemed wise. They could probably even be called rash and impulsive.

Everything she'd initially told Logan was the truth. She hadn't wanted a puppy. Nor had she wanted the responsibility or the work. Nowhere in her protestations had she considered that she might come to love Bruce. Somehow, he'd carved a place in her heart. She cared about his well-being and his health and had thought she could provide him with a wonderful life.

It was all too evident that she couldn't because of Michael.

She had to protect Bruce. She didn't trust Michael not to take matters into his own hands if he thought she wasn't fast enough to obey him.

Today she wore another one of her newer dresses, this one a green-and-white pattern. Of all the garments made for her in the past few months, this one was her least favorite. If she got muddy paw prints on it she would not be overly disturbed.

The day was rainy, the storm clouds hovering over London as if in punishment. Thunder had been a constant accompaniment to the morning. Perhaps she would be better served by waiting until the weather was better, but she had a feeling that time was not a friend in this instance. She had to get Bruce somewhere safe, somewhere Michael wouldn't be able to touch him.

To her surprise, Bruce jumped into the carriage with no hesitation, settling beside her on the seat and staring out the window. He hadn't been this good a passenger on the trip from Scotland. Perhaps he thought he was going home. In a way, he was.

She'd expected Logan to live in a small flat and had even anticipated having to climb a few sets of stairs. If not that, she'd thought his residence might be a small house tucked away among other small houses. When Liam slowed in front of a townhouse that was the equal to Hamilton's home or even larger, she was astonished.

Painted bright white, it had at least a half-dozen black sash windows on the first and second floors. A wide set of six stairs, bordered on each side by a black wrought iron railing, led to the front door, shielded by a small portico with two columns on each side.

She remained where she was until Liam opened the door and unfurled the steps. She stared up at the black door with its enormous fan-shaped brass knocker.

"Are you certain this is the address?"

"Yes, Miss Eleanor," he said. "The London streets aren't difficult once you get the hang of them."

He held out an umbrella and she left the carriage, heading for
the steps. Evidently, being an MP paid a great deal more than she
thought.

Behind her Liam grabbed the large satchel she'd packed while
she held Bruce's lead and guided him up the front steps.

The door was answered only seconds after she knocked. Instead of a majordomo, she was greeted by a short, plump woman
with a round face and a mop of curly blond hair. The woman, who
looked to be about the same age as Eleanor's aunt, possessed a
rosebud mouth and a spot of color on each cheek.

"Aye, you'd be Miss Craig, would you?" she asked in a thick
Scottish brogue.

"I am," Eleanor said.

Logan must've informed his staff of her arrival. So much for
making this visit as secretive as possible.

Bruce preceded her into the foyer.

"Oh, I'm so sorry," she said, instantly noticing the track of his
paw prints. Here she was a guest and she already had reason to
apologize.

The woman surprised her by reaching for a bit of toweling
stacked on a long table against the wall. "Now, don't you worry,
Miss Craig. It doesn't take a genius to realize that with this mucky
day we're having, he'd be tracking himself in."

Less than a minute later, the mess had been cleaned up and
Bruce had his paws wiped as well.

"Isn't he a dear?" the woman said, ruffling Bruce's fur. "He puts
me in mind of those dogs that guard the sheep."

"That's exactly what he is," Eleanor said. "Or at least on his
mother's side."

"We'll go into the parlor where I've already laid a fire. It might
not be cold enough yet, but it'll warm your bones all the same."

"Would it be all right to bring Bruce?"

"Of course. He's a guest, too. Aren't you, Mr. Bruce?"

She could swear that Bruce nodded.

One of the woman's hands fluttered in the air while the other patted her chest.

"And here I am, not introducing myself properly. I'm the housekeeper for himself. Mrs. Campbell."

"It's nice to meet you, Mrs. Campbell."

The housekeeper smiled at her, such a bright and cheery expression that Eleanor couldn't help but smile in return.

"And I you, miss."

The drawing room was another surprise. The walls were a pale yellow, the furniture upholstered in dark blue. The tables were mahogany and less cluttered with statuary than those in her aunt's house. One wall was filled with paintings of Scottish scenes from Ben Hagen to Edinburgh, each framed in gold. The fireplace surround was black stone that reminded her of slate, but it was carved with thistles and vines. Overall, the impression was of a masculine, welcoming room honoring Scotland.

Soon enough she was tucked into an overstuffed chair, one of two in front of the fireplace. Mrs. Campbell pushed an ottoman close to her. "You go and put your feet up right there. I'll be bringing you some tea and some biscuits we made this morning."

"That really isn't necessary, Mrs. Campbell. I don't want you to go to any extra effort on my account."

"Don't be silly. The only guests we ever have here are politicians, gruff sorts all. It's a pleasure to entertain a young miss. A Scot by the sound of it, too, am I right?"

Eleanor nodded. "I am," she said. "I was born at Hearthmere, in the Highlands."

"Ah, not far from the Duke of Montrose's home. That's how you know himself, then."

Before she could answer, she heard a door close not far away. Bruce began to wiggle and whine, a sure sign that Logan was coming. In less than a minute he appeared in the doorway.

Mrs. Campbell glanced toward him, her broad smile making her face appear even rounder.

"There he is, then. Himself. And here I thought I was going to have to make you stop reading all those papers of yours and come and visit your guest."

"What would I do without you, Althea?"

To her surprise, when Logan reached the housekeeper he bent and kissed her on the cheek. Mrs. Campbell's face reddened in response.

"Oh, get away with you now," she said, obviously flustered. "I'll go and get that tea."

"And whatever you were baking this morning," Logan said. "It smelled delicious."

"Just a bit of shortbread with some currants. Sweet enough for you, I'm thinking."

"Do you have a sweet tooth?" Eleanor asked after Mrs. Campbell left the room.

Logan came and sat on the adjoining chair. "I do. Luckily, Mrs. Campbell does as well. Cook keeps us both well supplied."

Bruce forgot his manners and tried to crawl into Logan's lap. He only laughed and pushed the puppy down to the rug again.

"He's grown a great deal in two weeks," he said.

"A little over two weeks," she answered. "Fifteen days." With a little time she could probably calculate the hours.

He held her gaze for a minute before glancing down at Bruce again. "Yes, fifteen days."

He looked tired, but from the newspaper reports there was reason for it. There was speculation that Mr. Disraeli would not be reelected as Prime Minister. Mr. Gladstone had more support. When she said as much to Logan, he smiled.

"You're remarkably well informed, Eleanor. I think you read more than one newspaper every day."

She had, at least in the past fifteen days. Because of him she'd taken to reading everything she could find. She wanted to know what he was doing during the day, what he thought, and what he said.

Her father would've liked him, and her uncle as well. Logan was a man of convictions and sometimes fervently defended them. He never forgot that he was a Scot or that his loyalty was owed first to his homeland. Occasionally, he went toe to toe with an English politician who made no secret of his disdain for the other members of the Commonwealth: Wales, Ireland, or Scotland. According to the newspapers, Logan lost no time or opportunity excoriating the man. He'd gotten a reputation for being fiercely defensive. Some reporter had labeled him the Savage Scot.

Eleanor thought that it might be the perfect nickname for Logan.

"But you didn't come here to talk to me about politics, did you? You said you needed my help."

There was no good way to explain her idea, what she hoped he would agree to do. All she could do was tell the truth. If that didn't work she would resort to begging.

Anything to save Bruce.

Chapter Twenty-Five

*"J*need to find a home for Bruce." Eleanor willed her voice not to quaver. "A good home with someone who will love him."

Logan didn't say anything for a long moment.

"It's become impossible for me to keep him," she continued. "I need you to take him. Please."

She hadn't meant to be emotional, but she didn't want to lose Bruce. What she was doing was for his safety.

The puppy came and sat on her feet, looking up and tilting his head slightly, almost as if he were trying to understand. She bent and scratched that area he liked so much just in front of his ears.

"What's wrong, Eleanor?"

He really shouldn't sound so sympathetic. Or so kind. She really would start to cry.

"I think he's in danger," she said.

The words were probably disloyal but they were the truth. Was she supposed to lie about Michael?

"Tell me."

She took a deep breath, repeating what Michael had said. Even as she repeated the words she heard how ugly they sounded. What kind of man threatens a puppy?

She wasn't all that surprised when Logan said the same thing.

"The man is an ass," he added.

"I'm sure he didn't mean it," she said. Her tone lacked conviction. "He just doesn't like dogs."

Logan sent her a quick glance. She could read its meaning well enough. His opinion of Michael had dropped even further.

"I need to protect Bruce," she said. "That's the most important thing."

"I'll take him," he said.

Three words, but they summoned her tears.

"Now what have you done, Logan McKnight? Made the poor thing cry?"

Bruce chose that moment to bark, a sound of pure puppy happiness because of the smell coming from the tray one of the maids was carrying.

"Now don't you start, wee one. If you behave yourself, I'll give you the bone I fetched you from the kitchen. Not another sound out of you, though."

Mrs. Campbell directed the maid to put the tray down on the table between them, then waited until the girl was gone before putting her hands on her hips and glaring at Logan.

"He's been very kind," Eleanor said, pulling out a handkerchief from her reticule and blotting at her eyes. "Truly, Mrs. Campbell. If anything, I was weeping at his kindness."

"Then it's sorry I am for my words," Mrs. Campbell said, nodding at Logan.

He smiled back at her. "If you brought me shortbread we'll call it even."

She reached for the plate, but handed it to Eleanor first. She declined with a smile.

Logan waited until the housekeeper left the room again before turning to Eleanor.

"He's a bastard. Not only for what he said about Bruce, but for making you cry."

"He didn't make me cry," she said. "You did. I didn't lie to Mrs. Campbell. I was hoping that you would save Bruce and you have. I didn't know what else to do."

He startled her by moving to sit on the ottoman. Bruce tried to get into his lap again and Logan picked up the puppy and held him at eye level. "You'll mind your manners, Bruce. Or it's to the back you'll go."

Bruce licked his nose.

Logan laughed, then put the puppy back down on the rug before turning to her. Reaching out, he grabbed both of her hands.

"I'll give him a home, Eleanor. You needn't worry about him anymore."

"Could I come and visit him from time to time? He's such a dear little thing and I've grown to love him."

He looked down at her hands.

"I won't be a bother," she said.

"Of course you can come and visit him," he said. "I think, under the circumstances, however, that it would be easier if you came when I wasn't here."

Perhaps it would be easier for him, but not for her. Even a chance to see him would be enough to make her anticipate the day.

That confession would never be said, couldn't be said. It's not just that the words were disloyal, but that they were wrong. She was engaged to another man. She was going to be his wife. She couldn't fall in love with Logan McKnight. She couldn't.

She shouldn't have come. She shouldn't have made the situation even worse. If she hadn't been so worried about Bruce's fate she wouldn't have.

"Logan . . ." Her words ground to a halt. She couldn't say to him, *Let me into your life. Let me be a part of it, however small. Talk to me about your day. Tell me of the legislation you want to get passed. Who did you argue with today? What did you learn?*

She had no right to any of his time, his thoughts, or his experiences.

The best thing to do was return to her aunt's home and never look back. She wouldn't return to see Bruce. She wouldn't communicate with Logan. She would face her future and think of him as a distant memory or perhaps even a dream.

Otherwise, it would be too painful.

She'd never questioned her own bravery. Yet she knew that

leaving without a chance of seeing Logan again would require more courage than she'd ever demonstrated. More than leaving Hearthmere.

Perhaps she wasn't brave enough. She couldn't lose both of them. Not just yet.

"What day would be best for you?" she asked.

"Wednesdays."

"Then I'll come on Wednesdays," she said. "In the afternoon."

"And I'll be absent on Wednesdays."

She nodded. What else could she say? If he didn't want to see her again she understood. It would be easier for both of them. Yet she'd still be able to see Bruce, until such time as even that would be difficult. She didn't know if she would be living at Abermarle or London after the wedding. Wherever it was, it would be solely at Michael's discretion.

"Thank you," she said, grabbing her satchel. She placed it between them. "Bruce's blanket is in there, along with his rope toy. He appropriated one of my shoes and I included that, too."

It shouldn't be so difficult to turn over Bruce's belongings, but somehow it was.

"Stay for tea," he said. "Otherwise, Mrs. Campbell will get her feelings hurt."

She had the feeling that he would do anything rather than allow Mrs. Campbell to be hurt. Was he that considerate of all the employees in this surprisingly large house? She suspected he was. Just another facet of this man. This amazing, fascinating, enchanting man.

It would have been easier if she'd never met Logan. She would never have come to love Bruce. Neither would she be feeling the pain of losing him. If Logan had never come into her life, she wouldn't have anyone to compare Michael against and find him lacking. She would have no one to long for, wishing that circumstances were different.

Yet if she'd never met him she would never have known what this emotion was that she was feeling now. She would never have felt the lightness in her heart when she thought she might see him. She would never have known what it felt like to be truly alive as she only did in his presence. Or the freedom of being herself with someone.

"Then I change my mind," she said. "I'll take one of those pieces of shortbread."

He handed her the plate with a smile before moving back to the chair.

For a half an hour they managed to talk of innocuous things like his niece and nephew or his recent trip to Scotland. The conversation could have been held between two strangers, not people who'd come to know each other well. She drank her tea and ate the biscuits, and when her cup was empty and the biscuits eaten, she stood, smiling down at a sleeping Bruce. The minute she started to walk toward the door he would wake, but the image of him dreaming on Logan's carpet was one she'd always remember.

Bruce would have a home here with someone who would care for him and treat him well. Most importantly, he would be safe.

Walking away, however, would be difficult.

"Will you let him sleep on your bed?" she asked. "He always settles in at the foot of my bed."

"If you want."

Logan came to stand in front of her. Before she could turn and grab her reticule, he pulled her into his embrace, wrapping his arms around her. They stood like that for some minutes as she rested her cheek against his chest and closed her eyes. She doubted that she would ever feel as safe with anyone else again. She would always remember these moments with the fire crackling behind them and the soft breathing of the puppy at their feet.

Heaven must be like this.

"You don't have to marry him, Eleanor. You could always change your mind."

"No, I can't," she said.

He pulled back, dropping his arms. "Is becoming a countess such a lure?"

"You know it isn't."

"Then what is it? Why go ahead with the marriage?"

He didn't understand. What was left of her family was thrilled with the union. Her aunt would finally be related to an earl. Granted, it was a feat she would have preferred her daughter achieve, but a niece was a close enough relative. Hamilton's business empire would be positively affected. Daphne and Thomas could tell everyone that they had a countess in the family. Even Jeremy's life would be bettered.

If she didn't go through with the wedding she'd not only disappoint everyone, but she'd have to live under a cloud of disapproval for the rest of her life. She couldn't imagine a worse fate.

Family is everything, Eleanor. It's the same with horses.

Her father's words and his belief.

Family is everything. Perhaps it was even more important than her own wishes, hopes, or dreams.

Chapter Twenty-Six

Every Wednesday afternoon for the past month Eleanor had Liam drive her to Logan's house. If her driver thought it odd that she made the same trip repeatedly, he never mentioned it. Nor did he gossip among the rest of the staff. No one looked at her strangely or giggled when she passed.

Every Wednesday she met Liam down the street a bit, so no one in the house knew that she'd left. As long as she wasn't needed for a fitting, her presence wasn't required, especially when it came to her own wedding preparations. Deborah and Daphne were making all the arrangements themselves with occasional input from Michael.

No one ever asked where she'd been on those Wednesdays, even when she stayed longer than she planned, talking to Mrs. Campbell or walking Bruce in the square. No one seemed to notice her absence or demand an accounting.

It was as if, in addition to being mute, she was now invisible.

One day she would probably be caught. She wasn't foolish enough to think she could escape detection forever, but until then she was going to continue to visit Bruce every Wednesday.

Neither her aunt nor Daphne asked about the puppy. If they noticed his absence, they didn't remark upon it. Jeremy never made mention of anything but his own concerns, but she expected Hamilton to say something. He didn't.

Not one of them asked if she missed Bruce. Or if a place in

her heart felt empty. Those maids who'd made a point to pet the puppy or give him a treat wouldn't meet her eyes. At first she didn't understand until one of them clarified the issue for her.

"Did you have him drowned, Miss Eleanor? We're all wondering, but we didn't want to ask."

She wanted to tell them what she'd done, but all she was able to say was, "He went to a good home, I promise. Someone loves him and will care for him."

Everyone knew that Michael had decreed that Bruce be gone and like magic he was gone. The dog had annoyed him and the problem had been rectified. What Michael wanted, Michael always got.

Did he dispose of people that easily, too?

Surprisingly, Michael hadn't asked about Bruce. He never commented on his absence. He'd given her an order and expected her to obey it.

She could tolerate any number of fittings, comments from Daphne, or criticism from her aunt as long as she had Wednesday. Wednesdays made the rest of the week bearable.

Although Logan said that he wouldn't be there, each time she arrived at his house, her heart beat faster. He might change his mind today. He might come into the drawing room when she was with Bruce.

He never did.

She missed Bruce as much as she'd thought she would. Every night she looked at that spot at the end of her bed where he'd curled into a little ball and she wondered if he was doing the same in Logan's home.

He seemed happy there, but even more important, he was safe. Logan would always provide a home for him, either here in London or in Scotland. She knew that without being told. He would never take out his anger on a defenseless animal, a point she kept coming back to time and again. What kind of man was she marrying? What did it matter if a man had a title if he had no character to accompany it?

Michael was exceedingly personable and had a great number

of acquaintances. Surprisingly, they were not of the aristocracy. Instead, they seemed more sycophants than friends, congregating around him to offer him praise and compliments. Or to occasionally solicit money from him. They even did so in front of her. At first she'd been amazed, but then she realized that they considered her a nonentity. She couldn't help but wonder if Michael felt the same way.

Her fiancé labeled people by two categories, harmless and annoying. The hangers-on were mostly harmless. Logan was considered annoying, as in, *that annoying Scot*. From time to time Michael asked her if she'd seen him again, making her wonder if her aunt had said something to him about the letter after all.

She always responded with her own question. "Why would you ask me that?"

He always looked irritated, enough that he didn't realize she hadn't answered.

Every week she took a treat to Bruce, along with a toy. It could be something as simple as a coiled and knotted rope or something she'd knitted in the evening.

Whenever she arrived, Mrs. Campbell opened the door. Seconds later she could hear Bruce running from the back of the house to greet her. On those occasions he forgot his manners completely and jumped up on her skirt, licked her hands, and was so excited that he was wriggling and whining.

"He does the same thing to himself," Mrs. Campbell said the first week. "You would think that you two are the only people on earth for this one. I've never seen the like."

Now the housekeeper smiled down at the puppy before leading the way to the parlor.

Every week it was the same. Mrs. Campbell brought a tray of tea and refreshments, even though Eleanor told the woman not to bother.

"I'll not have anyone say that himself skimped on his hospitality," she answered. For that reason, Eleanor always took a cup of tea and more than one of the delicious biscuits. Sometimes, she even had a slice of plum pudding. Evidently Logan liked it as well, which was why Cook often made it.

Mrs. Campbell always spent some time with her, then left her alone with Bruce. Eleanor thought it odd to be so comfortable in this parlor even without Logan here. His home was welcoming, and it wasn't simply the furnishings or that a fire was always lit during rainy weather. It had something to do with Mrs. Campbell's smile and that of the maid who brought the tray into the drawing room.

She realized, with a start, that the servants at her aunt's home didn't smile all that often. At least not around Deborah or Hamilton. The three girls who made a point of stopping by to see Bruce when he'd lived there were cheerful, but never publicly. Had Deborah issued an edict banning any sign of happiness? Was Eleanor supposed to act the same as Michael's wife? How awful it would be to never hear the sound of laughter during the day. Or to never have someone greet her with a smile.

The hour she spent at Logan's home was a holiday in her week, an hour of contemplation, joy, and entertainment. Bruce, despite his garrulous welcome, was learning his commands. Every week she wished things were different and he could live with her.

Once she was married in a few months she'd lose whatever small amount of freedom she had now. The Countess of Wescott couldn't disappear for an hour or two without explanation. She'd probably have to account for every minute of her day. Would Michael expect her to justify her purchases? Would he approve or veto her friendships, too?

She felt like a prisoner knowing that she would have to soon walk into the jail of her own accord.

Family is everything.

It was becoming harder and harder to remember that.

Today the future weighed heavily on her. The weather seemed to echo her mood. On days like today she enjoyed bundling up and going for a walk. It didn't matter if she got wet. Sometimes, she liked to feel that she was part of nature. If it thundered, even better. The sound mimicked her thoughts, chaotic and dark.

Once Mrs. Campbell and the maid left the room, closing the door behind them, Eleanor got down on the carpet in front of the fire, reaching into the satchel she brought and pulling out the new rope toy she'd brought. Bruce instantly wanted to play tug-of-war and she let him win most of the time.

Several minutes were devoted to going through all his commands to see how well he was learning everything. As busy as he was, it looked as if Logan had taken the time to continue Bruce's training. She didn't think that he would delegate such a task to anyone else.

"How smart you are," she said. "Has Logan taught you whistle commands, too?"

Bruce tilted his head and looked at her, as if trying to understand the question.

She hadn't given up practicing whistling. She was up to two notes now, of different pitches. A foolish duty she'd given herself. She would have no reason to learn how to train a dog that was half border collie. Not now. Not after Michael had gotten his way.

Bruce wasn't a fuzzy little ball of fur anymore. Instead, his ears no longer flopped over but stood at attention. A ruff was developing around his neck and shoulder area. His legs finally looked like they were growing into the size of his paws. His tail was fluffy and capable of standing straight up in the air or waving back and forth like a flag. The most surprising change was his nose, lengthening and giving his face a distinctive look. If she hadn't seen the changes herself, she would never have been able to match the dog to the puppy.

She tossed the rope, but instead of retrieving it when it fell, Bruce caught it in midair, catapulting his entire body up from the floor in an amazing feat of athleticism. Surprised, she tossed the rope again and he did it once more.

Did Logan know he could do that?

It was soon time she left and she reluctantly did so, thanking Mrs. Campbell, and bending to hug Bruce. He barked his good-bye, making her smile.

She went back out into the rain, not caring if she was drenched by the time she reached the carriage. It would only take minutes to get back to her aunt's house. Only minutes to make the transition from Eleanor of Scotland to the meek and malleable creature who was going to be a countess.

LOGAN WATCHED AS Eleanor made her way down the steps and into the carriage slowly, almost as if she didn't care that she was being pelted by the rain. She'd stayed an hour, just as she did every week, arriving at the time she said she would. Every week Mrs. Campbell welcomed her like a long-lost daughter, and every week she was gracious and grateful to his housekeeper. Every week, after she left, Mrs. Campbell would say something like, "Poor lass. You can tell it hurts her heart every time she has to say goodbye to the wee one."

Mrs. Campbell never called Bruce by his name. He was "the wee one" or "the furry one" or something in Gaelic. Every week Logan would reply with something noncommittal. Words that didn't fool Mrs. Campbell one bit.

Althea Campbell had worked for his parents, and it had been a test of wills between him and his sister as to who could convince Mrs. Campbell to come and live with them. He'd won only because the housekeeper had never seen London and wanted to experience being around the English for a while. He knew that he wouldn't be able to keep her here all that long. She would probably listen to Janet's blandishments and return to Edinburgh to his sister's household. However long she remained with him, he considered her an invaluable ally and a member of his family.

For the past four weeks he'd been gone when Eleanor came to see Bruce. Today, however, he'd been greeted at dawn by a courier from Disraeli. He'd wanted to dismiss the man and the pouch he carried, but the press of politics never diminished, despite what else might be happening in his life.

Disraeli was, even after having lost the general election, intent on making his opinion known. Because of his friendship with Queen Victoria he was also still interested in anything to do with Scotland, which meant that Logan had to opine on various subjects in order to satisfy Disraeli's curiosity.

Instead of the courier giving him the packet and disappearing, he'd repeated a statement obviously memorized from the Prime Minister, followed by a directive.

"I'm to remain here, sir, until there is an answer for Mr. Disraeli."

As if Logan didn't already have enough to do. However, one thing that Parliament had taught him in the past two years was that rank had its privileges. You might disagree with the former Prime Minister. You might hold contrary beliefs. You might believe that he was an idiot in certain regards, but you never forgot the man's position and you always accorded it the respect he deserved. If Disraeli insisted that his courier remain here until Logan had studied the issue, then that's exactly what would happen, however much it disrupted Logan's life.

"Can I interest you in tea?"

The courier looked surprised. "Thank you, sir."

He led the man to his study and told him to make himself comfortable, and that someone would be with him soon. The man nodded and thanked him again, which made Logan wonder if the man was treated as if he were invisible most of the time.

Now Logan was studying the issue, choosing to do so away from the bustle of his office. The fact that it was Wednesday no doubt featured in his decision to remain at home. When two o'clock came he'd been unable to work, however, knowing that Eleanor was in his house. All he had to do was descend the stairs to see her. All he had to do was open the door to the drawing room and there she'd be, Eleanor of the warm, enchanting smile, and the blue eyes that revealed all her emotions.

I won't be a bother. Her words on the day she'd brought Bruce to him.

What would she have said if he'd answered her honestly?

Oh, Eleanor, you're a bother even when you're not here. I think of you too often. I even dream of you. When I should be writing a speech I want to write a letter to you instead. When I'm speaking to a crowded room I want to be talking to you. When I'm on my way to Parliament I want to stop at Queen's Park. Nothing's been the same in my life since that day on the hillside. There you were, all arrogant and magnificent, terrified and refusing to admit it, pushing your way through the sheep as regal as a queen. I think I fell in love with you then.

She wouldn't have liked his honesty. She would probably have begged him not to say such things. But they were his words, his thoughts, his heart. He'd never asked her for anything in return.

He'd been sure it would be hard to see her again and know that she wasn't his. She'd never be his. He had no right to touch her, to say those things to her. To love her.

That didn't stop him from missing her. He wanted to see her every day. He wanted the right to hold her hand at any time, to ask her thoughts and opinions. He wanted to pull her into his embrace whenever they were alone. He wanted to kiss her and more.

She was adamant, however, about marrying Herridge.

The man would be a terrible husband for Eleanor. Logan wished she could see that. She was bright, intelligent, and fearless, but it would only be a matter of time before Herridge browbeat her, changed her permanently into the person she called London Eleanor.

There was nothing he could do. Logan had said as much as he could to Eleanor and it hadn't altered her decision. If he had any power beyond that of words he would've done something to prevent this marriage. She was marching headlong into disaster and he was powerless to prevent it.

Even his uncle held a similar opinion about Herridge.

A man might think that a title exempted him from courteous

behavior, but the truth was that it magnified his actions. Few people cared about a simple mister, but tell a tale about a peer and they were all ears. Consequently, Michael Herridge was well known for the kind of man he was. If he had been stripped of his title, Logan doubted he'd be welcome in any of the drawing rooms in London. He'd be nothing more than an embittered man who insisted others adhere to his wishes and wants. There wasn't a charitable bone in his body or one that demonstrated any concern for another human being, even a future wife.

Eleanor deserved better.

Logan disliked being helpless. He'd wrapped his heart in wire and there was no way to free it. Eleanor was the only one with the power to do that and it was all too obvious that she was going to marry Michael Herridge.

Logan had no one to blame but himself. He should never have taken the puppy to her. If he hadn't, if he'd found Bruce a home somewhere else, he wouldn't have gotten to know her. He wouldn't have fallen in love. He wouldn't be standing at the window, watching as his beloved drove away.

Mindful of the courier still in his study, he forced himself to return to the task at hand, knowing that there was plenty of time to behave like a lovelorn idiot later. Right now, Disraeli was waiting on him.

Chapter Twenty-Seven

 ❧

$\mathcal{A}$ few nights later, Eleanor was preparing to attend a ball being held by one of Michael's distant cousins. The purpose was to introduce his daughter to society. Tonight's function was a preseason ball, given for the debutante to acquire some practice and poise before the start of the season.

She'd experienced a similar event a few years ago. Unfortunately, she had to follow in Daphne's footsteps, and while London society had oohed and ahhed over her cousin, they welcomed Eleanor with somewhat less enthusiasm.

There was a decidedly rigid standard for beauty in London. Blond hair was preferred over brown. Unusually colored eyes were always admired rather than plain blue. It also helped if one's father or guardian was sufficiently wealthy. It was amazing how beautiful a certain girl could become with the hint of wealth in the background.

Eleanor sincerely hoped that the girl tonight was attractive enough not to be shunned, but had the sense to realize that whatever attention she received for the next several months wouldn't be for herself as much as her father's rumored fortune. From this point on, Francesca would be the object of attention from young men of good families but few financial resources.

She also hoped that Francesca had friends who would last beyond the season. Eleanor hadn't seen Jenny Woolsey since the announcement of her engagement. It was as if the girl had simply melted away along with her friendship.

The other girls she'd known, most of whom had gone on to become wives, were less true friends than companionable rivals. Every man worth marrying was considered a prize. At the end of her first season, when she'd not received an offer, she was considered not quite damaged goods but certainly slightly used. She was all for skipping the second season, but her aunt was determined. Deborah considered Eleanor's lack of success in the marriage mart almost a blot on her social record.

No doubt Michael's earldom and the fact that he was distantly related to Francesca's father would have some influence on how warmly the girl was welcomed into close-knit London society. That's why he was making an appearance at this preseason event. They would stay long enough for Michael to be seen and admired and for her to be critically reviewed.

In other words, the night was going to be ghastly. She would much rather be at home, curled up in a chair with a good book. Unfortunately, her schedule looked to be filled with a flurry of social engagements. The months until the wedding would be occupied with pre-celebrations, everything from lunches to dinner parties to balls.

The wedding ceremony was expanding in size and scope with each passing day. Even Hamilton was taking a growing interest, no doubt because he was paying for it. On three separate occasions she'd attempted to discuss the expense with him, but he refused to address the matter with her.

"It is of no consequence, my dear," he said. "You mustn't worry about it."

Nor was her aunt reserved about spending money. It seemed as if the wedding was less a religious ceremony than it was a way to demonstrate the Richardses' wealth. Eleanor truly didn't need all the dresses the seamstress was making. The trousseau was already occupying three trunks with more ordered.

The gown she was wearing tonight was a lovely creation, something that had been sent from France and altered by Mrs. Fournier. Of watered silk, it was a shade of peach that flattered her complexion and brought out the blue of her eyes.

Michael would no doubt approve. Getting her aunt's nod, however, had always been more difficult. Before she descended the stairs, Deborah made her turn slowly, raise her skirts to show her matching slippers, then don her elbow-length gloves. Only then did Deborah smile.

"You will do us credit, my dear. Jeremy will meet you downstairs."

Even though she and Michael were an engaged couple, her aunt believed that it was necessary for them to have a proper chaperone when they attended social events. For that purpose, her cousin was pressed into service when Deborah or Hamilton couldn't attend with them. Jeremy normally obeyed Michael's every directive, being less a chaperone than simply an extra person in the carriage. If Michael attempted to do something untoward, Jeremy wouldn't lift a hand in protest.

Such was the power of being an earl.

Eleanor couldn't help but wonder if she'd acquire a similar ability as a countess. Would she be able to wave her hand in the air and have something instantly done? If so, it would explain why so many people believed that a title was such a great honor.

She walked slowly down the curving staircase, wishing that she enjoyed going to a ball. She would much rather sit somewhere and listen to the music than cavort to it. If tonight went as some of the entertainments in the past month, she'd meet a great many people, some of whom were related to Michael. Some of them would attend their wedding. Some of them might possibly make judgments as to whether she was good enough to become the Countess of Wescott. If they knew her true feelings about the matter, there was every possibility they'd be shocked. After all, who wouldn't want to be a countess?

She didn't.

The majordomo was in the foyer, but there was no sign of Jeremy. To her surprise, Michael's carriage had already arrived. No one was inside, which meant that he was probably waiting for her in the drawing room. She turned and walked in that direction, but was sidetracked by voices coming from Hamilton's study.

Rather than interrupt the two men, she hesitated in the hall-way, trying to decide if she should wait in the drawing room or go back to the foyer.

Michael's words made the decision for her. She remained where she was.

"His inspection was answer enough for me. The horses will be sold, as will all the furnishings. I've plans for the house, too."

"If that's the way you feel, then of course it's the right decision. I doubt that Eleanor will have the same opinion, however."

"She has an idiotic attachment to the Hearthmere bloodline. I trust that you'll leave such matters to my discretion."

"You have to understand," Hamilton said, "that it is her home. Hearthmere means a great deal to her."

"That's strictly emotion talking, but I don't expect any less from a woman. I don't want to be bothered by property in Scotland since I have no intention of ever traveling there. I've already found a man I'm going to send to appraise the furniture. He'll deal with the staff as well. As soon as we're married I'll finalize the sale."

She stood there, frozen, her hands at her midriff. She'd seen Michael yesterday and the day before. Not once had he brought up Hearthmere. Nor had he said anything about an inspection.

They only talked about Scotland occasionally. Whenever she brought up the subject of her country he would brush her comments aside.

"I don't care for Scotland," he'd said once. "You must understand that."

"You haven't seen the best parts of it," she'd responded. "Hearthmere, for example, is magnificent with its rolling hills and mountains in the background. If nothing else, you should see the horses. No finer horses have ever been raised in Scotland or England, for that matter."

"I can assure you, Eleanor, that no horses anywhere shall ever cause me to wax eloquent about them. Nor, as I said, am I fond of Scotland. I have no intention of traveling there."

Hearthmere was her legacy. Her father had left it to her because he'd known she would keep it safe.

Michael couldn't sell it. He couldn't sell the bloodline. It was hers.

Turning, she walked back to the foyer, nodding to the majordomo again. She would stand here and wait, however long it would be. If the majordomo waited with her, that was fine. An audience would guarantee that she didn't succumb to what she was feeling.

She would shock the entire household if she did what she wanted to do. She wanted to pick up something heavy and throw it, preferably through the glass at the side of the door or a window. Or scream. That would startle everyone. She rarely made a noise of surprise or disdain, anger or frustration. She was a nonentity: silent, exquisitely proper, and barely there.

Five minutes later Michael appeared, resplendent in his black evening wear. He truly was an attractive man. Yet his physical appearance meant little to her now, especially knowing what she did about his character.

He greeted her and she forced a smile to her face, thanking him when he complimented her on her appearance. Jeremy suddenly appeared on the stairs, joining them as they left the house and entered the carriage.

She needed to talk to Michael, but not in front of her cousin. However, when they arrived at the home of his relative, it wouldn't be the time or the place. Nor did she think she could wait until after the ball.

"I can't agree to selling the bloodline," she said, hearing the emotion in her own voice. "The horses are my father's legacy. I don't know what kind of inspection you ordered, but I won't sell them. Hearthmere horses are known throughout the world. It would be foolish to dismantle the stable now."

For a long moment he didn't answer her. The exterior lantern cast shadows on his face as they made their way through the crowded London streets. Even nightfall didn't make the traffic lighter.

Jeremy looked fascinated with their conversation. By tomorrow every member of her family would know exactly what they said.

"Eavesdropping is a vulgar practice, Eleanor."

She ignored his comment as well as his contempt. "If I hadn't, would you have told me what you wanted to do?"

"I see no reason to involve you in my plans, Eleanor."

"Hearthmere is mine."

"Until our marriage. Then it will be mine."

"What?"

"Your property, your inheritance become mine, Eleanor."

"It can't. You have to be . . ."

He cut her off. "I have no intention of discussing the matter with you."

She wished there was more light in the carriage. She wanted to see the expression in his eyes. Were they as flat as stones? Or did they hold any emotion?

First Bruce, now Hearthmere. Michael had as much as given her an outline of their marriage and her future. He would make unilateral decisions and she would be expected to simply accept them. He would decree and she would submit.

No.

She'd been disturbed about Bruce, but she'd told herself that perhaps there was a reason for Michael's antipathy to the puppy. Perhaps something like her own experience with the rabid dog had colored his reaction.

Now she knew it was nothing that decent.

Michael Herridge was simply a bully. An attractive, well-dressed, wealthy, charming, and titled bully.

A strange place to have such an epiphany, but perhaps it was fitting after all. They were always on their way to some social event or another. They rarely sat and talked. She'd spent more time with Logan than she ever had with her fiancé.

Even worse, she would have gladly traded one man for the other.

Chapter Twenty-Eight

$\mathcal{E}$leanor was on her way back up to her room when her aunt called her into the Ladies Parlor.

"What is the matter with you, Eleanor? You've been sulking all morning."

She hadn't felt like speaking to anyone and had retreated to the park for a few hours. If she'd still had Bruce she would've cuddled with him for a little while or even told him about this aching feeling of betrayal. Her conversation with Michael still replayed in her mind.

"Are you ill? You were out very late last night."

"Michael wanted to remain at the party."

He'd been in an expansive mood, greeting people with a smile, exerting all the charm she knew he possessed. As for her, she'd been in a daze most of the night. She remembered meeting some people, but couldn't recall either their faces or their names. All that she could think about was what Michael was planning.

"Well, then, that's understandable."

Was anything Michael did acceptable to her aunt? Could he do nothing wrong?

Eleanor came and sat on the chair opposite the couch where her aunt was sitting. There was a book on etiquette on Deborah's lap. No doubt she was going to impart some knowledge to her later on how to be a countess.

"Tell me you haven't quarreled with him."

"No, I haven't quarreled."

"I sometimes think the man is a saint to put up with your disposition."

"My disposition?"

"Such as right now. You're acting almost sullen. When I ask what's wrong, you won't answer me. Are you ailing?"

"I'm not ill, Aunt Deborah. I'm heartsick. Michael's going to sell my horses. My father's horses. The Hearthmere bloodline."

Deborah shook her head. "The worst thing your father ever did was leave Hearthmere to you. You've become fixated on it. If Michael thinks it's best to sell them, then of course that's what you must do. I'm certain it's a wise decision on his part."

"It's my inheritance. He has no right to sell them."

"Of course he does. He's going to be your husband."

"Does that mean he can do anything he wishes and I have no say?"

"Of course. Now go and take yourself off to your bedroom. It's a good thing Michael isn't here. If he saw you looking as you are right now he would immediately regret his offer."

Eleanor stood and left the parlor without another word. Once in her room she sat at her secretary and wrote a letter to Mr. Babbage. Her father's solicitor had called upon her from time to time, even after she moved to London with her aunt's family.

"Your father was a friend of mine," he'd told her during their last meeting a year ago. "I consider it a sacred duty to ensure that you are well and happy, my dear."

She had hastened to reassure Mr. Babbage that she was both, even though she would much rather have remained in Scotland.

"Your aunt has not proven difficult, has she? She's still kept to the letter of our agreement, I hope. You return home a month each year, don't you?"

"I do. Thank you for that, Mr. Babbage. I don't know what I would do if I couldn't go back to Scotland for a little while."

His gaze had been compassionate, but he hadn't said anything further about her visits. Thankfully, he'd always understood her love for Hearthmere.

The man was getting up in age. Would he agree to meet her in London once again? She didn't feel as though the question she needed to ask him could be conveyed in a letter.

For the next week she kept her normal schedule, including her visit to Bruce. Each week it was more difficult to leave. Each week she wanted to stay at Logan's house. If nothing else she wanted to leave him a note and ask him to meet with her. She missed their interludes in the park. They seemed to be her happiest times in London.

Fortunately, she had no social events during the week. She didn't know how she would have been able to bear being in Michael's company for even one minute, let alone an entire evening.

One of the maids delivered the post on the following Thursday. In it was a letter not from Mr. Babbage, but from his son, who had followed in his father's footsteps and was a solicitor as well. He would be willing to meet with her at her convenience. To her surprise he included a London address for her to respond.

She sent Liam there an hour later, asking if the solicitor could meet with her soon. Thankfully, he agreed on the following day.

The Royal Meadows Hotel was only three years old, but its tearoom was reputed to be the most popular in London. She'd heard that unescorted ladies were welcome there, even accompanied by young men. No one would think anything of her meeting Mr. Babbage's son.

The walls of the tearoom were decorated in a soft peach color while the tables were covered in a pale gray cloth. Each table was adorned with silver place settings and a small bouquet.

She stood at the entrance, wondering if she should take a table or wait for the solicitor where she was. She'd never met Mr. Babbage's son. How was she to recognize him? Thankfully, she didn't have to concern herself with that problem. A young woman, attired in a dark blue dress with a white apron, approached her.

"Are you Miss Craig?"

Eleanor nodded.

"If you will come with me, Miss Craig."

She followed the woman across the tearoom to a table by the window. The man sitting there stood and greeted her with a smile. She shouldn't have worried about recognizing Mr. Babbage. He was the image of his father, down to his receding hairline and round face.

"Miss Craig?"

She nodded again.

"You look exactly as my father described you."

He introduced himself as he pulled out the adjoining chair. Eleanor sat, spending some time arranging her skirt. A delaying tactic since she wasn't entirely certain how to begin this conversation.

"How is your father?" she finally asked.

"Exceedingly well, thank you, except for a touch of gout. It was only happenstance that I was visiting him when your letter arrived. I hope you don't mind my being here in his stead. He doesn't travel lately, because of the gout."

"Please send him my best wishes."

"I will. Thank you."

He poured her some tea from the pot already on the table. She occupied herself with adding sugar to her cup. There was no delicate way to broach this subject. She was simply going to have to be blunt.

"Are you familiar with my father's will?"

"My father and I have discussed its particulars. Do you have some concerns about your inheritance?"

"I am engaged to be married, Mr. Babbage," she said after taking a sip of her tea. "Unfortunately, my soon-to-be husband believes that he has the right to sell my horses."

He turned his gaze to the crowd. The tearoom was filled with well-dressed women and some men. Consequently, it was noisy, the conversation often punctuated by laughter.

When he directed his attention back to her he said, "You do not wish the horses to be sold, I take it?"

She shook her head. "I do not. I've done everything I can to continue my father's legacy. Yet my fiancé, who knows nothing of racing and cares even less, wants to sell the bloodline. Does our marriage give him the right to dismantle another man's dream?"

"I'm afraid it does," he said, his voice soft and laced with compassion. "He cannot sell Hearthmere or do anything with the property or the land without your consent, but the contents? Yes."

"Contents?"

"The furniture, any items of decorative value, and unfortunately the horses."

She stared at him for a moment. A cavern opened up in her chest. The echo of her heartbeat seemed to come from far away.

"Is there nothing I can do?" she asked finally. "Is there nothing you can do? Have I no power as my father's only heir?"

His eyes darted left to right, and lit on the china, then the window. Finally he settled on the tip of one shoe peeping out beneath the tablecloth.

She waited with some impatience for him to speak. When he did, she almost wished he'd kept silent.

"As a woman you have no standing. Upon your marriage, your father's estate essentially becomes the property of your husband, without the right to sell the structure and the land, as I mentioned. That's simply the law."

Her stomach was queasy. "You're quite sure?"

"I am, yes."

She couldn't help but wonder if the elder Mr. Babbage might've had a different answer for her.

As if he'd heard her thoughts, his son added, "My father would've told you the same thing, Miss Craig. It's settled law."

In other words, Michael could do anything he wished and she couldn't stop him. He could empty Hearthmere of all the antiques, the French furniture her great-great-grandmother had purchased, and the paintings her grandfather had so enjoyed. He could decimate the Clan Hall and sell all the volumes in Hearthmere's library.

She waved away the tray of pastries she was offered. She wasn't hungry. There was a terrible taste in her mouth, like ashes or dust. She wanted to apologize to her father for being unable to protect his legacy.

Picking up her reticule she clutched it with both hands on her lap. "Are you quite sure, Mr. Babbage? There's nothing I can do? Nothing at all?"

He smiled at her, an expression that was oddly charming, making him seem boyish.

"Do not marry, Miss Craig. That way no one will have any say in your inheritance."

"Except my aunt," she said.

"Your aunt has no legal standing in regard to your inheritance. Nor could she keep you from Hearthmere," he added, surprising her. "The arrangement for you to visit Scotland for one month out of the year was a social concession more than a legal one. As a single woman you would have autonomy over your inheritance."

Was she willing to go that far? Was she willing to be a pariah to her family?

Family is everything.

What about her father, though, and his life's ambition? Didn't that count for anything at all?

She thanked Mr. Babbage for meeting with her, stood, and made her way to the front of the hotel where Liam was waiting.

"Back home, Miss Eleanor?" he asked before she got into the carriage.

"No, Liam. Take me to Mr. McKnight's house, please."

She couldn't bear to return to her aunt's home. Or hear more gushing praise about Michael.

Her family had heralded this marriage. At first she'd been bemused about the engagement. As it continued, she began to feel the first twinges of unease. The situation with Bruce had crossed a line. Now the prospect of selling Hearthmere pushed her onto the edge of a cliff.

Michael cared nothing for what she thought was important. All he'd demonstrated since they'd become engaged was that his wishes and wants were important, but hers were to be ignored.

For the great honor of making her his wife, his countess, she was to understand that she was only a vessel, a woman who would give him heirs but nothing more. She wasn't to have an opinion. She wasn't to have a dog. She wasn't to disagree. She wasn't to own anything. She was to turn her back on her country, her inheritance, and see Michael as an object of adoration, nothing less.

How could she marry someone like that? How could she consider a future with someone so selfish and insular?

She couldn't.

Gain a husband, lose her inheritance.

Even worse, marry and be miserable.

Chapter Twenty-Nine

To Eleanor's surprise, Mrs. Campbell didn't open the door. Logan did. He stood there, attired not in his customary suit, but in a white shirt and dark trousers. He was also not wearing shoes.

He was the one she'd come to see, but she was startled at his appearance at the door. So much so that she looked down, then back up at him, then down once more, uncertain what to say.

Thankfully, Bruce's arrival made it unnecessary for her to comment. She bent and petted him, smiling as he wriggled and whined in response.

"Where's Mrs. Campbell?" she finally asked, straightening.

Bruce was truly learning his manners because he sat between them, looking first at Logan and then at her.

One of Logan's eyebrows arched upward as he answered. "It's her day off. In fact, most of the servants are out this afternoon. If you've come for tea and biscuits, I'll have to provide them."

She told herself to say something. Anything but stand there staring at him like a dolt.

"I haven't come for tea or biscuits or to see Mrs. Campbell. I came to see you. I was hoping you would be here. I needed to see a friend."

His face didn't change. He didn't look any happier to see her, but he did step back and open the door wider.

She entered the house, knowing that if Mrs. Campbell wasn't here and the servants were gone then she shouldn't be here, either. She kept silent.

He led the way down the corridor. She'd never come this far into his house before. He entered a spacious and sunny kitchen. Herbs in green pots lined two large west-facing windows. The windows on the opposite wall revealed his closest neighbor, bushes planted between them to afford some privacy.

She hesitated at the doorway, looking around her. The cupboards were painted white, as was the long table in the middle of the room. She could imagine a dozen or so people working away, companionable and earnest in their tasks. Laughter would occasionally punctuate the conversation because Logan's home was a happy place. The fireplace at the other side of the kitchen looked large enough to roast a boar beneath its arched bricks. A half-dozen wrought iron trivets and pulleys held pots, now empty and ready for the next meal.

A white ten-plate wood-burning stove with two ovens took up most of the space against another wall. A pump and sink area were not too far away. All in all there was enough room in this kitchen to prepare meals to feed a small army.

After filling the kettle with water, he placed it back on the stove, but didn't turn to look at her.

"Why do you need a friend?"

She wandered over to the window.

"Michael is going to sell the Hearthmere bloodline."

He had his back to her and it seemed like he was staring down at the stove, anything but look at her.

"Are you angry?" she asked. "If you are, I can't blame you. You're right, you did ask me to come only on Wednesdays. Forgive me. It's just that I wanted someone to talk to and I knew you'd understand how important the horses were to me."

He turned and faced her. "What are you going to do about it?"

"According to my solicitor, there's nothing I can do. A woman has no rights to her inheritance after she marries. I have two choices: to marry Michael or to never marry."

The idea occurred to her that maybe she wasn't here to get his observation and opinion after all. She wanted to feel valuable and important to someone. She wanted someone to think she was worth caring about. Logan always had.

He walked toward her slowly, almost as if giving her time to escape. She didn't want to be anywhere but here.

She walked into his embrace and when his arms went around her she felt as if she were home. A foolish thought, one that was compounded by the knowledge that she was behaving in a shocking manner. She shouldn't be here. He shouldn't be placing his hand against her cheek or tilting up her head to look into her eyes.

He was the answer to every prayer she'd ever had, and that thought was both sacrilegious and foolish.

Joy spilled through her because he was holding her and she was returning the embrace. He might kiss her, and that was part wish and part anticipation.

If she was doomed to perdition by her behavior, at least let it be for something that she truly wished to do. Being here was what she wanted, what she'd always wanted.

She pulled back, then stepped away. Not because she wanted to, but because she didn't want to put him in a difficult position. Logan was an honorable man, and being with an engaged woman would test that honor.

The words were difficult to say, but they must be said. "I should leave."

He nodded. "Have tea at least."

Logan walked back to the stove, reaching for something between it and the cabinet. It turned out to be the large round tray she'd seen every Wednesday. In the next few minutes he equipped it with two cups and saucers, a large white teapot, and a dark blue knitted cozy. In addition, he cut them both a piece of clootie dumpling, explaining that he liked it as much as plum pudding.

"It reminds me of my childhood," he said. "I used to tell myself that when I was grown I would eat as many clootie dumplings as I wanted. And if I grew fat as a stoat, no one could tell me no."

"You haven't grown fat as a stoat," she said.

"That's only because Cook refuses to make it that often, for my own good."

"I suspect you have a great many people who care about you, Logan. And only want good things for you."

She was one of them.

The fact that he knew where the cups and saucers were and where the teapot was stored impressed her. If Hamilton ever wandered into the kitchen—an accident, to be sure—she was entirely certain that the man would be confused. Logan, however, acted comfortable in the space. And Michael? She didn't want to think about him right now, especially here in Logan's house.

"You gave me tea in Scotland," she said.

"In a shepherd's cottage. I will guarantee you that this tea is better."

"Do you ever cook your own meals?"

"Occasionally. Why do you look so surprised?"

She shook her head. "No reason."

"What about you? Would you die of hunger if your cook suddenly quit?"

"No, but I doubt if I could make a lot of the complicated dishes she does. I can bake bread, scones, and I have a few recipes I memorized from the cook at Hearthmere."

"I can make a great oatmeal," he said. "And a venison steak."

"I could add boiled potatoes. And maybe a few greens. Or buttered squash."

"See, the two of us wouldn't starve."

The idea of fending for themselves, alone, without anyone interfering, was an idyllic notion, one that she tucked away to think about later.

They moved into the drawing room, Bruce following. When Logan set the tray on the table, the puppy sat patiently between the chairs, waiting.

"Mrs. Campbell always brought him a treat, too," she said.

Logan smiled. "Then a treat he shall have." He left the room.

In his absence she noticed the stack of papers beside one of the chairs.

"I've interrupted you," she said when he entered the room again, closing the door behind him. "You were working."

"I was reading and I was bored. You came at just the right time."

He gave a bone to Bruce, but only after he showed off his manners.

They sat, each in one of the chairs before the fire. Logan spoke about his sister, Janet, and how she could never take her tea without cream.

"Her husband only drinks coffee and I think it's a testament to their love that she accepts his choice. Otherwise, I'm sure she would have forced him to drink tea and like it."

"Some days I prefer coffee," she said. "Today it's tea."

"For me it has a lot to do with the weather. For some reason, on cold and rainy days, tea is perfect. Maybe that's why England has so many tea drinkers."

They spent nearly an hour talking about subjects great and small. Legislation that Mr. Disraeli was intent on getting passed, the election, and how Logan was coping now that someone else had been PM.

Bruce seemed utterly content to sit on the floor between them, occasionally raising his head when his name was mentioned. Today she saw a hint of what he would be like fully grown, his intelligent brown eyes seeming amused.

She could imagine sitting here like this every day. Logan would discuss his work. She would share the advances to the breeding program at Hearthmere. Mr. Contino had recently written her about his need for an addition to the stables and she was predisposed to agree to his idea.

Yet that was foolishness, wasn't it? Logan had never told her that what he felt for her was something special and unique. Nor had he ever once mentioned that he wanted her in his life on a permanent basis.

What she wanted and what was going to happen were two entirely different things.

Chapter Thirty

*H*er tea done, Eleanor stared down at her cup. She'd come and told Logan what choice faced her. Staying longer would only hint at scandal.

Eleanor knew she should leave. Right now, before she said something foolish. Telling him how much she'd needed to see him these past weeks wouldn't be wise. Those words were better kept to herself.

The emotion she was feeling, the same one that kept her awake at night and summoned her tears too quickly, had its roots in friendship and respect. Yet it was so much more.

She loved him. She adored him. This man was the most important person in the world to her.

Keeping silent didn't diminish the power of what she felt.

She bent and spent some time petting Bruce, who rolled onto his back, asking for a belly rub. She missed the puppy, missed having him in her life. He was a four-legged friend, a companion, and a warm and funny reminder of Logan.

What a wonderful person he was, offering both her and Bruce a haven.

A strange time to begin to cry.

"Eleanor, what's wrong?"

Logan moved to sit on the ottoman, reaching out and taking her hands in his. A minute later, when she still couldn't stop her tears, he startled her by standing and pulling her into his arms.

"Eleanor, stop."

She couldn't. It was as if all the sadness she'd felt since giving up Bruce had accumulated in a well deep inside her. Whether she wished it or not, the well was emptying.

He gently put his arms around her. "Please, Eleanor."

She nodded, but it didn't seem to have any effect on her tears. They continued. Resting her cheek against his chest felt like coming home.

"I hate to see you cry."

"I never cry in front of other people," she said, her voice sounding watery.

"What would you call this?"

She pulled back, swiping at her face with her hands. "Do you think this is funny?"

His smile evaporated. "This is the least amusing situation I've ever been in."

"I'm sorry."

"For what?"

"For crying. For coming here." *For needing you.* "Thank you for giving Bruce a home." *And me a haven.*

"I like having him here. He reminds me of you."

She'd thought the same thing. Logan had annoyed her, then become a friend. Now he was so much more, but she couldn't say that, could she?

Every Wednesday when she'd come to see Bruce, she'd hoped he would be here. To see, to touch, to talk to. She hoped he'd be waiting for her. When he hadn't appeared, she sat in his house and accepted his hospitality. It had both comforted her and made her miserable.

They were standing too close. She placed her hands on his chest. He covered her hands with his.

Her arms went around his waist. He lowered his head, the warmth of his breath causing shivers down her back.

His hands were suddenly on her waist and then upward on her sides, almost at her breasts. She could feel them through her clothing, as if his fingers were on her bare skin.

She should move. Now. Before anything else happened, she should step back, apologize for coming, and leave. This visit had already been too long. At least on Wednesdays, Mrs. Campbell was here. Now no one stood between them and scandal. They were bending, if not breaking, all the rules of propriety.

It was so hard to move. She wanted to remain exactly where she was, friended and protected, safe and valued.

The tick of the mantel clock measured the moments. Still, she didn't step back and walk toward the door. His arms were still around her, his stance as immobile as hers.

Finally, he pulled back. He didn't speak for the longest time, his eyes searching her face.

"I want to kiss you."

Her heart felt as if it stopped, then started again. "Do you?"

"Yes, in violation of every whisper from my conscience. You should leave."

"And if I don't?"

"Then we'll both be fools."

"Is it really important to be wise?" she asked. "I haven't been very happy lately, but I've been very wise." She placed her hands on either side of his face. "Can't we both be fools together, Logan? Please kiss me."

A second later she was back in his arms, his mouth on hers.

She wanted to stop time itself, memorize these moments so that she could always recall them.

He hadn't kissed her often enough. They hadn't done this as many times as she'd wanted, as often as she'd thought about. In her dreams his kisses had led to even more scandalous things. Then, he touched her everywhere, learning her, causing her body to heat and her mind to simply stop.

She wanted to match the dream to reality, make all of that happen. She wanted to stroke her fingers over every part of him.

Long moments later he ended the kiss, pulling back, but keeping her within his embrace. They were both breathing hard but they still didn't separate, as if each needed the other to keep standing.

When he spoke his voice was harsh. "Stop me, Eleanor, because I'm not certain I can stop myself."

"Must we stop?"

She'd never been as brave as she was at that moment.

"You don't know what you're saying."

"Yes, I do. I know what happens next. You forget what Hearthmere is. We breed horses. Growing up there I couldn't help but learn about nature."

His cheeks were bronzed, his smile wry. "So I'm a stallion now, is that it?"

"Yes," she said, smiling.

Her hands rose to her collar. She unfastened one button and then another. This bodice had entirely too many buttons, a thought she'd had this morning when dressing. At the time seduction hadn't occurred to her. If it had she would have chosen another outfit.

"What do you think you're doing?"

"Undressing," she said. "Unless you want me to simply toss my skirts over my head."

"Eleanor . . ."

"Logan." *My love.*

Once her bodice was unfastened, she grabbed her skirt with both hands, pulled it over her head, and threw the garment onto the nearby chair.

Bruce barked at it, thinking this was a new game.

She laughed, glancing at Logan.

"I would say that we should put him out in the hall," she said, "but I know Bruce only too well. He would bark to be let in."

"That he would." Logan hadn't moved. His eyes were still fixed on her.

Her fingers went to her corset cover, removing it without one hint of embarrassment. That garment joined her dress on the chair. Bruce barked again.

"I have to admit, however, that when I considered this moment, I never thought that a dog would be witness to it."

"You considered this moment?" he asked.

She nodded. "In a general way. When I was growing up. I think girls always visualize their first time. It's exceedingly important to us."

His hands reached out to hold hers.

"Eleanor . . ."

She pulled free, unfastening the busk of her corset before letting it fall. There were only a few garments between her and nakedness.

His gaze hadn't left her, but he was shaking his head slowly from side to side.

"Oh, yes," she said. "I sincerely wish to be deflowered. Isn't that what they call it? I want you to be my lover."

He didn't respond.

Good, she didn't need him to speak. All she truly wanted was for him to kiss her again. Kiss her and then rid her of her virginity.

When he didn't move, she went to him and began to unfasten the buttons of his shirt. His hands came up to stop her, but she shook her head.

"No, on this I am quite insistent. Pretend that I am one of your constituents and I'm demanding that you act on my behalf."

"My constituents are men, and I doubt one of them would come to me with this demand. If they did, I would have to respectfully decline."

"Then just pretend I'm a fellow Scot who has it in her head to be loved by you. No one is here. No one would know."

"I would know," he said.

She dropped her hands and stepped back, looking up at him.

"I've never felt this way with anyone, Logan. If you truly wish me gone, say it now before I humiliate myself further."

"You don't understand, Eleanor."

She turned and reached for the corset on the chair. She would simply get dressed, get back in her carriage, and pretend that this afternoon never happened.

He placed his hand on her upper arm and gently turned her to face him.

"You don't understand. This moment is the culmination of a great many dreams, but I can't take advantage of you."

"Take advantage of me? In what way? Didn't I kiss you back? Did you take my clothes off, Logan? Or did I? How would you be taking advantage of me?"

"By allowing you to be rash."

She was heartily sick of everyone deciding how she should act.

"I'm not a child," she said, "to be lectured about my behavior. No one compelled me to kiss you, Logan McKnight. I did so because it was something I wanted. Loving you is something else I want. My great mistake was in thinking it was something you wanted as well."

"Eleanor."

"Oh, don't say my name in that way. As if you're an elder statesman and I'm some naive, foolish chit. I misunderstood. I thought you were as enchanted by our kisses as I was."

"Of course I was."

She shook her head. "Evidently not."

He didn't say anything. She stepped forward once again, wrapping her arms around his waist and laying her cheek against his chest.

"Must loving me be so difficult for you?"

"I am holding on to the dregs of my honor with more strength than I knew I possessed."

"And if you loved me, you'd regret it?"

"Would you?"

"Never. How could I ever regret anything so wondrous?"

"How do you know it would be wondrous?"

"Because of the way you kiss me. The way you touch me, gently and tenderly. I want the memory of you loving me, Logan. I want that experience. But I won't beg you anymore. Your honor is evidently stronger than my need or my wishes."

"What about Herridge?"

That question just ratcheted up her temper. "What about him? He has nothing to do with this, with us."

"Doesn't he?"

She blew out a breath. "Right now, Logan, I'm Eleanor from Scotland. I'm not the pale imitation who lives in London. I'm not the silent, acquiescent nobody who fades into the background. I know exactly what I want, and it's this afternoon with you. Don't talk to me about honor. I don't care about honor. I only care about what I feel here and now. Words can't possibly measure it."

She pulled his head down for a kiss. This, this was what she wanted. To feel this connection, this closeness, this gate to another place, another experience she'd never had.

When the kiss was over she stepped back and looked up at him.

"Don't tell me you feel differently."

"Damn it, Eleanor, how can I?"

He pulled her into his arms, so tightly that a thought couldn't come between them. She laughed. Then he kissed her and every thought simply disappeared.

He helped her remove the remainder of her clothing. She continued to work on his buttons. When they proved to be stubborn she wanted to say one of the oaths she'd heard the stable boys use. Logan smiled and replaced her hands with his. In seconds he'd removed his trousers and the rest of his clothes.

$\mathcal{H}$IS HANDS WERE shaking and that had never happened to him before now. The voice of his conscience was getting louder. He should kiss her on the forehead and leave the room. He should say something conciliatory, something that would explain his bizarre, ravening behavior.

She smiled at him as he helped her off with her petticoat, holding out his arm as she stepped delicately out of the pool of lace.

There was no fear in her expression. No hesitation, either. No doubt her conscience was speaking loudly to her as well. Yet she was more adept than he at silencing it.

"Eleanor . . ."

She reached up and placed two fingers on his lips. Just that wordless gesture as well as the look in her eyes. One that said as clearly as speech, *Don't banish me, Logan. Allow us this pleasure, please.*

He should have taken her to his room, but then the threat of scandal would be even greater should the lone maid see them enter or leave. He couldn't imagine a less romantic bower than his drawing room, but at the moment it simply didn't matter. All he cared about was Eleanor.

Bruce yawned, bored by their antics.

Logan bent and scooped Eleanor up into his arms, struck by how perfect she felt there. Gently, he lowered her to the sofa, grateful that it was long and wide enough for their lovemaking.

He knelt there for a moment, confounded by his own wonder. Her skin was alabaster, the perfection of her body only hinted at beneath the style of her dresses.

She was exquisite from her full, rose-tipped breasts to her perfectly curved hips and down the long expanse of her legs. He reached out one trembling hand and placed it on her abdomen, following up that gesture with a kiss. Eleanor put her hand on the back of his neck before trailing her fingers down his shoulder.

Rising up, she kissed him. In that moment his conscience was silenced. He could no more dress and leave this room than he could command night into day. A sense of rightness flowed through him, a feeling that he was destined to be here on this day with this woman.

He wasn't going to waste any more time on second-guessing or questioning.

SHE THOUGHT SHE'D feel vulnerable being naked but the opposite was true. A sense of power rushed through her, as if in shedding her clothing she also dispensed with the person she'd become in the past few years. The woman she was now, fearless Eleanor, was the woman she'd always wanted to be.

Never once had she considered that she might want to touch a man everywhere, that she might need to do so with an urge she'd never before felt.

In her imaginings about her wedding night, about those nights her husband would demand his rights, she believed that allowing him into her bed would be an act of duty.

This was different. There was no duty in this loving, only excitement, and the thrill of being human and alive. She felt as if her body was burning up, her breasts full, her nipples taut and acutely sensitive.

She'd never imagined that she would feel a surge of joy, or gratitude that flowed through her like heated wine. She was grateful for being a woman, for Logan, for this perfect afternoon, for the solitude and seclusion, and especially for the freedom to give herself to this man.

$\mathcal{H}$IS HANDS STROKED her everywhere, learning her, memorizing her for when she was no longer with him. He knew, with a precognition alien to him, that he would never be able to forget this blissful afternoon.

His lips closed over one nipple, pulling gently. When she moaned, the sound was tied to something within him. While he explored her she did the same with him, her hands finding places he'd never known were sensitive to touch: his buttocks, the small of his back, his throat. She kissed her way across his body in a way that surprised him given her innocence.

$\mathcal{E}$LEANOR NEVER THOUGHT that when she lost her virginity, it would be on an overstuffed sofa, or that she would be carried away by passion. She felt desperate and hungry for him, something she hadn't expected. She wanted to be kissed all over and he did that, making her marvel at all the sensations her body could produce. Kissing her ear made her shiver, but when Logan touched her breasts with his fingers or mouth, heat raced through her body. His hand skimming down her leg sent icicles down her back. His fingers trailing a path behind her knee made her smile. Each touch caused a bell to ring in her mind, a rounded sound that made note of that particular feeling to recall it in the future.

Whatever he wanted she would give to him. She was both his acolyte and his accomplice.

Let this feeling last; end this waiting now. Two needs fought each other.

WHEN HE ROSE over her, Logan didn't ask if she was sure that this was what she wanted. They were eons past that point. He was driven by an incalculable need and nearly desperate desire.

He entered her slowly, grateful that she welcomed him by lifting her hips, cradling him between her legs with a gentle rocking movement. Her hands gripped his shoulders; her fingernails marked him as hers.

Time slowed before racing. His blood pounded in his ears. Every muscle, every nerve was focused on completion, on the sounds Eleanor was making deep in her throat, on her hardened nipples grazing his chest.

He had never needed anything more than this joining, this coming together. Nothing would ever mean as much or destroy him as completely.

Her body bowed beneath his, her hips rising to demand more of him. A lone keening cry left her lips as his vision grayed. Seconds later he collapsed next to her and only then did his conscience wake from its imposed slumber.

Chapter Thirty-One

Eleanor kept her eyes shut a long time, feeling Logan beside her. They were skin to skin from head to toe. His hand rested on her waist; his leg was between hers.

She wanted to cry again, but she didn't understand the tears. She didn't regret what she'd done. How could she? She'd always remember these moments with Logan.

If she hadn't already decided to end her engagement, this act might have been one of disloyalty and betrayal. Instead, it was an affirmation of the freedom she'd decreed for herself.

Perhaps all the cascading emotions were responsible for her sudden wish to weep. Love for him overwhelmed her. She was suffused with sadness because she had to leave soon. Then there was the joy because of the perfection of their coming together.

She'd expected pain, but there had been none, only an uncomfortable feeling of fullness that had eased within moments.

This, then, was passion. You lost any sense of yourself. Your body heated. Your soul incinerated. If anything came between you and the object of your desire you would simply step over it or around it or kick it out of the way. Mere mortals didn't have a chance against such an overwhelming set of sensations.

She opened her eyes, turning her head slightly to find that he was watching her.

What words were appropriate at this moment? She didn't know because what she wanted to say was forbidden.

I love you.

She placed her hand on his cheek, rose up, and kissed him lightly. Would it be permissible to say thank you? Would he understand how much she appreciated that he'd put aside his honor in order to give her this experience?

"I have to leave," she softly said. "I've already been gone for some time. I'll be missed." Especially since she was supposed to be feeling ill, too sick to be attending a fitting.

When she was questioned about her absence, she would say that she needed to get some air. She would find some excuse.

She doubted that would be necessary for long, however. The actions of this afternoon would soon fade beneath her news. When she told her family that she wasn't going to marry Michael, no one would remember her absence.

She wasn't going to lose everything that her father had built up for years. She wasn't going to turn over the management of Hearthmere to anyone else. Nor was she going to allow the horses, the very bloodline her father had perfected, to be sold. She was going to choose a single life rather than becoming a countess and she wasn't going to regret one single moment of it. Nor was she going to regret this afternoon, either.

She'd thought about her decision for hours. *Disappointment* wasn't a strong enough word to describe what her family would feel, but it was the only way to keep Hearthmere intact.

She sat up, reaching for her shift, conscious that Logan was still behind her, naked.

Finally, he sat up beside her. Did he feel the same reluctance to speak?

She finally found her corset cover, but she'd lost one garter. Logan dressed and helped her look for it, but it was nowhere to be found.

Bruce had moved and was now sitting to the side of one of the chairs.

"Did you take my garter, Bruce? Did you think it was a new toy?"

He tilted his head and gave her a little whine.

"Where is it, silly?"

He came and licked her fingers.

"Never mind," she said. "I just won't wear my stockings." Her skirt was voluminous enough that no one would know.

She put her two stockings and the remaining garter in the bottom of her reticule. Standing, she wished she had a mirror, the better to put her hair in some order.

"You look beautiful," Logan said.

She turned and gazed up at him.

"There's a faint flush to your skin," he said. "And your lips are pink."

She wanted to go to him and kiss him once more. That would only make her departure harder. She wanted to stay here for the rest of her life, and wasn't that a silly notion?

"I have to leave," she said once more. If she didn't get back soon she wouldn't need to inform Michael of her decision. Gossip would end their engagement.

Logan nodded. "This shouldn't have happened."

How do you stop a whirlwind? That's what it had felt like. As if she would die without touching him or being touched.

"Will it help?"

"Help?" she asked, not understanding.

"Will this afternoon help you get through your wedding night, Eleanor?"

She was so shocked by his comment that she could only wordlessly stare at him.

"I trust it shall. I hope you have a long and happy marriage, Your Ladyship."

He didn't stay to hear her answer. Instead, he strode from the room, leaving the door open behind him. Bruce remained at her side.

How could he have said such a thing? After a moment she realized why. He thought she was still going to marry Michael.

She hadn't told him any different. By not informing Logan of her decision, she'd given him the impression that not only was she disloyal, but that she was incapable of her own sense of honor.

She could race after him and tell him what she'd decided. What would he think of her then? Would he believe that she expected a declaration of some sort from him? Or think he was obligated to her in some way? She didn't want to leave with him thinking the worst of her, yet she didn't know what else to do.

If she was going to return to Scotland and live her life alone, she should begin right now.

LOGAN KNEW HE'D been a fool and he wasn't given to being foolish. Despite what the newspapers called him, he couldn't adequately represent his constituents if he was truly a firebrand. No, he wasn't normally rash. However, whenever he was around Eleanor he was given to acting unlike himself, almost as if he reverted to being a boy.

He should never have seduced her, if that was the correct word for it. It was more like a mutual seduction. Any words he'd uttered in caution had been buried beneath passion. Eleanor hadn't been the least reluctant. Nor had he. In fact, he couldn't remember ever being as overwhelmed by desire. He could only thank Providence that it was the servants' day off.

There was always one maid who rotated with the others. She remained here in case he needed something. Hopefully she hadn't come looking for him in the past hour.

All of his servants were Scottish and each one of them was loyal. No gossip would reach anyone about Eleanor. He couldn't guarantee the same when she returned to the Richardses' house. He could always ride out the storm of controversy. She, less so. Society always blamed a woman in a situation like this. His own reputation might be enhanced by a hint of scandal. For the last two years, ever since he'd become a member of Parliament, he'd been the brunt of teasing from various contemporaries for his lack of romantic entanglements. Even Disraeli had made a comment about his bachelor life.

He shouldn't have said what he did to Eleanor. Yet he couldn't bear the idea of her still marrying Herridge. She'd said she had a choice, but she hadn't indicated that she was going to end her engagement. They needed to have that conversation again or discuss her circumstances more fully. It was his business now. What he felt for her gave him the right to argue against marriage to Herridge.

What would he do if she insisted on going through with the wedding? What if becoming a countess was more important to her than anything else? The woman he'd come to know wouldn't care about a title, hadn't cared about one.

Letting her leave was a mistake. Letting her leave as she had was even worse. His words had spread a pall over an otherwise unforgettable afternoon.

He would make a point of being here on Wednesday when she came to visit Bruce. Would she come? If she didn't, he'd get his answer then. She regretted their afternoon of passion.

Chapter Thirty-Two

To her surprise, Liam didn't leave his driver's perch to open the carriage door for her. He glanced at her, then pointed toward the carriage. She couldn't understand what he was mouthing to her, but before she had a chance to ask, the door opened on its own.

Michael sat there, his arms folded and his face empty of any expression.

Eleanor hesitated, then continued descending the steps.

The last thing she wanted was to confront Michael right now. However, it needed to be done. The sooner this difficult encounter was over, the better.

Did he know that she wasn't fully dressed? She fervently hoped that he couldn't tell she wasn't wearing stockings, or that they were tucked into her reticule. Although he couldn't know what had transpired in the drawing room, he did know that she'd been in Logan's home. That fact alone was enough to label her as shocking since she'd broken several rules about comportment and propriety.

Perhaps he'd be so incensed with her that he'd break their engagement, thereby sparing her the necessity of doing so.

There was nothing else to do but join him and she did so, entering the carriage, and settling herself opposite Michael.

"What are you doing here?"

"It's a question I might ask of you, Eleanor."

She sat back against the seat. "Evidently you browbeat my driver to allow you into my carriage."

Michael gave the command to Liam and they began to move.

"Don't be ridiculous, Eleanor. I don't have to browbeat anyone. They all know who I am."

Michael had always had a high opinion of himself.

"You've been a very busy woman today. First the hotel and now McKnight's residence."

She stared at him. "How did you know I went to the hotel?"

"I've had you followed for a considerable time."

"What do you mean, you've had me followed?"

"You've been different ever since Scotland. I wanted to know why. I decided that today was as good a time as any to confront you about your behavior. Why were you with McKnight?"

She couldn't form an answer. He'd had her followed? Why, because she was a Scot and therefore beneath him? What a pity a mirror couldn't bear him children. Otherwise, it would be the perfect mate, endlessly reflecting his image back to him.

"I came to visit Bruce," she said. "Remember? The dog you refused to let me keep? Logan gave him a home, but I missed him. I wanted to see how he was doing."

"One day a week? Such devotion, Eleanor, and to a dumb animal."

She felt more affection for Bruce than she did Michael. Although it was neither the proper time nor the place, the words must be said.

"I've decided we won't suit, Michael. I can't marry you. I wouldn't be the wife you want and, in turn, I would be miserable." She could not, for the life of her, imbue her voice with any compassion or fondness. She wasn't that much of a hypocrite.

He didn't say anything, but his mouth thinned. There was no expression in his blue eyes. They might have been a pond frozen over in winter. He still had his arms folded in front of him, his knuckles now white.

She continued, "I can't accept your decision about Hearthmere. You have no right to sell my father's horses or to empty my home. I won't tolerate it."

"You won't tolerate it? Who are you to dictate to me? There will be no change of plans. You'll marry me and you'll learn to be a docile, obedient wife, even if I have to beat it into you."

"No."

"Oh, yes, Eleanor. You aren't going to shame me in front of the world. No one rejects me, Eleanor. No one makes me a laughing-stock."

"You can let it be known that you were the one to break the engagement," she said. "After all, most people were surprised when you chose me in the first place. You can just say that the longer we were engaged the more you were convinced that I was the wrong choice."

"Not an untruth, Eleanor. However, I wouldn't have waited this long before making my decision. All of my acquaintances know that. Besides, I've introduced you to them. That doesn't lend credence to my changing my mind."

She'd never anticipated this reaction. She'd thought he would be angry, perhaps even enraged. But to refuse to listen to her?

"We will be married and you will become an exemplary wife. You'll be a paragon of virtue, an example for others. You'll never see McKnight or that cur again. You'll never go anywhere without me. You'll never act contrary to my interests."

"You can't force me to marry you," she said, wondering if, somehow, he thought he could.

"You'd be surprised at what I can do, Eleanor," he said, his smile chilling.

Once they were at her aunt's house, Michael grabbed her wrist and nearly pulled her from the carriage. He kept his hand clamped on her as they mounted the steps and into the foyer.

"Send Jeremy to me," Michael told the majordomo as he pulled Eleanor behind him. More than once she tried to break free, but Michael's grip was too tight on her wrist. He didn't seem to care that he was hurting her. Nor did he slow when she stumbled. She was certain he would have let her fall and then dragged her down the corridor.

He entered the gray parlor and nearly flung her from him. She hit the sofa, righted herself, and turned to confront him.

She rubbed her wrist where it was red and burning.

"What is it, Your Lordship?" Jeremy asked, entering the room.

Michael was the only person Jeremy addressed with any level of respect. Even Hamilton, who funded all of his ventures, wasn't treated with this much obsequiousness.

"Watch her," Michael said. "Do not let her leave this room. Do you understand?"

Jeremy nodded.

"I'll be back in a few minutes. I don't want her to leave."

"She won't," Jeremy said.

She looked from her cousin to Michael and back again. Did they honestly believe they could keep her prisoner? What utter foolishness. Michael may not like the idea that she'd broken their engagement, but he was going to have to accept it.

Once Michael left the room, Jeremy moved to stand with his back to the door, his arms folded.

"You can't be serious," she said. "Step aside, Jeremy."

Her cousin didn't budge. One corner of his mouth turned up, and she expected him to say something caustic, but he remained silent.

"Please."

He still didn't speak. Nor did he move.

She was powerless against his stubbornness. He was several inches taller and many pounds heavier than she was. Her only chance to get out of here was to appeal to his reason or his sense of justice.

She wasn't entirely certain that Jeremy possessed either.

"He can't keep me here, Jeremy. He can't force me to marry him."

"What do you mean?" Jeremy asked, frowning at her.

"I've ended our engagement," she said. "Michael isn't taking it well."

"What do you mean you ended your engagement?"

"Just that. I'm not going to marry him. He was going to sell the horses, Jeremy. He was going to gut Hearthmere. He doesn't have the right to do that."

He shook his head. "You really are an idiot, aren't you?"

She hardly thought it foolish to choose her own future.

Before she could say anything, Jeremy continued. "You have to marry him. The entire family is counting on it, Eleanor. You have to."

"No, I don't."

"Mother isn't going to be happy. What's Hamilton going to do then?"

"What do you mean?"

"His business is failing. Too much competition. He's sunk the last of his cash into your wedding. He thinks your marriage to Herridge will bring him investors and additional capital."

She stared at her cousin and wondered if he was right. Had Hamilton been in financial difficulty all this time? Had it been a closely guarded secret? Was that the reason everyone in the family was ecstatic about the upcoming wedding?

A close family association with an earl might bring about the investors Hamilton wanted. If nothing else it would give his business a certain cachet.

The door opened. Michael entered, nodding to Jeremy. Aunt Deborah and Hamilton were next, not looking at her as they moved to the sofa.

They were all here, unless Deborah had sent for Daphne.

Eleanor stood in front of the fireplace, wishing that someone had thought to light a fire against the chill of the day. Hamilton certainly had the income not to have to worry about such paltry expenses.

Unless he didn't. Unless Jeremy was right and everything Hamilton had bragged about in the past year had been a falsehood.

Evidently Michael had informed her aunt and Hamilton that she'd changed her mind about the engagement. She could see the effect of his announcement on their faces.

Both of them looked shocked. Or perhaps the word was *horrified*. Deborah's eyes were wide in her pale face. Hamilton's hands were shaking and he, too, looked almost waxen.

"Michael and I will not suit," Eleanor said, hoping they would understand her decision. "He doesn't want to marry me any more than I want to marry him."

Michael waved his hand in the air as if to dismiss her words. Neither Deborah nor Hamilton paid any attention to what she was saying. It was as if she was invisible, but it had always been that way, hadn't it?

The only person who'd ever seen her was Logan. With him she could be herself without criticism or censure.

"I've no wish to be seen as a laughingstock," Michael said. "This wedding will take place as planned."

He turned to Hamilton. "Until the wedding, Eleanor will need to be closely watched. She must be brought to accept this marriage. Is that understood?"

"Of course, Your Lordship," Hamilton said, nodding. "It will be as you wish."

She glanced at Michael. "What makes you think that I'll change my mind, especially after all the things you've said to me?"

Aunt Deborah stood and approached her. "You silly girl. How can you be so foolish?"

"I can't marry him, Aunt Deborah. He'll destroy Hearthmere."

The slap was hard, stinging, and unexpected. Her aunt had never struck her before. She placed her hand against her cheek and stared at the older woman.

"You'll do as you're told. We're not in Scotland anymore, Eleanor. You don't get to dictate to others."

She never had. She never would. Yet her aunt was beyond any kind of convincing. She grabbed Eleanor's upper arm with talon-like fingers and nodded to Hamilton.

He left the drawing room only to return in moments with the majordomo and two footmen.

Eleanor might've been able to pull away from her aunt's grip, but she was powerless when both footmen each grabbed an arm and dragged her up the stairs. Instead of her own room, she was taken to one of the guest chambers. It wasn't until they closed the door behind her that she realized why. This door was equipped with a lock.

She was well and truly a prisoner. In nine weeks she'd be released, but only for another jail: either Michael's townhouse in London or his country estate.

Chapter Thirty-Three

Logan waited all Wednesday afternoon, but Eleanor never came. He stood at the window, watching every carriage coming into the square. None of them were hers. None of them pulled up in front of his steps. The door didn't open; she didn't emerge.

At his feet Bruce whined. He glanced down at the dog and said, "I know. I'm waiting, too."

Mrs. Campbell was worried and didn't hesitate to let him know.

"She's never missed a day. She cares for the wee one as if he's her own bairn. She wouldn't miss a Wednesday without sending word."

He only nodded, not trusting his voice. Bruce spoke for him with one solitary bark, as if agreeing with the housekeeper.

It was obvious to him that Eleanor regretted what had happened between them. That's why she wasn't here. Yet her affection for Bruce wasn't feigned or false. Would she give up seeing the dog out of pique? She also knew that Mrs. Campbell prepared for her visit. Would she simply stop coming without some kind of notice?

That didn't sound like Eleanor.

He made some excuse to Mrs. Campbell, but he didn't feel comfortable about the situation. Perhaps he should send word to her, ask her point blank if she was returning. Or should he go even further and appear on her doorstep?

His appearance at the Richardses' home wouldn't be welcomed.

Nor did he want to make the situation worse for Eleanor. Instead, he pushed his concern to the back of his mind.

He made it through the next week, keeping himself occupied with new legislation and assisting Disraeli. The next Wednesday he worked from home deliberately.

When Eleanor didn't appear, Mrs. Campbell came to him.

"You know I'm not the sort to see omens and signs. It's a feeling I've got, though, and you need to hear. I think something's wrong. She's a dear girl and she wouldn't be doing this to Bruce unless she had no choice."

He nodded. He had the same feeling. "Even if we're right, I'm not sure what we can do about it."

"Then I think we need to figure out something," she said.

"Aye." He smiled at his housekeeper. "That we should."

ELEANOR WALKED TO the window. In the past two weeks this room had become her prison. The view overlooked part of the roof and beyond to the small lawn in the back of the house. From here she could see the path that she'd taken to Queen's Park. She could almost see the girl she'd been months earlier with Bruce at her side, eagerly escaping through the gate, waiting for Logan, her heart beating fast in excitement and eagerness.

He'd loved her and she'd gloried in it. Perhaps she should feel some regret. Society had labeled it sinful to love without restraint, to feel that much for a man. If she had the chance she'd do it again and never feel a pinch of shame.

The memory of that afternoon was the only thing keeping her sane.

She'd tried screaming the first day, only for Deborah to bring a footman in to bind her wrists and jam a gag in her mouth. A day of that was enough for her to agree not to make a sound if the gag was removed. She doubted anyone could hear her anyway. This room was on the end of the block of townhouses with no nearby structures.

For two weeks she hadn't been allowed any books or periodicals. She had been given her nightgowns, but no other change of clothing. No fire was allowed. No hot water was brought to her. The surroundings might be luxurious, but she was treated like a prisoner in all other ways.

In the morning her aunt visited her. At noon it was Daphne. In the early evening it was Hamilton, who carefully averted his gaze from her, dressed as she was only in a nightgown with the bedspread as her robe.

The family visits were not designed to ensure her health or well-being. Instead, each of her relatives was determined to make her see how wrong she'd been. Her wedding to Michael would end all of Hamilton's worries about his company's future. It would immediately elevate Deborah and give Daphne status. It would help Jeremy in his search for a position to give him meaning and purpose in life.

Couldn't she see what damage she was doing by refusing to marry the earl?

They didn't want to discuss the situation or hear what she felt or thought. The first day each of them was almost kind. Deborah didn't appear angry anymore. Her tone was measured, without a hint of irritation.

The second day they were more insistent. Her aunt grew increasingly annoyed at Eleanor's silence. She'd already realized that she might as well save her words. No one wanted to hear them.

On the third day she wasn't brought breakfast. Nor was the noon meal forthcoming. The bell pull beside the fireplace had been disconnected in the kitchen, so she couldn't signal for any of the servants.

When Hamilton arrived in the evening he was accompanied by a maid who carried a tray containing a bowl of lukewarm soup and a thin slice of bread.

"Your aunt thinks that if you are only allowed one meal a day, Eleanor, you will soon come to see how foolish you are being."

"Should I be grateful that I'm not being tortured, Hamilton?" she asked.

To his credit, he looked uncomfortable. She couldn't help but wonder if this new punishment was her aunt's decision or if Michael had any say in what happened to her.

They didn't understand. It was possible that they would never understand. It wasn't just Michael's dislike of her country, the sale of the Hearthmere bloodline, or his contempt for anything she cherished. It was obvious that he felt nothing for her or he wouldn't approve of what was happening.

She didn't want to have anything to do with Michael Herridge. She didn't want to become the Countess of Wescott. She yearned to be herself, to be Eleanor Craig of Hearthmere. She wanted to marry a man not because of what he might be able to do for the family, not because of his wealth or position or title, but because he stirred her heart. Because he was kind and witty and thought of others. Because a quick glance from him made her heart warm.

Michael might be able to dictate where she was kept, what she ate, how she was dressed, but he couldn't alter her thoughts or soften her will. She was a Scot and plenty of her countrymen had already demonstrated their obstinacy in the face of tyranny. She could do no less.

The days passed and she kept track of them by using one of her hairpins to scratch the wood inside one of the empty dresser drawers. No one would come for her; she knew that only too well. She'd given Logan no reason to think that she had changed her mind about Michael. He had no inkling of her decision not to marry.

He would think that she was simply preparing for her wedding. Would he wonder about her at all? Would he remember that magical afternoon and think—as she sometimes did—that it felt like a dream?

At the beginning of the second week she wondered if she was strong enough to hold out after all. She was nearly faint with hunger almost all the time. The maid never came by herself but was always accompanied by Hamilton. If she'd been alone Eleanor might have begged her for more food. The girl had a look on her face that indicated she would've been willing to help.

There were days when Eleanor wondered if it was worth leaving her bed. In the morning she always bathed with cold water, standing in front of the dresser, then drying with the thin piece of toweling she'd been allowed. After that she changed to a fresh nightgown and sat on the edge of the bed in a square of sunlight.

She fell back onto the habits of her childhood, kneeling beside the bed and praying as she hadn't since leaving Scotland. The prayers were simple yet fervent. *Save me, God.*

Deborah, Daphne, and Hamilton came every day to lecture her. Deborah looked like she was losing her temper most of the time. Eleanor always moved away from her aunt, choosing to stand against the wall in case Deborah wanted to strike her again.

"You're a fool, Eleanor," Deborah said yesterday. "You can make this so much easier on yourself by simply agreeing that you made a mistake. Of course you're going to marry Michael and do so happily. The world will see you as an ecstatic bride. All you have to do is agree that you were wrong. That's all, Eleanor. It's so easy. Three simple little words. *I was wrong.* Tell Michael that it was all a mistake."

What her aunt wanted was impossible. The only way she could say those words was to reject everything her father stood for, everything he worked to create all his life. She couldn't turn over Hearthmere to Michael. She couldn't allow the house to be gutted and the horses sold.

What kind of man was Michael that he would go along with his future bride being punished? Even worse, if he agreed to this treatment now, what would he do when she was his wife and she displeased him? Keep her chained in the attic and fed bread and water?

For days Eleanor wrestled with the idea of telling her aunt about Logan. She hadn't wanted to involve him, but the more time passed the more she realized that her relatives were in thrall to

Michael. Telling Deborah about that afternoon might be the only thing that saved her.

She waited until her aunt closed the door and approached the bed. Sometimes, she was so dizzy when she stood that it was better if she just sat on the edge of the mattress.

"I'm not a virgin," she said.

"What are you talking about?"

"I'm not a virgin. You asked me if I felt something for Logan and I do. I've been with him."

Deborah stared at her. "You're lying."

"No, I'm not. I was with Logan the day Michael brought me home."

"Does he know?"

Eleanor forced a smile to her face. "He wouldn't want me if he did know, would he? I'm going to tell him, Deborah. This marriage you want so desperately isn't going to happen."

Deborah came so close that Eleanor was certain the older woman was going to strike her again. She closed her eyes, willing herself to absorb the blow without a sound.

It didn't come.

"You fool," Deborah said softly. "You're a spoiled, obstinate girl who's trying to ruin us all."

Eleanor opened her eyes at the sound of the door closing and the snick of the key in the lock.

A few hours later her aunt was back, a cup in her hand. She pulled up the lone chair and sat, facing Eleanor on the bed.

"Drink this," she said, holding it out. "It will make you feel better."

Eleanor was always so hungry and thirsty that she took the cup eagerly.

"It's a special tea," Deborah said. "Something to make you stronger."

Had her admission worked? Had her aunt realized that the truth would change Michael's mind?

She began to drink the tea. It was hot and liberally laced with sugar, but it still tasted terrible, a strong mix of herbs and something that reminded her of licorice. When it was finished she handed the cup back to her aunt.

"Listen to me," Deborah said, very softly. "I'll not repeat this, Eleanor, so it's important that you listen well."

She looked at her aunt, nodding.

"Hamilton knows some unsavory people. Regretfully, so does Jeremy. The type of person who would think nothing of taking a few pounds for a despicable task. Breaking a leg, for example. Or even garroting someone."

Her voice was low and menacing, the match to the look in her eyes. There was no pity there, no compassion or empathy. At that moment Eleanor believed Deborah, knew that her aunt would stop at nothing to achieve her aims.

Had she always been as ruthless?

"I've given you something to ensure that you don't carry a bastard, Eleanor. You'll begin to feel the effects shortly. If you mention being with Logan to Michael I will have McKnight killed. It will be ridiculously easy to do."

She could only stare at her aunt.

"As for your wedding night, you've been on horseback since you were a child. Michael knows that. He won't be able to tell you're not a virgin unless you tell him. It's your choice, Eleanor. McKnight's life or your marriage. Which is it to be?"

Once upon a time, when Deborah had first come to Hearthmere, Eleanor had wondered if her aunt would become her second mother. That had never happened.

Now she knew it never would.

Chapter Thirty-Four

"Who did you say you were again?" the majordomo asked.

"Mrs. Campbell. Mrs. Althea Campbell. A native of Inverness. I promised my cousin that if I ever made it to London I'd look up Miss Craig. He was a great friend of her father's, you see. Long did they know each other. In fact, my cousin helped him with his horses."

"Miss Craig isn't accepting visitors, I'm afraid."

The majordomo was as autocratic as any London servant. Fortunately, he also had a voice that carried. Logan didn't have any difficulty hearing the two from his position inside the carriage.

"Is it sick she is? Oh, no, how dreadful. I'll be sure and send word that she's ill. He'll be so upset, what with how fond he was of her father. Will I be able to leave her my card? Or this note I have for her?"

He expected the majordomo to refuse, but to his surprise the man took both the card and the envelope containing the carefully constructed letter they'd written. It was an innocuous message, in case it didn't reach Eleanor. In it, Mrs. Campbell had expressed her wish to meet Eleanor and waxed eloquent about a nonexistent cousin. If Eleanor did happen to read it, it would only confuse her, perhaps enough to ask for Mrs. Campbell to return.

Until they'd arrived this morning and Mrs. Campbell had knocked on the door of the Richardses' townhouse, they hadn't known where Eleanor was. Logan had gone to Queen's Park for two straight days at different times. She hadn't been there. At least the majordomo had indicated that she was still in London.

What he didn't know was if she was avoiding him. Or had someone kept her from her usual Wednesday visits?

When Mrs. Campbell returned to the carriage, they exchanged a look.

"At least we know she's still in London," Mrs. Campbell said.

"Do you think she's ill?" he asked.

She shook her head. "I don't think so. I think something else is going on."

He glanced at his housekeeper. "Are you sure you aren't using some Celtic intuition?" he asked, only half teasing.

She shook her head. "No, there was something in his eyes. Something that bothered him. I think you need to find out what it is."

"Short of taking a battering ram to their front door, what do you suggest I do?"

She tilted her head slightly and eyed him. It was the same look Logan had gotten from a determined ewe when he'd been a shepherd for a few days. The ewe had been stubborn, just like Mrs. Campbell.

"You're a handsome man. A house this big would require a staff near the size of ours. Lots of young girls, some of them silly. Silly enough to want to please a handsome man by getting a note to Eleanor. Or confiding the truth in you."

"So you want me to engage in a flirtation with the servants?"

Mrs. Campbell leaned forward, reached out, and patted his knee. "It might take more than one day. Not that you don't have an excess of charm when you want it, you understand. It's just that they might have put the fear of God into their staff to not speak of anything that goes on in the household."

"Have you?" he asked, genuinely curious. "Put the fear of God into the staff?"

"I've no need. Our people are Scots. They've no wish to share our secrets with the English."

He wasn't certain he had all that many secrets, except the one from the other day. Hopefully no one knew about what had transpired in the drawing room.

Despite Mrs. Campbell's words about his supposed charm, Logan didn't accomplish much. Hedges in the back of the house sheltered the small yard on two sides. Anyone strolling by would immediately be looked on with suspicion. He'd already crafted a story for himself if he was questioned. He was going to pretend to be a new resident in the neighborhood.

The first day he occupied himself by peering through the hedges. If the mission hadn't been so important, he would have felt ridiculous. As it was, he was willing to do anything in order to find out what had happened to Eleanor.

From what he saw, the maids were occasionally in the back lawn, either hanging laundry to dry or taking out refuse. He heard how irritated two of them were about the new household assignments. Two of the upper maids had been rotated, which was, from what he could tell, a demotion of sorts. They weren't pleased and already talking about other households that needed help.

He only learned two things. First, the maids gossiped. Second, only a few of them were young. Most of them—at least the ones he'd seen—were in their middle years. He wondered if that was a conscious decision. Had Eleanor's aunt chosen older servants so they were less of a temptation to the males in the family? From what he'd seen of Jeremy, Logan wouldn't be surprised if that young man took advantage of a woman employed by his mother.

He remained where he was for some time, realizing it wasn't an easy feat finding an ally in the Richardses' household. Every time one of the servants entered the yard they were accompanied by someone else, so he couldn't lure one of the maids away without calling attention to his presence.

Finally, he returned to his carriage and his housekeeper. Hopefully, Mrs. Campbell would have some additional ideas to gain the trust of the Richardses' maids.

FOR TWO DAYS Eleanor was nearly senseless. She lay in bed motionless except for bouts of nausea. She felt like she was going to die. The morning of the second day she didn't care if she did.

Deborah returned often to check on her, insisting she drink some tea, and bringing a maid to change the bowl next to the bed. Finally, she helped Eleanor dress in a clean nightgown.

She didn't trust her aunt's new solicitousness. Was Deborah planning on giving her more poison? If she died there'd be no marriage.

That was her last thought before she succumbed to sleep again.

On the evening of the second day Hamilton arrived with a maid bearing her one meal. Eleanor couldn't stomach the thin soup she was given. Even a digestive biscuit made her sick again.

Please. It was a word she repeated often in her mind. She wasn't exactly sure what she was asking for. Freedom, perhaps. Or a respite from sickness. Or something to eat. *Please.*

She dreamed of food. Food and Logan. They appeared equally in her dreams. If she had her way she'd do nothing but sleep. She wasn't hungry when she slept. Or as frightened.

Time was running out. She was getting sicker and sicker. She'd lost. Her aunt would do anything to break her. She knew that now. She also knew that Deborah was going to win.

LOGAN HAD HIS driver park the carriage on the other side of the square. He walked with his head down, the gait of a man lost in his thoughts. In his pocket he had a note to Eleanor and more money than he normally carried. After conferring with Mrs. Campbell, they'd decided that since spying on the servants for two days hadn't worked, the best way to get any information about the household was to bribe one of the maids. Somehow he was going to have to get one of them alone and tell her the truth— that he was desperate to learn what had happened to Eleanor.

There was one maid, younger than the others, who might be persuaded to tell him what she knew.

As he headed for the row of hedges and the back garden, he glanced up at the windows of the house.

A figure in a second-floor window had him stopping and retracing his path. Stepping back, he looked up again.

At first he didn't recognize the woman standing there in her nightgown, the morning sun making the garment almost diaphanous. A second later he realized it was Eleanor, but not the woman he'd seen weeks earlier. Her face was too thin and pale. Her hair was lank and hanging below her shoulders. She was looking out at the distance with no expression on her face. She might have been a ghost for all the life she demonstrated.

He waved his hands above him, but she still didn't see him. He moved closer to the house and dug around in the flowerbeds until he found a few pebbles. He'd always been a good pitcher as a boy and hopefully his skill hadn't deserted him after all these years.

Stepping back, he tossed a fair-sized pebble at her window and hit it at the first try. She flinched, startled. He threw another pebble, aiming this one a little higher. She looked down finally and he raised his arms, stepping back so she could see him more clearly.

Placing both hands against the glass of the window she fell to her knees. She shocked him further by beginning to cry.

It took him a minute to understand the words she was saying. *Help me.* She repeated the words over and over, her hands still pressed against the glass.

Why didn't she open the window to talk to him?

It was midmorning and she was still attired in her nightgown. Under normal conditions a woman would have hidden behind the curtains, waved to him, perhaps. Or smiled a little shamefacedly, knowing she'd been seen in her nightclothes.

Eleanor didn't do any of that. She hadn't stopped crying or mouthing the words he couldn't hear. *Help me.*

"I will. I will, Eleanor."

Uncertain, he stood there for a moment, trying to decide what to do first. He suspected she was being held against her will, but legally he didn't have that many options.

Hamilton and Deborah could be seen as parental figures. As a single woman Eleanor had few protections, especially since she lived in their house. The law was murky on this point, especially if the couple stated that she'd been recalcitrant in some way and they were simply attempting to discipline her.

Had they discovered what had happened in his drawing room?

Shame washed over him. He should have paid attention to his initial worry and not allowed so much time to elapse before coming here.

He thought about knocking on the door and demanding entrance, but he didn't know how many footmen Richards employed. He could be overpowered within moments which would make the possibility of rescuing Eleanor more difficult.

No, he needed a plan. A more secretive plan. Perhaps something even illegal.

Forcing a smile to his face, he sent Eleanor a kiss. Finally, Eleanor nodded, then put her hands together as if she were praying.

Chapter Thirty-Five

Logan was here. Logan was here. Eleanor repeated those three words to herself silently.

She'd prayed for a miracle and God had delivered Logan to her, standing outside in his coat, impervious to the wind that blew his hair askew. When she'd seen him her knees weren't able to support her weight and she'd dropped to the floor. The window had been nailed shut so she couldn't open it. Nor had she taken the chance of shouting for fear that she would be heard by the footman outside the door. Every time the door was unlocked she saw him, standing at attention as if on military parade. Not one of them had ever met her eyes.

None of the servants had ever been left alone with her. If they had, she would have pleaded with them to get word to Logan or Mr. Babbage or the authorities.

Logan had seemed to understand that she needed his help. All she could do was keep praying that she was right.

After he vanished she sat where she was, her cheek against the warm glass. Had she misinterpreted his signal? Was he really coming back? *Please, God, don't let this have been a hallucination, a vision I've imagined out of desperation.*

She hadn't realized that her aunt's greed overwhelmed every other decent impulse including any familial feeling for her. Maybe Deborah only had a certain amount of love to share and it was reserved for Daphne and in lesser amounts for Jeremy and perhaps her husband.

Deborah didn't seem to realize the barbarism of her actions, being so focused on the possible result. Every morning when she came to convince Eleanor to give up her rebellion it was the same speech, the same false concern, the same attempt to play on Eleanor's emotions.

"Don't you care about your family?"

"We've given up so much for you, Eleanor. How can you be so selfish now?"

"Three little words, Eleanor. Just three little words. Just say it: *I was wrong.*"

Family is everything.

No, it wasn't. She'd learned that one day when Deborah lost her temper.

"You owe me, Eleanor. I gave up my entire life in Edinburgh so you wouldn't be disturbed. I had to move my family to Hearthmere because you were a spoiled little orphan. You have no idea of the sacrifices that William and I made for you. You couldn't be bothered."

"I was eleven years old, Deborah."

"You were a tyrant, Eleanor. Someone who saw us as her servants. You were the Queen of Hearthmere and you spent more time thinking about those damnable horses than us."

She stared at her aunt, stunned. She'd never once considered that Deborah, William, and her cousins had been unhappy at Hearthmere. She'd been so miserable in that first year after her father had died that she hadn't seen anyone else's discomfort. Yet she'd been a child, one who'd been grieving.

"You never said anything. Not one time."

"And if I had? What would have been the result? Your solicitor would probably have sent us packing back to Edinburgh with no money at all."

Her aunt suddenly smiled. "But you have the chance to make it up to us now, my dear girl. All you have to do is become a countess. Isn't that the silliest thing? Anyone else would be leaping at the prospect. You'll live in a beautiful home, you'll be wealthy, you'll be in a position to help your family. Don't you want to do that?"

No, she didn't want to do that and even less now after she'd been a prisoner in this room. She couldn't help but wonder what excuse they'd given for her absence at all the social events she'd missed. Had they told everyone she was ill? Or had a family emergency necessitating a visit to Scotland?

She turned back to the window. *Please, God, don't let it have been a hallucination. Please let Logan have been here. Please let him have cared enough to find me.*

With the hem of her nightgown she wiped the glass clean of her fingerprints.

If she ever escaped this room the first thing she would do was make sure that Logan knew what she felt. Loving him, being in love with him, had been the only thing that had kept her sane and hopeful.

All she had to do was keep herself strong until he returned. She didn't know how he was going to rescue her, only that he was. All she had to do was last until it happened.

Please, God, give me the strength.

LOGAN GAVE HIS driver directions to a part of London that was a great deal more dangerous than this fashionable square.

As a member of Parliament he had occasion to meet a few less reputable members of society. He'd been involved in several charities, some of which were geared to giving criminals a second chance at an honest life. Some of the men so honored took advantage of their new opportunities. Some didn't. A few straddled the line, appearing to be honest, hardworking individuals while keeping their less honorable talents honed should they be needed in the future.

One of those was a man by the name of Peter Cook, a cracksman who'd been recently released from jail. He'd been hired as a footman because of Logan's recommendation and had been fired less than a month later. Unfortunately, Pete had been tempted by the silver and had stolen several pieces of flatware. It was only Logan's intervention that had prevented him from going back to jail.

The man owed him.

Luckily, Pete was at home. His wife, a short, petite woman with bright blond hair and a surprisingly pleasant smile, ushered him into the small flat.

"I'll just go and get him," she said, her accent one of East London. "You have a sit. I'll tell him you're here."

He didn't sit, but stood in the middle of the room, surprised at the tidiness. They didn't have many possessions, but what they did have was dusted and shined. The sofa sagged in the middle and the lone chair looked to have a busted spring or two. However, both pieces of furniture were obviously cared for, because the cushions had been brushed and plumped and there were lace doilies on the arms.

"I married above me," Pete said from the doorway. "Molly keeps everything nice for us."

Logan turned to face him.

Pete was a young man, probably twenty-two at the most. He was tall and lanky and always looked like he was wearing clothes two sizes too small for him. His wrists protruded from the yellow shirt he wore now. His gray trousers ended at his ankles. Even his face was bony, his high cheekbones leading to a sunken look and his chin knife-sharp.

"I can see that."

"But you didn't come to inspect my lodgings, did you?"

Logan shook his head. "No. I'm here to ask for your help."

"Do you need a footman?"

"I should think you've given up that line of work, Pete."

Pete grinned. "Maybe you're right."

"I need a cracksman. Someone who can get into a house after it's been locked for the night."

"No," Molly said, popping up from behind Pete. "I'll not have him taken away again. Not with me having a baby."

"How do you think we're going to afford the baby?" Pete asked without turning. "You are thinking of paying me, aren't you? This isn't something you expect me to do as a favor, is it?"

"Yes, I'm definitely paying you," Logan said, reaching into his pocket for the money he'd taken to the Richardses' house. He pulled it out and would have handed it to Pete, but Molly stepped between them.

"No," she said, staring up at Logan. "What am I to do with him in jail?"

"If you want my assurances, Molly, I'll give them to you freely. Pete won't suffer for tonight's work."

She didn't look like she believed him and he couldn't blame her. People in this area of London had learned to suspect everyone and everything. He'd probably feel the same way if he'd had their upbringing.

Instead of giving Pete the money, he handed it to Molly, watching as her eyes widened. He didn't know what the going rate was for breaking into what was probably a well-guarded home, but he suspected he'd overpaid.

"Make your decision," he said, glancing at each of them. "It has to be done tonight."

He could almost hear Molly's thoughts. She was conflicted. In her hand was enough money to care for her coming child, yet Pete might be put in danger.

"He won't suffer, Molly."

She reluctantly nodded, tucked the money into her pocket, and kissed her husband.

Ten minutes later Pete joined him in the carriage, the destination Logan's home. He had at least eight hours before they could rescue Eleanor, but he didn't trust Pete to show up on time. In addition to being an excellent cracksman, Pete also had a fondness for gin. Logan preferred to keep an eye on the young man until it was time for the rescue plan to be put into operation.

Mrs. Campbell insisted on being present during the strategy meeting in his study. To his surprise, Logan discovered that his housekeeper had the impulses of a criminal. He hadn't considered, for example, that the family might have a footman guarding Eleanor's door. Nor was he able, unfortunately, to pinpoint exactly where her room was on the second floor. It might be the third door from the stairs or it might be the second. When he said as much, she only nodded.

"You'll have to take Bruce, then." She explained further. "Bruce will find her faster than opening doors. Just give him the garter that she left here. That's all he'll need."

He didn't know what to say, stunned as he was by her comment. She'd found the garter in the drawing room, but hadn't said anything to him until now. If she expected him to immediately launch into an explanation, she was going to be disappointed. He had no intention of saying anything, especially with Pete and two stable boys sitting across the table grinning at him. He wasn't going to discuss the matter in the future, either.

"Besides, Bruce is as close to her as she is to him," she continued. "He'll be an asset."

Logan wasn't entirely certain of that. He'd trained the dog in the past few weeks to bark on command and to not bark when he gave a certain hand signal. Tonight's activities required total silence and he wasn't sure Bruce could be obedient, especially if he was excited.

"He'll do fine," she said when he explained his misgivings to her. "So would I," she added.

"I am definitely not taking you with me," he said.

She rolled her eyes. "The poor girl will need someone with her. Someone to provide a little comfort."

"I'm bringing her back here. You can provide comfort then."

He was adamant. He was not going to involve his housekeeper in such a risky operation. Unfortunately, Mrs. Campbell was a great deal more stubborn than he'd ever realized.

When she finally left the room he turned to the two stable boys he'd recruited.

"What I'm proposing isn't exactly legal. I believe it's moral and justified, but I'm not sure the authorities would see it that way. Your decision won't affect your position here. If you don't want to participate tonight, your job will not be in jeopardy."

To his relief, both men decided to accompany him. Hopefully, their force of four would be sufficient to rescue Eleanor.

His plan was to have Pete open the front door and then take one of these stable boys around to the side of the house and gain access to the roof. Pete wasn't put off by heights. He'd told Logan stories of thefts he'd committed by scaling the outer walls of a house, getting to the roof, then dropping down to a bedroom window. That's exactly what Logan wanted him to do tonight.

While Pete was trying to reach Eleanor's window, Logan and the second stable boy would go up the stairs and find her room. He agreed that Bruce might make finding Eleanor less difficult, if he could keep the dog quiet in the meantime. The last thing he wanted was for Bruce to start barking once they were inside the house.

Pete pulled out a dark shirt from the satchel he'd brought, donned it, then looked at Logan.

"If you have something dark, Logan, now's the time to wear it. Or red. That shows up as black at night, too."

He didn't have either, but he'd be wearing the jacket to one of his suits. In addition, he had a dark-colored sweater that he would loan the stable boy accompanying Pete. At least that way they wouldn't be seen by an alert neighbor.

That wasn't enough, according to Pete. They needed dark cloth to make into masks. Mrs. Campbell helped there, providing a bolt of dark blue cloth used for the maids' uniforms.

Just when Logan thought they were prepared, Pete opened the

satchel again. Inside were two curious tools, each consisting of an iron ball connected to a rope.

"For if someone comes after you," he said, demonstrating that the rope was to be wound around Logan's hand. With a certain movement the iron ball became a controlled projectile.

"Have you ever used it?" Logan wasn't about to kill anyone on this adventure. He'd leave the weapon behind and claim forgetfulness.

"Once," Pete said, but thankfully didn't furnish any details.

There were a dozen picklocks in the bottom of the bag, a crowbar to remove iron bars, two chisels, a long knife, a rope ladder, and something Pete identified as a cutter.

"If I can't get through the lock, I can usually get through the door."

The last item was a small square lantern with a hole on one side no larger than a shilling. It was designed to illuminate the way without being seen by the Watch.

"I didn't think about the Watch," Logan said. He had a great deal to learn about breaking the law.

"I did." Pete grinned at him. "Places like this think they're too big to be burgled what with all the maids and footmen roaming around. I'll admit, it does set me back a bit, but there's no place that's safe. No place."

Logan tucked that information away for later.

"The Watch normally patrols on the half hour," Pete said. "As long as we're quiet then we should be all right. They're not as alert as you think."

Logan would remember that, too.

Mrs. Campbell entered the room again and placed a bowl filled with ashes on the table. Pete thanked her with a grin, but Logan only glanced at his housekeeper.

"You'll be smearing that on your face," she said, pointing to the bowl. "Even with a mask. It's a full moon out, which isn't going to help us."

As if she heard his unspoken question she smiled. "Me da was a bit of a smuggler. Border raids they were. He always said that the old ways should be remembered, just in case they were ever needed again."

"You went with him, didn't you? On more than one raid, I'd bet." He was certain of it when she only smiled at him again and left the room.

The door opened once more and Bruce raced into the study, bumping into the leg of the table before colliding with Logan. He hadn't spared time for play or training today and the dog was feeling the lack.

There was an hour to go before they would leave. He'd use it to tire Bruce out a little, so that he wouldn't be so excited about a carriage ride and entering the Richardses' home.

Chapter Thirty-Six

Before they left his house, Logan took William into his confidence. His driver had been with him for years and must've known that something unusual was going on. Now he told William the entire story.

"Be prepared to get out of there quickly," Logan said. "I have no idea what we're going to face, only that I need to get Miss Craig to safety."

"Aye, sir. I'll stand at the ready."

Once they were dressed in black, their faces covered in soot, and their masks in hand, the four of them piled into the carriage. Bruce settled down on the floor on top of Logan's feet. He didn't whine and he hadn't barked since Logan opened the door and encouraged him inside. Hopefully his lessons had taken and he would remain silent once they were inside the Richardses' house.

He hoped his constituents didn't find out about tonight's activities. Then again, Eleanor was a Scot being held in an English house. He had the feeling that the men who'd voted for him would understand his actions completely.

The order of interrogators changed. Instead of Daphne arriving around noon, Hamilton appeared. Of late her aunt's husband looked more and more reluctant to be here. Eleanor wondered why. It certainly wasn't pity for her condition or her imprisonment. Hamilton could put an end to it with just a word. Why didn't he? Either it was love for Deborah or his own greed.

Eleanor was leaning toward greed.

Family is everything. No, Papa. It wasn't. Not this family. Not this collection of people. Not her aunt and her cousins. Not Hamilton. Certainly not Michael.

Hamilton sat on the lone chair, studying her. At first she'd been self-conscious during his inspection. Now she didn't care.

She'd not been allowed a brush and her hair was a tangled mess. The past three days she hadn't been given any water to bathe. She was surprised the maid came in to collect the chamber pot every morning.

However, today she was marginally stronger. She'd seen Logan this morning. He was coming to rescue her. All she had to do was make it for a few more hours. She would be saved.

Unless she'd imagined him.

It wouldn't be the first time she'd seen something that wasn't there. One morning she'd awakened, startled to see a table against one wall. A feast had been arranged for her, from ham to roast chicken to flaky, delicate salmon. The smells of the food had awakened her fully. Until she'd walked to the other side of the room, she'd thought everything was real.

She dug her nails into her palms. She had to believe. It was the first time in days that she had any hope at all. Logan wasn't a hallucination. He was real. She had to hold on to that thought.

"Your silence does you no good, Eleanor," Hamilton said. "Let me help you. This situation can't be comfortable for you."

She knew better than to listen to his blandishments. His voice was soft and almost kind. She could almost think that he was a compassionate man. Yet people should be judged by their actions, not simply their words. Hamilton had agreed to keep her here. He hadn't done anything to help her.

She remained silent. Her silence always made him leave faster because it frustrated him. Hamilton was not a man given to patience.

If Michael had visited her—and seen her as she was right now—he would have ended the engagement himself.

Had Deborah encouraged him to stay away? *She's in no fit state, Your Lordship. She's still stubborn, still refusing to listen to reason. A few more days. A week, no less, and she'll come around.*

She could almost hear her aunt's words.

"Don't do this, Eleanor," Hamilton said. "You're upsetting everyone."

She let his words wash over her. She closed her eyes and willed herself back to Queen's Park. The leaves were falling gently to the ground, obscuring the grass. Bruce ran through them with a puppy's eagerness and daring, his joy easily interpreted. In her mind he barked excitedly, so that she couldn't hear Hamilton's voice.

He finally left.

Her sole occupation during the day was staring out the window, measuring the progress of the sun across the sky. Sometimes she guessed which cloud might produce rain and if fog would obscure her view in the morning.

She slept, as she did most afternoons, simply to pass the time. Sometimes, she put her pillow down on the floor and slept in a square of sunlight like a cat.

When she woke the sky was dark and so was her mood.

She had imagined it, after all. If Logan had been real he would have been here before now.

Help me to bear this. Help me to have the strength to outlast them.

Why was she fighting? Was death preferable to marriage to Michael? No, because if she died he would win.

She would have to agree to the marriage. She would have to excoriate the feelings she had for Logan, burn them until they were no more than ash. Then she would blow the ashes away until they were gone as well.

From this point on she would forever be Eleanor of London. She would never again return to her homeland. Why return if Hearthmere was only a shell of itself? The horses would be gone, the house stripped of its furniture and everything valuable. Even the Clan Hall would be emptied.

She would never forgive Michael for destroying her heritage.

Tomorrow she would send word to Deborah that she was done, that the near starvation, the near nakedness, the sickness had worked.

However, she would never call the woman aunt again. With her marriage to Michael she would do everything in her power to eliminate or diminish any advantage her marriage might bring to her aunt, Hamilton, Jeremy, or Daphne.

If she had her way they would never be invited to a function at Abermarle, never attend a dinner at their home in London. She would never recognize them in public and if she was to be a countess then she would be an icy personage, someone to fear.

They would have won yet lost. She knew that, but they wouldn't. Not for a while.

At six her stomach began to rumble. They had left the mantel clock, so Eleanor always knew the time, the better to anticipate her one meal of the day, no doubt.

She heard the key in the lock and her stomach growled again. In the first few days it had been almost constant. With a few more days perhaps she wouldn't feel hunger at all.

Her cousin sailed into the room, pointing to the table beside the lone chair.

"Put it there," Daphne said to the maid.

The girl did as she was told, stealing a look in Eleanor's direction. There was kindness in the girl's eyes and perhaps a little pity, too.

Eleanor glanced at the tray only once, knowing that she wouldn't be allowed to eat until after Daphne left. The lecture always came first.

There was a bowl on the tray with a spoon and a napkin. A cup and a teapot. No bread and she suspected that the soup was the same pale gruel she'd eaten for the past three days. One day, perhaps, they would only bring her a bowl of water and expect her to subsist on that.

"Have you stopped being foolish?" Daphne said, sitting on the edge of the bed. "Is today the day that you finally get some intelligence, Eleanor?" She shook her head. "My two children, young as they are, have more sense than you."

"Do you starve them, too?"

Daphne smiled. "If you'll agree, Eleanor, I'll have a feast prepared for you. You must be hungry."

Eleanor didn't answer her cousin. She would surrender to Deborah, but she wouldn't concede anything to Daphne.

Daphne stared at her for a moment, then stood. Going to the door, she addressed the maid. "Take the tray away."

"But, Mrs. Baker, Miss Eleanor hasn't eaten anything."

"Did you hear what I said? Take the tray away."

The girl nodded and moved to retrieve the tray, sending Eleanor a quick glance. No, she hadn't misinterpreted the pity, but what good was pity now?

Eleanor closed her eyes, refusing to look in her cousin's direction again. Instead, she would remember this morning and seeing Logan again. Even if she'd imagined everything, he'd been a comforting sight. Perhaps she could will him to come to her in her dreams.

He'd hold her hand and tell her that it was going to be all right, even though she knew, very well, that it wasn't.

Chapter Thirty-Seven

William stopped the carriage on the other side of the square. Tonight there was more traffic than there'd been this morning. They could easily be taken for guests at one of the well-lit houses. Although it was around midnight, parties often lasted until dawn.

They stayed in the carriage for some minutes, watching the Richardses' house. No lights shone in any of the windows. Either they were out or the household had retired for the night. Logan and Pete, accompanied by Bruce and the two stable boys, kept to the shadows, avoiding pools of lamplight as they crossed the street, heading for the house.

Pete only spent a few seconds opening the lock on the front door.

"It's a cheap one," he whispered. "I've got a better lock on my flat. You would think that someone with all that money would take care to protect what he had."

After Pete opened the door, he and Sam melted into the darkness, off to the roof.

Before they went inside, Logan and Phillip took off their shoes. They'd have to make their way up the staircase, taking care to stay on the far side of each step in order to avoid any sounds.

Bruce kept to Logan's heels, silent and alert. He whined once, but when Logan held his hand down at his side, fingers splayed, he stopped.

They stood in the foyer for a few minutes, listening. He'd guessed that the family had retired, but Logan didn't know if anyone read late into the night. When they didn't hear anything they moved cautiously up the staircase, Bruce still at Logan's side.

Gas sconces were lit in the upper hallway.

Granted, the light made it easier to see, but it also indicated that someone was awake in the house. Either that, or they were taking a chance with fire. Perhaps a footman had been assigned that duty and had momentarily slipped away. Logan couldn't see anyone, but that didn't mean they were free and clear.

They moved to the landing. There were two hallways, not one, further compounding the issue.

He pulled Eleanor's garter out of his pocket and gave it to Bruce to sniff. He wasn't certain that the dog was as scent-trained as Mrs. Campbell believed. At the moment, however, Bruce was their best hope for a speedy rescue.

"Find her, boy."

Bruce raced down the hall to the left, leaving the two of them standing there. He sat at a door midway down the hall, looking at Logan, then back at the door.

Logan owed Mrs. Campbell an apology.

"What are you doing in my home, McKnight?"

Well, hell.

He turned to see Richards standing in the middle of the hall in his bathrobe. Now was not the time to enter into a debate about rescuing Eleanor. Nor was he going to stand there and allow Richards to call the Watch.

There was only one thing to do.

"Eleanor! Are you in there? Eleanor!"

The voice that answered was weak, but it was hers. Bruce began barking uncontrollably which was probably enough to bring the rest of the household down on their heads.

Before Richards could say anything or anyone else appeared, Logan lunged at the door. The first attempt didn't do anything but bruise his shoulder. The second time Phillip added his efforts. Together they managed to damage the jamb sufficiently that the door could be opened.

Eleanor was beside the bed, one hand holding on to a nearby table as if to keep herself standing. She wore the same nightgown he'd seen earlier this morning, but that was all. No slippers. No robe.

She looked as if she'd lost weight since he'd seen her last. Her face was gaunt and pale. Her hand shook as she extended it toward him.

Logan made his way to her side, pulled the bedspread free, and wrapped it around her shoulders.

What had they done to her?

"I thought I dreamed you," she said, her voice faint. "I thought you were a fantasy, but you aren't, are you?"

She looked down at Bruce sitting at her feet, tongue lolling out of his mouth. He looked especially pleased with himself, as if he'd rescued Eleanor single-handedly.

"Bruce?" The tears in her voice were difficult for him to hear.

He scooped her up in his arms and carried her from the room, Bruce following.

Richards had been joined by his wife and a few maids and footmen. If they all rushed him he and Phillip wouldn't have a chance. Logan had a feeling, however, that they wouldn't. People like Richards and his wife operated in secret. They disliked witnesses to their cruelty. Right now they had a half dozen of their servants overseeing their actions. He doubted they would say or do anything.

He was right about Richards, but not Deborah.

"I don't care that you're an MP, McKnight. You have no right to come into our home and remove my niece from it. This is a private matter and you have no business interfering."

He turned, Eleanor still in his arms.

"I can't say whether what you've done is illegal or not, Mrs. Richards. I know, however, that it's morally reprehensible. Perhaps we should allow the public to learn of your actions and let them decide."

The woman took a step backward, her hand at her throat, her other hand at the belt of her wrapper.

"You're threatening me? Who do you think you are?"

A man in love. A man with a well-developed sense of right and wrong. A man who was more than willing to see the Richardses ruined. Instead of answering Deborah, he smiled.

In the next moment she gathered up her courage again, because she advanced on him. Bruce's growl was loud and threatening enough that Deborah stopped.

"He's never bitten anyone," Logan said. "Not yet. I imagine, though, that he'd like a taste of you."

Deborah's eyes widened and she wisely didn't take another step. He and Phillip descended the stairs, Bruce following. Phillip grabbed their shoes as they left the house.

No one stopped them.

He spoke to Phillip as they headed for the carriage. "Go and tell Pete that we have Eleanor," he said. "Don't worry about being quiet. I'm all for letting this whole sordid mess being made public."

No one left the Richardses' home to summon the Watch.

Once in the carriage, Logan held Eleanor in his arms instead of settling her on the seat beside him. He didn't want to release her. She was still trembling and that made him hate Richards even more. He wanted to ask what they had done to her and why, but now was not the time. His first task was to get her somewhere safe.

Pete entered the carriage. "We made it to the window just in time, only to see the two of you crashing through the door. A fine sight it was, although I think you'll be sporting bruises tomorrow."

"You're right there," Logan said.

"And Bruce was a hero, too," Pete added. He bent and ruffled the fur between Bruce's ears.

Eleanor smiled, the first time since leaving the bedroom.

Thankfully, the trip back to Logan's house was short and uneventful.

Chapter Thirty-Eight

It was a little past midnight, but Mrs. Campbell was waiting for them when they arrived home. She opened the door as Logan got to the top of the steps, Eleanor still in his arms.

Mrs. Campbell bit back whatever she might have said without their audience. Pete and the two stable boys had followed him into the house and were now standing in the foyer.

Eleanor had her cheek pressed against his shoulder and her eyes closed. When he was a child he'd done the same thing, reasoning that if he couldn't see the terror, it didn't exist.

"Let's get her upstairs," Mrs. Campbell said, bustling in front of him.

He turned to the other men and asked them to wait.

"You've a courier," Mrs. Campbell said as she opened the door to the guest room. "I've put him in the drawing room."

"From Disraeli?"

She shook her head. "Your uncle."

His uncle had been in poor health for the past three months. Logan sincerely hoped that the courier's presence didn't mean what he dreaded: his uncle's death and even further complications.

It was obvious his housekeeper had readied the room for Eleanor. A bowl of potpourri was on the bedside table. A gas lamp was already lit, with the bed turned down and a warming pan in the middle of it.

He gently set Eleanor on her feet at the end of the bed and helped her sit.

She smiled wanly up at him, which only made him want to beat her relatives senseless. He'd never been a violent man, but then, he'd never faced a situation like this, either. He didn't know what had happened since he'd last seen her, but it hadn't been good.

Her hair was dull. Her face was too pale. Even her lips looked bloodless. Her blue eyes were flat without a hint of their usual liveliness. One hand came out of the cocoon he'd wrapped around her to hold the bedspread in place. She was still trembling.

"Off you go, then," Mrs. Campbell said. "We'll be fine on our own. You need to go and see the courier and rid us of all those strangers in our house."

Mrs. Campbell had never sounded more like his mother than she did now. Would his mother have bossed him around with such fearlessness? From what he'd learned from his uncle, probably.

"You're safe here," he said to Eleanor. "No one can hurt you."

To his horror, she began to cry, soundless tears dripping down her pale cheeks. He gently wiped them away with his fingertips. Then, despite the presence of Mrs. Campbell, he bent and kissed Eleanor on the cheek.

He didn't want to leave her, but his housekeeper was right. He had other duties to handle at the moment. Besides, his place was not here helping Eleanor bathe or dress.

Bruce didn't seem inclined to follow him, so he left the dog in the bedroom. Eleanor would probably welcome Bruce's loyalty. God knows her relatives hadn't demonstrated any.

He descended the stairs, leading the three men into his study. He got four glasses and poured a measure of whiskey into each of them before handing three of the glasses to the others.

"To a successful conclusion to tonight's activities," he said as a toast.

After going to his desk he opened his strongbox, taking out an amount he thought equal to the night's work.

Handing the money to each of the stable boys, he said, "Consider this a bonus. Thank you for your actions tonight. I don't think we would have been able to rescue Eleanor without you."

The young men look shocked, then gratified. The amount would make their lives a little easier, buy them something that they hadn't saved for, or allow them to give someone an unexpected present.

He watched as they left, then turned to Pete. He'd already paid him for his work tonight, but there was something that Pete needed more than money.

"I hope tonight is the last time you'll use your tools of the trade, Pete. I don't want Molly or the baby to have to get along without you."

The other man only nodded, but Logan noticed that he didn't promise. Nothing he could say would alter Pete's trajectory in life. Only Pete's determination would do that.

"Do you have a job waiting? Anyone who wants to employ you?"

"No, but it's early days yet," Pete said. His smile wasn't convincing.

"I'll hire you," Logan said. "Mrs. Campbell will be your boss and she's tough. One thing goes missing, though, Pete, and she'll skin you like a rabbit. Do you understand?"

"Never worked for a woman before, Logan. I'd like to think about it."

Logan nodded. He'd done what his conscience decreed. What Pete did with the opportunity was his decision.

He sent Pete back to his house in his carriage, thanking William for his work in tonight's adventure. His driver smiled and tipped his hat.

"It's been a while, sir, since I was in the army, but tonight felt like I'd returned."

Logan dreaded the last chore of the night. He entered the drawing room, apologizing for the delay. The man simply nodded and handed him an envelope.

"A letter from your sister, sir."

That was the worst news.

"How is he?"

For the first time the man smiled. "Stubborn, sir. Loud, as usual. Begging your pardon, sir."

"You've worked for my uncle for some time, I take it?"

"Ten years this next June, sir."

Logan didn't remember the man, but that wasn't unusual. His uncle had a great many far-flung enterprises and employed hundreds of men.

Alistair McKnight was larger than life, a bear of a man possessed of a bellicose temper and an opinion about everything. He took pride in being an iconoclast and holding a contrary view. If someone said the sky was blue his uncle would counter that it was mostly gray simply to be argumentative.

When Logan and Janet had first gone to live with his uncle, they'd thought that, due to his rank and position in life, he would turn over their care to other people. To their surprise, Uncle Alistair insisted on overseeing everything about their lives. When they were young he met with the nurse and the maids assigned to the nursery, then Janet's governess and Logan's tutors. Since Alistair was a widower and childless, he was considered by some matrimonially minded women to be a catch. His uncle had numerous romantic relationships, none of which he kept secret, but he never remarried. Instead, he was the best uncle/father anyone could have. He took on the children of his younger brother as if they were his own.

When Logan had gone to Edinburgh a few weeks ago, he'd visited his uncle and had been shocked at the change in the man.

"I'm not dead yet, my boy," his uncle said. "You be about your business. You've enough to do without worrying about me."

When you loved someone you worried about them.

Janet was closer and visited often. The fact that she'd sent him a letter meant the end was near.

Logan thanked the man and walked him to the door, turning the envelope over in his hands. He didn't want to open it, but it was a duty he couldn't avoid.

Mrs. Campbell startled him by appearing at his elbow. Her usually pleasant face was marred by a scowl.

"Eleanor?"

"I promised her a meal fit for a king. They were starving her. Can you imagine such a barbaric thing in this day and age? Just because she told them that she was going to break her engagement. The girl doesn't want to be a countess, Logan, and they punished her for it."

He pushed the information down where he could deal with it later. Right now Eleanor had to be kept safe and allowed to recuperate while he dealt with other family matters.

LOGAN HAD RESCUED her. Eleanor kept reminding herself of that fact as the minutes passed. He'd rescued her. This wasn't a dream or a hallucination.

Mrs. Campbell brought her a bowl of soup, but this was unlike anything she'd eaten in the past two weeks. This soup was white, thick, and filled with delectable vegetables and fish. She ate two bowls, but stopped herself from having a third considering how long it had been since she'd eaten. She was, however, tempted to eat some blueberry cobbler.

After she ate, Mrs. Campbell bustled around her, placing a clean nightgown on the bed. "Miss Janet leaves clothing here. I don't think she'd mind if you borrowed a bit."

Janet, Logan's sister. Eleanor wanted to say something, but words were frozen just beyond her lips. Her mind wasn't functioning well at all. All she could think of was that Logan had rescued her.

He had rescued her and Bruce had, too. Ever since Logan exited the room, Bruce refused to leave her side. His loyalty had never been in question. Not when he was with her. Nor when he'd come to live with Logan. He'd always greeted her with joy and excitement, as if knowing that his new home was for his protection, not because she was punishing him.

Seeing Bruce lifted her heart and reminded her that there were people who were good in the world. However, she felt almost guilty to be related to those who weren't.

Grief welled up in her, spilling out in tears she didn't seem able to control. Why was she crying? For the first time she was safe.

"Oh, you poor wee lamb."

Suddenly, she was being hugged by Mrs. Campbell. That just set off another storm of weeping, sobs that felt as if they came up from some deep cavern within her.

"We'll get you well, just you wait and see."

Eleanor could only nod in response.

"You tell me what you want to do. Would you like to eat something else? Or bathe? Or simply go to bed?"

Her answer was somewhat muffled since she was still being pressed up against Mrs. Campbell's considerable bosom.

"I'd like to bathe. If you have some hot water."

"We have better than that. We have a tub that's as deep as Loch Ness."

She pulled back. "Loch Ness?"

Mrs. Campbell smiled. "Maybe not that deep, but deep all the same."

The housekeeper stood, grabbed her hand, and opened the bedroom door. Bruce uttered a single bark as if to tell them he was following.

Chapter Thirty-Nine

Logan's home boasted a bathing chamber not unlike the two at her aunt's house. However, the one attached to Logan's suite of rooms had walls made of slate. Slate imported from Scotland. The tub, too, was stone, carved into a long boat shape and polished until it was smooth and silky to the touch.

Eleanor didn't bother protesting to Mrs. Campbell that she couldn't possibly take a bath in Logan's tub. She'd already come up against Mrs. Campbell's will of iron and knew she would lose. In all honesty, she really did want to submerge herself in a tub of hot water. Perhaps, in that way, she could finally get warm and clean.

As the taps ran and steam rose in the air, Mrs. Campbell grabbed one of the earthen jars from the counter and dumped the contents into the water.

Eleanor was immediately taken back to Scotland on a spring day with the smell of the wildflowers, grass, and pines in the distance.

The housekeeper left the room and returned with a stack of towels. After placing them on the counter, she reached into the cabinet against the wall and retrieved a jar of tooth polish along with a new toothbrush.

"You take your time," she said. "I'll come back in a little while to check on you. I'll knock first."

Eleanor nodded. She would've said more if she'd had the ability to form words. Or if Mrs. Campbell had stayed around to hear. The housekeeper closed the door behind her, leaving her alone.

She was safe. No one could compel her to do anything. She wouldn't be forced to marry Michael simply to survive. Thanks to Logan.

Three sharp barks startled her. She opened the door to find Bruce standing there. He pushed his way inside, tail wagging. She smiled, the first time she had felt lighthearted for days.

"You want to be my guardian here, too?"

He barked once, as if in assent.

It was evident that the housekeeper wanted her to understand that she was not alone. The next day Mrs. Campbell sent a contingent of maids to Eleanor's room every hour on the hour to do something for her. She had her nails done. One of the maids helped style her newly washed hair with heated tongs. Two other maids brought her a selection of clothing from Logan's sister. Often a maid arrived with some sort of wonderful selection of food from venison to fish to pastries.

"You have the most talented cook," Eleanor said to one of the maids.

The girl had smiled. "You're right, miss. Plus, Mrs. Campbell keeps her hand in. She makes pasties and all sorts of delicious things."

Eleanor couldn't have been cosseted any better unless she was the queen.

Logan hadn't visited her and at first she didn't question his absence. On the second day, however, she mentioned—as casually as she was able—that she would like to thank him for her rescue.

"He'll be back as soon as he can," Mrs. Campbell said. "He had to go to Scotland to see his uncle. The poor man isn't doing well."

How selfish she was to feel a surge of disappointment. Logan's uncle evidently needed him, far more than she did. Besides, hopefully the next time Logan saw her she would look much better and would have recuperated from her imprisonment.

By the end of the week she felt a great deal more like herself. She agreed to Mrs. Campbell's urging and wore one of Janet's dresses. She'd never met the woman, but she would be certain to write her a letter of thanks.

She wondered how long it would be until she could obtain her own clothes.

None of her family had sent word to her, which was probably a blessing. Nor had she heard from Michael, but she doubted she ever would.

Living in Logan's home was strangely comfortable. She didn't feel like a guest or an intruder. Instead, Mrs. Campbell treated her like she was a member of the family, someone who was cherished and valued simply because of who she was—not because of what she could do for others.

For a week the only demand of her was for her to list her choice of entrée for her meals. Did she want venison or beef? Chicken or pork? Would she like scones for breakfast or blood pudding or both?

Although she didn't belong here, it was the first place in London where she'd been so thoroughly and completely welcomed. Bruce kept her company whatever she did. He insisted on following her from room to room and even sleeping on the end of her bed.

The path forward was a little murky. She knew what she was going to do, but not exactly how she was going to do it. Deborah and the rest of the family didn't enter into her plans. They'd made their choice known. Any familial loyalty she might have felt for them had been burned away because of their greed. They'd chosen Michael rather than her.

One afternoon, after asking Mrs. Campbell if she might borrow some stationery, she was directed to Logan's study.

The room was not unlike the decorations in the rest of the house. Very tasteful with touches of Scotland. On one wall was a portrait of a man and woman dressed in clothing of an earlier time. She wondered if they were Logan's parents. Another portrait, hanging not far away, was of a lovely young woman with two children. A man around the same age stood behind them, smiling. This must be Janet because her eyes were like Logan's and her smile matched his.

A family crest, complete with lions rampant, hung behind Logan's mahogany desk.

She sat in his large leather chair, feeling dwarfed. She felt like she was trespassing despite what Mrs. Campbell said.

"Himself won't mind it a bit."

Mrs. Campbell had provided her with a sizable box of stationery, also left behind by Janet. The stack of ivory vellum sheets was perfumed with blotting paper scented by roses.

She had to write her family, but she didn't know what to say. How could she possibly communicate what she felt? Rage, grief, confusion, disbelief—they were all rolled up like a tangled ball of yarn. She couldn't possibly untangle it.

Perhaps it would be better to simply ask for her clothes. There, a task she could accomplish.

She wouldn't comment on the events that had transpired in her aunt's home. Nor would she allow herself to vent any of the rage she felt at her treatment. Neither Deborah nor Hamilton were ever going to know how dispirited she had been and how close she'd come to capitulating to their demands.

Logan had rescued her. Not only from that situation, but an abysmal future. How could she ever adequately thank him?

That was another task she'd give herself when the time came. For now she would finish the letter.

Bruce sat at her feet as if knowing that she needed a friend at the moment.

Mrs. Campbell knocked on the study door, then opened it. Something about the housekeeper's expression kept Eleanor silent.

"A woman is here, Miss Eleanor. She says she's your aunt. Shall I put her in the drawing room or say that you're not at home?"

"My aunt?"

Mrs. Campbell nodded.

Eleanor's stomach clenched. At least she was saved from having to post the letter to Deborah. However, she was not entirely certain that she wanted to come face-to-face with her aunt right at the moment.

Eleanor stood, clasped her hands at her waist, and prayed that she would be able to get through this confrontation. She felt as if she might be physically ill, a combination of fear, dread, and anger. She wished, irrationally, that Logan was here. Logan could protect her, true, but she wasn't a weakling. She would face her aunt alone.

Deborah was quintessentially English. Eleanor was a Scot.

"Show her into the drawing room, if you don't mind, Mrs. Campbell. Thank you."

"Shall I bring tea?"

Eleanor shook her head. "That's not necessary. This isn't a social call. Nor is it a pleasant one, I'm afraid."

She didn't doubt that Mrs. Campbell knew all about the entire situation, what her aunt had done and how Logan had rescued her. She knew she was right when the housekeeper came to her and gave her a quick, hard hug.

"If you need me, you just call out. I'll be close enough to hear. Would you like me to take Bruce?"

"No, I think I'll bring him with me."

She entered the drawing room with her smile moored in place and greeted her aunt with a modicum of politeness. Bruce startled her by refusing to enter the room fully, preferring to remain close to the door. Perhaps Deborah had that effect on him.

Deborah had chosen to sit at one end of the lushly upholstered sofa. Eleanor chose the opposite chair. For long moments they didn't say anything.

Deborah's lectures came back to her. All the speeches about how unfair Deborah's life in Scotland had been, about how privileged Eleanor had been treated at the expense of her family. All the talk about how Jeremy had been cheated of his rightful heritage. She had hoped to be able to get through this meeting without revealing how angry she was, but as she sat there, Eleanor realized that her rage was just below the surface.

It had burned out any other feeling she had for Deborah.

"I would like my belongings," she said when Deborah still didn't speak.

"They're in your carriage," Deborah said. "Your personal things, along with the dresses you brought from Scotland. You won't be receiving the garments that we paid for, part of your trousseau."

"That's fine," Eleanor said.

"Michael will make it known that he's broken your engagement because of your infidelity."

Eleanor knew that she'd never get an acknowledgement from Michael about what he'd done. It was altogether possible that she would never talk to him again. If they happened to meet in public she was certain he would simply turn and give her his back.

She didn't care about what Michael did or said.

"McKnight won't want you, you know. When people learn how shameless you are, McKnight won't want anything to do with you. You'll be a social outcast. A burden. An object of shame. He's a member of Parliament and sensitive about scandal. He won't want his name tainted."

Her aunt was quite possibly correct. A good thing she'd decided to leave England and live at Hearthmere. No one would care what the English gossips said there.

"I've always wanted your love and affection," she told Deborah, knowing this was the last conversation she would ever willingly have with her aunt. "I thought, for a time, that I had it, but only because I was going to be a countess. You've never truly felt anything for me, have you?"

Deborah didn't answer. Her only response was to stare at Eleanor as if she was some sort of circus exhibit, something too bizarre to be believed.

Eleanor wasn't going to get an answer, then. Perhaps she'd already received one, from the treatment she received at her aunt's hands.

"Do not come to us for recourse, Eleanor. We will no longer be a safe haven for you."

A safe haven? Deborah had never been a safe haven. Granted, she'd been family, but Eleanor had never felt safe or even much wanted here. Hearthmere had always been and would always remain her home. Not London. Not Deborah's house.

"From this moment forward we will disavow any relationship to you. Do not think that you can trade upon our good graces anymore. You are no longer part of our family."

Eleanor finally understood. Deborah was here for one reason only. Not to bring her clothes, but to deliver this message.

Eleanor felt strangely calm, almost relieved. "That's fine. You've never been part of mine."

Deborah leaned forward slightly, almost as if she wanted to physically retaliate.

Bruce moved from the door to stand in front of the sofa. His lips curled back to reveal impressive incisors.

"I should have had him drowned when you first brought him from Scotland," Deborah said.

The fur on Bruce's back rose as he began to growl at Deborah. Eleanor didn't admonish him. Instead, she stood and walked to the door, Bruce at her side.

"I think it's time you left," she said. "This visit has already been too long."

She opened the door to find Mrs. Campbell standing there, accompanied by two of the footmen. She couldn't help but smile at all three of them.

Addressing her remark to Mrs. Campbell, she said, "My driver and my carriage are outside. Could they stay here for a few days?"

"Of course."

"Mrs. Richards will be leaving now," Eleanor said, turning to look at her aunt one last time.

In one way Eleanor was gratified that her aunt had come to see her. She'd put an end to their relationship as finally as a deathblow. Her aunt had said it herself: *Don't count on us. Don't come to us.*

She wouldn't. Not ever.

Family is everything. She would have to create her own now. How strange to suddenly feel so happy and free.

ELEANOR RETURNED TO the guest room with Bruce at her side. Sitting on the chair beside the window, she spent several moments telling him what a good dog he was. He responded by trying to chew the toe of one of her shoes.

She gave him his rope toy instead, watching as the footmen brought up her belongings from the carriage. How strange that her entire London life could be packed into only three valises, but then, those things she truly prized were at Hearthmere.

After thanking the footmen and watching as they closed the door behind them, she was left alone with her thoughts.

She'd already decided to return to Scotland, but her aunt's words had helped firm up the timetable. Perhaps Logan would be harmed by her presence in his house. She didn't want scandal to touch him. She would leave before he returned from Edinburgh.

She had her carriage and driver. She had her valises, still packed. All she had to do was write a note to Logan thanking him and Mrs. Campbell for all their kindnesses and comforts these past difficult days.

The note was easy. Saying goodbye to Mrs. Campbell was much more difficult.

"And when were you thinking of doing this thing, Miss Eleanor?"

"I think tomorrow morning would be best."

Mrs. Campbell put her hands on her hips and glowered at her. "You can't be thinking of traveling so far in your condition."

"I'm feeling much better, Mrs. Campbell, thanks to you. It's been a week and I think I should leave."

"I'm thinking you should wait until himself gets back. He won't be happy to find you've gone."

"It's really for the best, Mrs. Campbell. Surely you can see that.

I'm a single woman. Logan is a single man. It isn't proper that I'm a guest in his home."

"This is England. The English will say whatever they want about the Scots, whatever the circumstances. It doesn't matter, they'll find something to gaggle on about. Don't you worry what anyone says."

"I want to go home," Eleanor said softly. "I truly, truly want to go home."

At Hearthmere she felt centered and real. At home she could learn to deal with this pain. Not only from the betrayal by her family, but from saying goodbye to Logan.

All she needed was the courage to leave.

THE JOURNEY HOME was without incident. Even Bruce had taken to travel, enjoying being able to stick his head out the window and see the passing terrain. Occasionally, he saw a flock of sheep or a few cattle. These always necessitated a few warning barks. Then he would look at her as if waiting for a sign of approval. She always gave it to him, telling him that he was a very good boy.

The sight of Hearthmere usually calmed her heart, and gave her a warm glow and a feeling of homecoming. Today, for the very first time, she felt a deep and disturbing sadness when looking at her home.

He wasn't there. He would never be there. While Hearthmere offered her sanctuary and belonging, it also promised her loneliness. That was the price she had to pay for keeping it intact. She hadn't realized, however, how very painful it would be.

At first everyone was surprised to see her, but that response only lasted a few seconds before she was welcomed, ushered into the parlor to be warmed and given some of Cook's scones.

"My, the puppy isn't so little anymore, is he?" Mrs. Willett asked, bending to give Bruce a pat between his ears.

He wiggled a little, enjoying the unexpected attention.

"Will you be staying long, Miss Eleanor?" the housekeeper asked.

"I will. In fact, I shall never leave again."

The older woman looked a little startled, but then the expression faded into a smile.

"You and your husband will be living here, then?"

"No," Eleanor said. "I've decided not to marry."

The housekeeper couldn't hide her surprise. Most women would not choose spinsterhood over becoming a countess.

"Can I bring you anything else?"

Eleanor bit back her smile. The poor woman couldn't think of anything to say and had fallen back on her role as housekeeper.

"Nothing, thank you."

In a matter of minutes she was alone with a blazing fire, seated in a comfortable chair, an ottoman only inches from her feet. She should rest from the journey. Or look over the ledgers. Go and visit with Mr. Contino. A dozen things needed to be done, each one of them better than sitting here brooding.

She didn't move, staring into the flames with Bruce curled into a tight ball at her feet. She'd only been home a little while, yet she missed Logan already. Somehow she was going to have to become familiar with this feeling. Hearthmere and the horses had always been enough to occupy her.

How strange that they seemed lacking now.

Chapter Forty

Logan's assault on Hearthmere was a frontal one.

He hadn't realized that the minute he traveled from Scotland back to London he would be turning around and retracing his steps. If he'd had an inkling that Eleanor was returning to Hearthmere he could have saved himself a great deal of time.

He took a few minutes to write Mr. Disraeli, informing him as to his future. He sent one of the footmen after Fred, made him privy to the events of the past few days, and had him deliver the note to the former Prime Minister.

Mrs. Campbell informed him of certain developments, none of which changed his foul mood. He was all for giving William a few days off, but the man insisted on driving him back to Scotland. A change of clothes, a hamper of food, and they were off once more.

She'd left him. No, she hadn't left him. She'd returned home. Mrs. Campbell's obvious eavesdropping had filled in some blanks of Eleanor's situation. She'd ended her engagement, a fact that had infuriated Herridge and her family. For that reason she'd been a prisoner at the Richardses' home.

Of course she wanted to return to Hearthmere, especially given the amorphous nature of their relationship. He hadn't said anything to her recently about how he felt. In fact, he'd been careful not to reveal his emotions. What had seemed right at the time now seemed foolish.

The sight of Hearthmere on the horizon made him realize why she loved it. The house nestled in a divot created by a series of rolling, gentle hills. Ben Hagen sat like a sentinel to the rear, overlooking the series of paddocks and fences.

The gray brick of the house stood out against the fading green of the winter landscape. The building looked as if it had originally been constructed as a sturdy manor house. Over the years two additional wings had been added on either side, yet the architecture wasn't the same. Nor were the roof lines similar.

However, the hodgepodge of styles managed to give the effect of a surprisingly charming house. Not as daunting an edifice as the McKnight ancestral home, but a more welcoming one.

Fences stretched over the glen and up into the hills. Most of the corrals were filled on this early winter day. In a matter of weeks the area would be covered with a fine layer of snow, but Hearthmere had been running for decades. They knew how to take care of their horses in all seasons.

His heartbeat escalated as they took the last rise toward the house. He had marshaled his arguments both while traveling to Scotland and on the trip back to London. Now he didn't need to convince Eleanor to break her engagement—she'd done that on her own. All he needed to do was to declare himself.

He'd been in battle. He'd fought the lesser war of standing for election. Every day in Parliament was a challenge of one form or another. Why, then, did he feel so unsure of this coming meeting?

Perhaps because nothing else had ever mattered as much.

ELEANOR WAS IN the library going over one of the ledgers when Mrs. Willett arrived.

"Miss Eleanor, you have a visitor."

"A visitor?" The last visitor she'd had at Logan's house had been an unwelcome one. Had one of her relatives followed her to Scotland?

Bruce stood, ran to the door and disappeared.

Suddenly, she knew exactly who it was. A moment later she heard his voice as he greeted Bruce. Logan was here. Logan was here. Why was Logan here?

"It's the man who brought Bruce," her housekeeper said. "I recognized him."

Eleanor stood and thanked Mrs. Willett, not informing the woman that she knew Logan quite well indeed. The other woman nodded, then melted away in that fashion of hers. It wasn't fair to wish that Mrs. Willett was more like Mrs. Campbell, but she missed Logan's housekeeper.

Should she remain here? She hadn't told Mrs. Willett to bring Logan to the library. All she'd done was stare at the woman. No, she should go and meet him and greet him with a smile. Offer him the hospitality for which Hearthmere was famous.

Only her feet wouldn't move.

Logan was here. Oh, dear. Logan was here. Why was he here? Had he come to lecture her about leaving London before he'd returned? Had he come simply to see how she was faring? That sounded more like him. Logan was here.

What was she going to do? How was she going to react? What could she possibly say?

I've missed you terribly, much more than I should have, perhaps. The days have been endless without you.

What would it be like when years had passed before she saw him again?

Suddenly he was at the door, Bruce beside him. The dog looked like he was grinning because his two favorite people were together again.

"Hello," she said, feeling like a fool. It was the only word that passed her lips easily.

"Hello," he answered.

She should ask what he was doing here. She should say something, anything.

I've been missing you.

Thank you for everything.

I love you.

No, she couldn't say that, could she?

"You look tired," she said.

"I am. I've traveled between Scotland and England a bit much lately. Why did you leave?"

He had always been direct, hadn't he?

"It was better."

"For whom? You?"

No, she'd been miserable.

"For you."

She had to point out some not so pleasant facts to Logan.

"I'm sure that word has gotten out that Michael ended our engagement because of that afternoon in your house. I'm equally certain that your name has been bandied about. I won't harm your career, Logan. I won't allow that to happen."

"You can't," he said, closing the library door and walking toward her. "Any gossip about me will only add to my allure. No doubt I'll have whispers following me wherever I go, but that isn't altogether a bad thing."

"It isn't?"

He shook his head. "I'm all for revamping the prison system in Scotland. It's not something most people want to hear about, but a little scandal might mean that the newspapers would be more willing to listen to me."

She stared at him in amazement as he smiled back at her. Nothing had the power to disturb Logan if he didn't choose to let it.

"There's a way you could spare me some of the gossip, although I doubt you and I will ever be totally free of it."

"Is there? What is that?"

"You could marry me," he said.

She could only stand there wordless.

He nodded. "It's the best answer, don't you think?"

Not one word came to mind.

"It's not the same in London without you," he said. "I doubt I'll be able to get any work done for worrying about you."

She really did need to say something, but she couldn't think of a thing to say.

"Nothing's really been the same since that day on the hillside. I keep hearing your voice and I turn and you're not there. I dream of you and I'm angry when I wake because you're not beside me."

"The same things have happened to me," she said. There, a few words she'd actually been able to speak.

He smiled. "See? We should marry."

"Is that a sufficient reason?"

"I don't know of one better. I want to live with you for the rest of my life. I want your problems to be my problems. I want to tell you when I'm annoyed and have you save me from those interminable political functions."

"You want to marry me because you're bored?"

His smile faded. He reached her, placing his hands on her waist, and drew her forward.

"I want to marry you because I love you, Eleanor Craig of Hearthmere. My life is worthless without you. I'm worthless without you. I want you and I need you and I sincerely doubt that I'll be able to live without you. I might even pitch a tent in your garden and have my secretary bring my correspondence there."

She reached up with both hands and placed them on either side of his neck, her thumbs just behind his ears. For a long moment she only looked at him, trying to find the words that would convey everything she felt.

"It would be very cold there, Logan. I couldn't, in all good conscience, allow you to live there. At the very least I'd show you to a parlor."

"Marry me," he said.

She felt buoyant, as if she was a cloud blown by the wind. The words that were so difficult to say were much easier now.

"I didn't expect you," she said. "You gave me a puppy, but you gave me so much more."

His smile was back in place.

"I love you, Logan McKnight. I love you for a dozen reasons

and more. I love you most of all, because with you I feel whole, as if you're the other half of me missing for so long."

When he leaned forward and would've kissed her, she shook her head.

"I need to finish this and when you kiss me I can't think of anything at all."

His smile disappeared again.

"I love you because you're kind and generous, intelligent and loyal. You treat people with dignity, even those who can't do anything for you. You make me laugh and think. You challenge me and comfort me, and having you love me was the greatest experience of my life."

She dropped her hands and took a step back. "But I won't marry you, Logan. I won't lose Hearthmere. It's part of me. It's my heritage, what's left of my family. Hearthmere is my responsibility. I can't abdicate it."

"You're worried that our marriage will give me control over your property?"

She nodded.

"And that I'd do something to it?"

She shook her head. "No, I don't think you would. But you could."

"Then I'll gift the contents of Hearthmere to you. A wedding declaration. I'll have my solicitor draw it up and you can have someone look it over if you wish. That way your inheritance will stay yours. A gift, and not subject to antiquated law."

To do that she would have to trust him. Words he didn't say, but they were there in his eyes.

She put one hand against his chest, right where his heart was. She could feel it beating powerfully beneath his jacket.

Did she trust him? He'd saved her in more than one way. He was her friend. Her knight. Her lover. Yes, she trusted him, more than she'd ever trusted anyone.

Once more he drew her into his arms.

"Marry me, Eleanor, and be my love. We'll have to live in London for a bit, of course, but we can make the city our own. Then we'll come back to Scotland and live in Edinburgh or here or in my home. Wherever you want."

She wrapped her arms around him and put her cheek against his chest. How could she possibly explain what she was feeling? She'd been overwhelmed by grief, knowing that she would never see him again. Now he was here and he was offering her the world.

What would life be like with him by her side? He'd dare her to do more, she suspected. Perhaps she'd take on causes of her own. Perhaps she'd even become more involved with Hearthmere's breeding program. No doubt that would shock Mr. Contino down to his tooled boots.

There wasn't time to think of other changes that would probably happen in her life because Logan was kissing her. Sensations overcame thought and she could only clutch his shoulders and hold on.

His kiss lit something within her, a ravenous need that was like hunger or thirst. She'd never thought passion could be fierce, but that's what she felt now.

Her hands slid beneath his coat and gripped his shirt. She wanted it off. She wanted all his clothing off.

When they broke apart they only stared at each other. Their faces were both colored by emotion, their breathing equally harsh.

"No, not this way again," he said.

He startled her by walking to the other side of the room.

"It's the only way," he added. "I can't be within five feet of you without kissing you, and we both know where that leads." He looked around the library. "There isn't even a sofa here. I'll not take you on the desk."

"Come to my bed, then."

"And shock all your servants? I don't give a flying fig for my reputation, Eleanor, but I care about yours."

She really wanted to kiss him for that comment, but he held up his hand as if he knew what she was thinking.

"Does that mean I won't be able to be in the same room with you until we're married?" she asked.

"Will we be married? You never answered me."

"Yes. Yes. Yes." She smiled at him, but he still didn't approach her.

She went to one of the patterned tin walls and touched the middle panel on the second row. Smiling, she watched his expression as the secret door opened.

"It goes to my bedroom," she said. "Not a direct route, but it will get us there eventually."

He began to shake his head.

"Eleanor . . ."

"Logan . . ."

Bruce settled the matter by entering the secret passage. She smiled at Logan once more before she followed the dog.

Less than ten minutes later Bruce was happily chewing on his rope toy while Eleanor was backed up against a wall in her sitting room being thoroughly kissed.

"Are you always so devious?" Logan asked when the kiss was over. He continued to nibble his way down her throat, which made it very difficult to speak.

"Only when there's a significant inducement," she said, reaching for his trouser buttons. How odd that she'd never been maidenly with him.

Her hands reached up beneath his shirt, her nails gently scratching his skin. He sucked in his stomach, which made her laugh.

"Are you ticklish? I would never have known it."

"Now, that's a dare if I ever heard one. Don't tell me you aren't."

He would take it as a challenge if she denied it. It was safer just to pull his head down for another kiss.

There was none of the hesitation of before. None of the conversation or rationalizations. Only hunger. They were wild for each other and she didn't care if he knew how she felt.

He couldn't undress fast enough. Nor could she. Her fingers fumbled on buttons and tabs. Whoever had designed the newest style of dress evidently wanted to preserve a woman's virtue. She was half tempted to simply raise her skirts up and be done with it.

His hands were as active as hers, flying over tabs, bows, and the busk of her corset. She heard something hit the floor and guessed that she'd been a little too fevered in unbuttoning his shirt. She pushed his jacket from his shoulders while still kissing him.

Off, off, she wanted all his clothes off. She needed to be next to him, her skin against his. The day in his drawing room, the day that felt as if it had happened ages ago, was the first time she'd ever felt as complete. Or happy. Or satisfied.

She honestly didn't care if the entire staff of Hearthmere knew that they were here, making love. Let them talk. Let them speculate. It didn't matter.

All that mattered was Logan lifting her up in his arms and carrying her to her bedroom. He dropped her onto the mattress, then joined her there a second later.

They rolled together, still wrestling with clothing. Shoes fell to the hardwood floor with a thud. His shirt went flying onto the floor. Her dress got wound around one of the four posters. She thought she saw one of her stockings land on the sconce near her vanity, but couldn't be sure.

They were laughing by the time they were naked.

She wrapped her arms around him and held him tight.

"I love you," she said against his shoulder before kissing his skin. "I love you, Logan."

He pulled back and looked into her eyes. He'd charmed her when she hadn't wanted to be charmed, bedeviled her when they were opponents, if that's what they had been. With him looking at her now, she realized that he didn't have to say anything. Still, he gave her the words, soft and sweet in Gaelic and then in English.

"I love you, Eleanor. My dearest love."

The world, which had been alien to her so very long, slipped into place, into its rightful order.

She put one hand on the back of his neck, the other on his cheek. She'd never thought she could feel so much that it was painful. Her heart was filled to overflowing. Her mind was so engrossed with thoughts of him that she had no room left over to think about anything else.

His skin and hers were touching and yet they still weren't close enough. She wanted to melt into him.

Every care that he had she wanted to smooth away. Every worry, every concern, every aggravation—anything that marred his life—she wanted to erase, expunge, and eliminate.

If she had ever given a thought to the reason for her life, she would have an answer after this day. To be here. To touch this man. To love him.

He was kissing her from her throat to her feet, paying special attention to her breasts.

Their loving was like a whirlwind, passion, need, desire, laughter, and desperation all mixed up together.

She slid over him, kissing and nipping her way down his body. His hips arched as she took him into her mouth, shocking herself with her actions.

There wasn't anything to stop her from doing whatever she wished. She could explore, experiment, and test the limits of her own behavior. Logan would only congratulate her on her courage.

All the various places on his body that intrigued her from the last time were places that she investigated now: the beautiful curves beneath his arms, the breadth of his chest, the triangle of hair at the base of his manhood. Her fingers stroked along the curve of the arch of his foot, up his ankle, and through the dusting of hair on his legs.

Everything about him was special and perfect and masculine. There wasn't one thing about Logan that she would change.

She wanted him atop her, unwilling to wait any longer. She'd never known this hunger, this need. When he entered her, it was as if they'd been lovers forever. Her body already knew his. He lowered himself over her, then raised her hips with one arm so that they were even more tightly joined.

Neither was dominant, but each surrendered.

Joy had only been a word until this moment. As pleasure swept through her, she clung to him. One thought managed to pierce the haze that surrounded her: this was home. This was family. Not Hearthmere. Not even Scotland, but being in the arms of this man.

Chapter Forty-One

An hour or so later there was a knock on the door.

Eleanor managed to put on her shift, corset, and dress. She tucked the corset cover and her stockings beneath a pillow, slid on her shoes, and made it to the door in record time.

"Yes?" she asked, opening the door a sliver.

"There's a man here to see you, Miss Eleanor. He says he's Mr. McKnight's secretary."

Although Mrs. Willett hadn't said it, the housekeeper evidently knew Logan was with her.

How very odd that she wasn't the least bit embarrassed.

"Would you please put him in my study, Mrs. Willett? Tell him it will be just a few minutes."

"Yes, miss."

"Fred has made good time," Logan said.

Eleanor turned and faced him. He wasn't in a hurry to find his clothing. For a moment she thought about convincing him otherwise. She loved looking at him naked.

"Did you expect him?"

He nodded. "Eventually."

"I'll go on down, then," she said. Although she would much rather stand here and watch him dress.

She left the room first, Bruce at her heels. Logan would follow in a few minutes. Until then she would make his secretary comfortable in the study. Hopefully, Mrs. Willett would bring tea.

"I'm Eleanor Craig," she said, entering the room. She glanced down at Bruce before introducing him to Fred.

"I've met Bruce before, Miss Craig."

That was a surprise.

"Please, have a seat. Logan will be here in just a moment."

"Thank you, Miss Craig."

Logan's secretary was a very tall young man with a prominent Adam's apple and a physique that made her wonder if Logan was working him too hard. He didn't look as if he'd eaten a full meal for years.

He was wearing a black armband. She would have offered her condolences on his loss, except that she didn't know enough to say anything. Had he recently lost a parent or a sibling? He didn't look old enough to have been married, but appearances were often deceiving.

This study had been her father's base of operations. Paintings of various Hearthmere horses lined the walls. The large desk in the middle of the room had been carved with bas-reliefs of running horses, the detail so perfect that she could almost feel their hot breath.

Opposite the desk was a seating area consisting of a small sofa and two chairs. Her uncle had installed the furniture here when he'd taken over the room. She went to sit on the sofa, wishing she'd given her appearance more care. Her hair felt as if it was falling from its bun and she was embarrassingly aware that she wasn't wearing stockings again. Hopefully Logan's secretary couldn't tell.

He chose a chair opposite her, gave her a quick smile, then placed his briefcase on the floor beside him.

The maid, carrying a tray, entered the room and placed it on the circular table in front of Eleanor.

The girl smiled, then whispered, "Shall I take Bruce out?"

"Not right now, Norma, but thank you." Eleanor turned to Fred. "Would you like a cup of tea?"

"Thank you, no."

She wagered that if she offered him one of the pastries on the tray he'd decline that, too.

Nor was he inclined to talk. Rather than force him into a conversation she sat as silent as he, occupying herself with petting Bruce.

At Logan's appearance, Fred stood and bowed slightly.

"Your Grace, I was able to convey your note to Mr. Disraeli."

Instead of answering his secretary, Logan turned to her.

"There's one thing I need to tell you, Eleanor, and it won't please you one bit."

"Your Grace?" she asked.

"That's the part that won't please you." Turning back to Fred, he asked, "Did he have a response?"

"Not directly, Your Grace. However, I don't think he was pleased."

"Your Grace?"

Logan turned to her. "My uncle passed away two days ago."

"I'm sorry. You never told me your uncle was a duke."

"The Duke of Montrose."

"He was the Duke of Montrose?"

Logan nodded.

"And now you're the Duke of Montrose."

Logan nodded again.

"That's how you knew Old Ned."

He smiled. "Yes. I used to steal away and go and visit him on the hills."

He'd never told her he was related to a duke, and now he was one.

"My uncle deliberately kept our relationship quiet. He thought it would harm me politically. The nephew of a duke being elected to the House of Commons."

No wonder he had a large house in London and never seemed to worry about money.

She was making sense of the news one tiny bite at a time. "Now you'll be elevated to the House of Lords."

"I will. You didn't want to be a countess. How do you feel about being a duchess?"

She looked up at him. His eyes twinkled. Despite Fred standing there, he came and stood in front of her, holding out his hands. She put hers in them and let him pull her to her feet.

Strangely, she didn't feel the panic that had accompanied the notion that she was to be a countess. How very odd. She was going to be a duchess.

Her aunt was going to be apoplectic.

"You agreed to marry me," he said. "Has that changed? Will you become the Duchess of Montrose and my wife? Will you share my life and accept my love?"

Then, in front of Fred, he kissed her. When they finally parted she felt dazed. Whatever title Logan bore was immaterial. He was Logan. Logan, her nemesis turned friend, her lover, and her love.

What other choice did she have?

"Yes," she said, smiling. She wound her arms around his neck and stood on tiptoe to kiss him again.

Bruce barked his wholehearted approval.

Author's Note

Eleanor's horse, Maud, was named for a poem by Alfred, Lord Tennyson: "Come into the Garden, Maud." The poem was later used as lyrics in a Victorian parlor song.

Before 1868, wills could transfer only moveable and personal property (such as money, clothes, and furniture). After 1868 it was possible for someone to inherit land and buildings by way of a will.

Women lost all ownership over their property when they married. Basically, a woman lost her identity to that of her husband. He absorbed everything she owned.

I'd like to think that Logan was so incensed at what had happened to Eleanor that he fought for the law to be changed. In 1870 it was. The Married Woman's Property Act stated that a woman's inheritance could not be taken from her by marriage.

Until then, a husband could not sell his wife's land or buildings, but he could dispose of everything on it, including animals, furniture, and personal property. She could not rent, lease, or otherwise dispose of her property without her husband's consent, so basically she lost all control of what she owned.

Women had few protections in Victorian society. There are stories like Eleanor's imprisonment that didn't, regretfully, have a happy ending.

The Second Reform Act of 1867 gave the vote to men who owned property or who paid a rent of at least ten pounds for their rooms. Nearly a million more men were allowed to vote thanks to the Reform Act.

Abyssinia is the same country as Ethiopia. Europeans called it Abyssinia while Ethiopia was always the name within the country. The Battle of Magdala took place from April 9 to April 13, 1868.

White wedding dresses became popular after 1840 when Queen Victoria wore a white lace-trimmed gown.

To Wed an Heiress

Rebellion drove Mercy Rutherford to Scotland to escape the possessive grip of her fiancé. But it's fate that lands her in the crumbling highlands castle of Lennox Caitheart. A dreamer with visions of inventing airships, he's most certainly mad. Handsome beyond words, he's also causing an irresistible flutter in her stomach beyond reason. When Gregory arrives to see their arranged marriage to its bitter end, Mercy desperately turns to Lennox with an offer of her fortune—and her hand in marriage.

The Earl of Morton has a reputation for being a daredevil eccentric, but even he is hesitant to engage in such a rash proposition—no matter how utterly beguiled he is by the wildly independent American heiress. And yet, with so much at stake, how can he possibly say no? But when their unconventional union grows into a passionate and inseparable love, more than Gregory's obsession threatens them. Now, Lennox and Mercy will have to risk more than their hearts to save it.